Silent as the Grave
Book 1 in the Guild of Truth Series

Mary K. Norris

CRIMSON
ROMANCE
Avon, Massachusetts

This edition published by
Crimson Romance
an imprint of F+W Media, Inc.
10151 Carver Road, Suite 200
Blue Ash, Ohio 45242

www.crimsonromance.com

Dedication

TO MY OPA, I MISS YOU EVERY DAY.

ACKNOWLEDGMENTS

I'd like to thank all my family and friends who believed in me
and supported me. My parents especially, you guys never let
me give up on my dream. Thank you. To my brother and sister,
you always believed in me and were there for me.
I'll never forget that.

Special thanks goes out to the Merki-Norris Clan for your
never-ending support. I'd also like to thank everyone at
Crimson Romance for giving me this amazing opportunity,
especially Jennifer Lawler, who took a chance on me and
believed in my book. Thank you everyone,
I wouldn't be where I am today without you.

Prologue

Felix smiled at the little girl one seat over. She was waiting for her mother to come out from the patient room where she was discussing whatever treatment their dog needed with Sydney. He could tell by the little ways she wrinkled her nose that the smell of dog food was getting to her. He'd long since become accustomed to the smell. A hard concept for him to wrap his mind around considering his nose was used to the aromas of fresh baked goods from working at the bakery.

The sacrifices he made for friendship.

The little girl returned his smile and continued to shift in her seat. A child could only remain in one position for so long.

"Hey." He leaned toward her conspiratorially. "You want to see a cool magic trick?"

The girl's honey-brown eyes brightened for a moment before her face saddened. "My brother told me magic isn't real and only dumb little girls believe in it." She hugged her arms to her chest in a gesture that told Felix she hadn't quite broken the habit of carrying a stuffed animal around with her.

He eased back from her and dug into his pocket. "Is that so?" He held up a quarter before letting it rest in the palm of his hand. "Ready?" The little girl scooted to the edge of her seat.

Felix grinned at her hopeful expression.

All too easy.

He waved his other hand and the coin vanished.

"Whoa!" The little girl was practically in his lap. "Where'd it go?" She grabbed his hand and flipped it over.

He held his hands up and shrugged. "It's gone. I told you." He waggled his fingers for effect. "Magic."

She continued to look for it. "Yeah, but that's what they always say, and then they pull it out from behind my ear." Her large, honey eyes lit up, snagging on the side of his face. "Or from behind *your* ear!" She clambered into his lap and grasped his head between her little hands.

Not this time, he thought as she tilted his head this way and that.

If he'd been able to return things after Erasing them, it would have made his life a helluva lot easier when his powers had first manifested.

Before the little girl could give him a headache, he gently pulled her away from his face, keeping her little arms and hands at a safer distance. It still amazed him how open minded children could be. It was a breath of fresh air. There was no judgment, no fear. He could blatantly use his powers, and this little girl didn't even bat an eye. She simply sat on his lap, eyes glittering.

"You want to know why those other people bring the coin back?" he asked her. "It's because they didn't really make it disappear, they only hid it."

"So you can't bring it back?"

He shook his head. "Nope."

"Not even if you really, *really* tried?"

His smile slipped. The question was asked in innocence, but that didn't stop his gut from sinking as he remembered all the times he'd desperately tried.

He shook away the lingering ghosts of his past and pasted that smile back onto his face.

"Not even if I really, *really* tried," he told her.

She considered him for a moment, and he half expected her to jump from his lap and tell him how lame he was that he couldn't make a damn coin reappear.

Well, I could always pull another one from my pocket . . .

But after a few more seconds the little girl nodded to herself and scooted closer so she could wrap her arms around his neck. "That sounds like real magic to me. Two years ago I had this one pet called Mr. Hobbles . . . he was a Junebug that I used to practice magic with . . ."

*

Emily's mom emerged from the patient room fifteen minutes later, clearly astonished to find her daughter in the lap of a complete stranger and positively glowing with excitement. She collected Emily from Felix, sprouting apologies and thanks for his patience with her daughter.

"Bye, Felix." Emily waved the entire time as her mother tugged her from the vet like their dog on its leash.

Once the door shut and they disappeared into a large SUV a soft snort drifted over from behind the reception desk.

Felix glanced over to find Niella, not bothering to hide her amusement. "I don't get it," she said. "What do they see in you? It's almost sad how easily they fall for you. That poor girl is going to have a crush on you well into middle school."

He shot her a grin. "I can't help it. At least I set the bar really high for her."

"You sure did," she said sarcastically. "Now all it'll take to get her engine going when she grows up is some cheap magic trick. Well done." Niella gave another snort and turned back to her paperwork.

"You'd be surprised how hard it is to find good magic shows nowadays," he said. "You laugh now, Niella, but just wait. Give it a couple more years and you'll be as head over heels as my youthful followers."

She didn't respond.

He gave her a few more moments but the retort never came. "Ell?"

He leaned forward in his chair to get a better view.

Her head was lolled onto her shoulder, her body tilting precariously over the side of her wheelchair.

Felix shot from his chair with a curse.

"Niella? Come on, I wasn't that boring." He gave her shoulders an experimental shake but he already knew she wouldn't wake.

She was Dreaming.

"Damn." He ran a hand through his hair. It'd been so long since she'd had a Dream in front of him, he'd forgotten how disconcerting the whole thing could be. He looked around the lobby, lost. What the hell was he supposed to do?

He thought about calling Sydney from the back rooms, but there was nothing she could do. Her powers only negated the use of others and would likely wrench Niella from her Dream. And he had a tingling suspicion that would hurt like a bitch. Besides, didn't they say never to wake someone from sleepwalking? Did the same concept apply here?

Gritting his teeth against this sudden helplessness, he kept his hand firmly on her shoulder to keep her from falling out of her wheelchair and remained where he was, kneeling beside her.

He couldn't imagine having to deal with having visions at random. All that information floating around through his brain . . . it made him grateful that he only caused things to vanish.

"Ell? Niella!"

Hazel eyes blinked at him. He grasped her shoulders more firmly.

"Damn, Ell. Don't do that to me."

A flash of anger passed over her face, and he could have groaned aloud.

Watch your mouth, idiot.

He knew better then to make it sound like she was able to control her Dreams. His heart sank further when she stared down at her mangled legs. Useless, she liked to call them.

He tried to steer her attention elsewhere. "Did you have a Dream? Anything we can do to help?"

Panic and fear flooded her face, and his whole body stiffened as her eyes sought his.

He could count on one hand the number of times he'd seen Niella frightened. His gut clenched. "Your Mirror Mate, she's about to be ambushed. A trap." She closed her eyes as if she was trying to rearrange all the fragments of her Dream into some kind of order. "There was a cage. Pain. She was able to manipulate sound. A Silencer. She's at a house."

She cursed under her breath and pulled paper from the reception desk. She scribbled something onto a scrap and thrust it into his hands.

"She's in danger."

Chapter 1

This was so humiliating. After moving out seven months ago, Cali was already crawling back to her parents.

That's what you get for trusting anyone.

Jessica had been her roommate, her sort-of friend, and she'd stolen Cali's painting and hawked it to the highest bidder to get the money and run.

Cali exhaled. "Figured." She'd been working on that painting for two months. It was supposed to pay for this month's rent. It was a little too convenient that it was Cali's turn to pay the full brunt when Jessica decided to take off. Her parents were going to love that.

Don't think about that. Remember the job offer you got back in April. Vander said you were all but hired. Use that to lure them in, then when their defenses are down, pounce.

It was as good a plan as any, but that didn't stop the nagging voice inside her that said her parents wouldn't do a damn thing to help her. While she knew her parents weren't the harshest out there, she still thought it a little heartless for them to force her to pay rent at eighteen or move out when neither her brother nor sister had to.

Jared and Garnet never got arrested.

It didn't matter. Her parents never helped her when she'd been behind paying them rent. Why would they help her now? She'd once had to pawn off a gold bracelet they'd bought her for her sixteenth birthday so she could make her payment. Granted, she'd splurged that month on new oils and brushes, but her parents never approved of her art.

And that bracelet was hideous, so maybe they did you a favor.

Either way, she'd see this through till the end. She kept her head high as she unlocked the front door.

The drapes were pulled shut, casting the house in darkness. She squinted against the sudden change in lighting, giving her eyes a second to adjust.

A lone shadow lay hunched in the hallway.

The back of her neck prickled. "Hello?"

The lump didn't move. Gripping her side bag, she pushed the door open wider with her shoe. The sun spilled into the hallway, not quite reaching the far end where it led into the kitchen.

Get a grip, Cali. How do you know that thing isn't a new piece of furniture Mom and Dad bought?

She squinted against the sun's reflection cast on the wood floor and hesitantly made her way in.

Her heart stopped. "Whoa."

The body slouched up against the wall was surrounded by a pool of bright red blood.

That's a lot of blood.

She was going to be sick.

Don't panic, don't panic, don't . . .

She sucked up her fear and approached. What if he was still alive?

With all that blood? Yeah, right.

The man couldn't have been any older than thirty-five. He had brown hair and plain features, nothing to make him stand out in a crowd, unless one factored in the current piece of wood sticking out of his chest.

Dropping her bag, she inched closer. Was that a stirring spoon?

All panic fled as concern took root in her gut. She called out, "Mom? Dad?" The prickling at the back of her neck intensified, and nothing but dead silence greeted her.

Movement at her feet had her jumping back with a shriek. The dead man slumped forward, his body caving in on itself. The skin started to sink in as if aging decades right before her eyes. This most definitely wasn't a sign of rigor mortis, and with morbid fascination she watched as the body continued to shrivel until all that was left started to crumble and turn to ash.

Cali wanted to scream, but her throat closed up, her eyes fixed to the sight before her.

She had to find Mom and Dad.

Trying to control the trembling of her limbs, she edged toward the kitchen, keeping as far from where the man had been as possible.

"Don't freak," she told herself. "There has to be some sort of reasonable explanation. You're not going insane."

But how did she know that? Didn't all the research say that a person never knew when they were crazy?

She shook her head and stopped dead in her tracks as she entered the kitchen. "Mom!" She rushed to her mother's prone form on the floor, her father within arm's reach. "Holy shit." She checked her mother's wrists, felt no pulse, cursed and fumbled around at her neck.

The pulse was slow but steady.

Cali sagged in relief, her muscles turning to jelly. She crawled to her father and checked his throat. She'd never been good at taking radial pulses.

"What the hell happened here?" The kitchen hadn't been touched. There was no sign of a struggle. It was as if some kind of assassin had snuck in, incapacitated her parent's and then gotten stabbed in the chest. But by whom?

The light coming through the open threshold flickered.

With a sinking sensation, she realized she'd left the front door wide open.

*

It couldn't be real.

Felix took the next corner a little too sharply. He'd always hoped—hell, he'd dreamed of finding the one woman who was meant for him. That one person he wouldn't have to hide himself from, but after so many years he'd simply given up. He'd stopped looking for any sort of companionship ever since Collette—

He cut the thought off as soon as he'd had it, but that didn't stop the memories.

Jasmine. Dead.

The bullet scar along his left shoulder stung. He ignored the phantom pain and sped through a yellow light. He'd learned the hard way that his life would never permit him to date or get close to any normal girl.

And if this girl was another *normal* person to save?

Was it possible Niella had Dreamed wrong? He doubted it, but it tempered his excitement. He needed to stay level headed. There was no point getting riled up over a fantasy that'd been haunting him for four years. The only living proof he'd been given had been shot down the very same day. By him.

He turned down the last street and scanned the houses for their numbers. It wasn't necessary. The house had the front door wide open.

His hands tightened around the steering wheel.

Was he too late?

He parked on the curb one house up and ran from his car. His eyes caught a large, navy blue van two houses down. The hair prickled at the back of his neck.

He stepped through the front door.

Silence greeted him. The drapes were drawn shut, casting the house in shadows, the sun carving a shaft of light through the dim hallway.

Something shimmered at the end of the hall. He gently shut the door. He took measured steps deeper into the still house. No matter how quiet it was, that didn't mean he was alone.

The hallway led into a kitchen but before he stepped through the threshold he squatted down next to the shimmering pile of ash. He passed his hand right through it. "Illusionist."

A chill swept down his spine. This was not another vigilante rescue mission. The seriousness of Ell's prescience crashed down on him. He'd just run head first into something he had no concept of.

Other people with powers were involved.

Movement darted past the archway that connected to the kitchen. The shape female.

Felix jumped to his feet. "Hey." She was reaching for a drawer, and he had a pretty good idea what was inside. He grabbed her before she could get her hands on something pointy.

Her body jerked. Felix hissed as a jolt went straight through his system.

"Don't touch me." She started to struggle but he dropped her instantly, having no idea what had ripped through his body.

She stumbled. Dark brown hair covered her face until she whirled on him, her hands held like claws near her chest, ready to strike.

She faltered when she caught sight of him. He was pretty sure his face held the same expression.

She was tall.

It was the first thing he fixated on. And why not? Sydney didn't even reach his shoulder, and Niella was bound to a wheelchair. He'd met tall women before, when they came into the bakery, but none of them was this tall.

Not without high heels, anyway.

She had to be at least five-ten. Her shoulder-length, dark chocolate hair was cut in an edgy fashion with side bangs. Her eyes were polished onyx and her skin had a faint golden tinge, as if she'd just begun enjoying the So Cal summer sun. She had on a loose-fitting tee and jean shorts with sneakers. It emphasized her lean build. Felix's whole body tightened. It looked as if she'd been made for him.

Her eyes finished their own appreciative assessment of him. His appearance had caught her off guard. The thought made him smile.

When she noticed his attention all emotion was wiped from her face. She regarded him coldly. "Who are you?"

He gave a bow from the waist, making sure to keep his eyes locked with hers. "Felix Del Valle."

Her eyes raked him again. His blood rushed south.

Calm. Stay calm.

She took a step back from him and glanced down the hall toward the front door. "Did you kill that man?"

He frowned. There was no man . . .

Then he remembered. The Illusion.

He ground his teeth. Niella was right. This was some kind of trap. Someone was setting her up. But for what, he didn't know. "No, but I need to get you out of here." Every instinct inside him raged for him to protect her. "You're in danger. This is a trap, some kind of set up. There was a dark blue van parked two houses down. I thought I might have been too late, but either way I don't think we have much time."

She looked at him like he was crazy and stepped back. He wanted to follow. He wanted to be near her, to smell her hair and touch her skin.

She glanced over her shoulder. Felix followed the movement and spotted a man and a woman on the floor.

Shit.

"There's no way I'm leaving my parents," she said.

He didn't blame her, only now his chances of getting her to leave with him went from slim to none. There had to be something he could—

His gaze shot back to the girl's parents. He stared hard, knowing he hadn't imagined it.

It came again. The slightest shimmer along their shoulders, like an image struggling to stay in focus.

An Illusion.

The air left his lungs. "Son of a bitch."

That could only mean two things. One, the Illusionist was getting tired. Two, he was still close by.

He swung his attention back to the girl. She jumped back.

He ran a hand through his hair. How the hell was he supposed to explain this?

"Look, your parents aren't real."

Her eyebrows rose and her foot darted out behind her, seeking an escape.

Great start, Felix.

He took a hesitant step sideways, trying to ease his way over to where the Illusion of her parents resided. If he could get her to reach out and touch them then she'd see that they weren't real. The Illusion was fading, the power draining, which meant they were going to lose their solidity.

She watched his progress with blazing eyes, but she didn't retreat. He took that as a good sign.

When he got within a foot of the Illusion he stopped. She looked ready to strike if he so much as sneezed at the Illusion wrong. "I'm not going to harm them," he tried soothing her. "But you have to believe me when I tell you they're not real. If you'd simply touch them you'd know." He started to lower himself. All he'd have to do was show her, then she'd see . . .

"I've already touched them. I felt for a pulse. It's there—faint— but there. And if you so much as harm one hair on my father I'll make that trick you pulled with the stirring spoon on the man in the hall look downright enjoyable."

Felix halted his hand where it was inching out to touch the shoulder of her father. "Stirring spoon?" What the hell had been back in that hallway?

She didn't elaborate on what she had seen and Felix didn't ask. There was no time. He could sense the minutes ticking by.

There was another faint glimmer from the Illusion. Time was running out. If the Illusion dropped then he had a feeling their time was up.

"Would you just watch?" he bit out. "Nothing is going to make sense to you right now but if you'd simply watch, it would really cut down on all the explaining I'd have to do."

He looked up and found she'd retreated a few steps.

He lightened his tone. "Please."

He didn't wait for her to respond. He eyed her father and slowly lowered his hand. If the Illusion remained solid, he was so totally fucked.

His hand slid right through the back of her father's shoulder blade. He sighed in relief and kept his hand where it obviously sat in the middle of the Illusion's body.

He looked up to explain. "I know it looks—"

She'd made a break for it.

He exhaled. "Fucking hell."

*

Cali didn't wait. As Felix's hand reached out for her father she took it on blind faith that he bore no malicious intent toward her dad. Besides, it was the perfect opportunity. Felix was distracted, and Cali had spotted the portable phone on the bench by the front door. As much as it pained her to turn her back on her parents, she had to contact the police. Her parents were unconscious and defenseless, and she was alone with a murderer.

And just what the hell had happened back there when she'd first laid eyes on him? God, when he'd introduced himself with that elegant bow, his brilliant blue-green eyes locked with hers . . . the effect had been positively electric.

Her fast-acting lunge only carried her as far as the hall before a pair of warm, firm arms wrapped around her waist. "Yeah, I don't think so." His breath brushed against her neck, causing a shiver to run down her body. Her knees buckled.

Felix's arms locked around her as they went down with a grunt. He twisted at the last minute, his firm chest cushioning her fall.

One of her hands landed on his sternum. She felt his heart kick start beneath her palm.

She snatched her hand back as if burned.

His eyes locked with hers. "You don't understand—" he started to say but she refused to listen. She needed to get out of his arms. His touch did something to her, made her feel things best left unnoticed.

That strange prickling at the back of her neck started up again.

She'd never been very good at fighting, but she'd spent a lot of time with her older brother when she was little. He'd been a wrestler, and she'd been famous for her flexibility that allowed her to maneuver out of his holds.

Felix must have seen the determination in her face because he quit talking. His arms wrapped tight around her back. She ignored the flutter in her chest and twisted her limber body out and under his arms.

He swore. "Look, I don't want to hurt you," he pleaded as Cali shot to her feet. He was behind her in an instant, his fingers curling around her wrist like a vise. She ducked the left side of her body, going down to one knee while simultaneously turning her torso and arm out and around, breaking his grip. His other hand shot out in an attempt to make up lost ground. She pushed up with her bent leg, throwing her right shoulder back to pivot out of his reach.

She collided with the stair banister, and pain spiked up her spine as the wood hit one of her vertebrae.

Felix winced, hesitating in his pursuit.

It was all the opening she needed. She dove for the phone. Her fingers closed clumsily around it as her momentum drove her into the living room. It was one of those sunken rooms that she swore she'd never get in her own home specifically for this reason. She'd forgotten the drop-off was there. She tried to stop herself from landing on her face but her foot met nothing but air.

A yelp whooshed out of her as her stomach smashed into the hard back of her dad's favorite leather chair. She took in a pained gulp of air and rolled as Felix grabbed for her.

"Would you stop already?" He sounded beyond frustrated. "You're my Mirror Mate. I'm not going to harm you."

Ignoring him, she hit the *talk* button on the phone, her finger shaking over the 9. The button gave the appropriate *beep* before Felix caught her in his arms again. Cali swirled around, having no qualms about fighting dirty, and kicked him in the shin as hard as she could. His blue-green eyes widened in pain.

She expected him to release her, but instead her kick must have disrupted his equilibrium because he lost balance, and together they fell onto the beige leather couch.

She kept the phone above her head to keep it from getting crushed between them. She squirmed against him but only succeeded in pressing her body closer to the hard planes of his.

Heat pooled low in her gut.

She brought the phone close to her face and hit the 1.

"I said stop." One of his arms snaked out from under her, giving a showy wave, and just like that the phone *vanished*.

"Holy shit."

Cali stared at her hand, waiting for the phone to reappear. It didn't. Her shock started to diminish as the realization that Felix was still atop her sank in, his tall, powerful body pressing hers into the material of the sofa.

He was a magician.

It was the only explanation her mind could come up with.

"How—?"

Her mouth went dry as her eyes bored into his oceanic ones. The prickling on her neck increased as all sound seemed to fade from existence except theirs. Her breathing was loud and harsh, and she could've sworn she heard the pounding of Felix's heart like thunder.

A look of awe came over him as his gaze fell to her lips. She licked them instinctively but they continued to tingle. "What's your name?" he asked her.

In the strange stillness of the house, his words reverberated in her ears louder than normal.

She found her own gaze dropping to his mouth and forced her eyes back up to his. They met with a spark.

"Cali Crazar," her traitorous mouth spoke.

A boyish grin tugged at his mouth. "Cali." He seemed to test her name on his tongue. "Cali from *Cali*-fornia."

She glared daggers at him and he laughed.

"How did you make the phone disappear? Are you a magician?" A murderous magician, she tried to remind herself. *Don't forget you still have no idea who this man is.* But she couldn't dispute the fact that if he wanted to hurt her he would have done it by now.

Amusement sparkled in his eyes. His thumb reached out and brushed her lips. Her heart pounded against her ribs, her nipples hardening where they were pushed against his firm chest. "No, I'm most definitely *not* a magician."

She didn't believe him. He had to be. Phones didn't simply vanish, and dimly in the recesses of her mind she recalled that there had been no sign of the dead body in the hallway when she'd gone for the phone.

Strangest. Day. Ever.

Felix's head dipped close to hers.

Alarms shot through her brain.

Pull away. Spit in his face. Do something!

She couldn't, even if she wanted to. Something inside her simply responded to him. She couldn't resist. She'd wanted him as soon as she'd laid eyes on him, and that want frightened her.

The warmth of his lips ghosted over hers. Heat rolled through her body.

The front door burst open.

Chapter 2

In the silence of the house the crash sounded like an explosion. Cali winced as pain tore through her ear-drums.

Above her, Felix's face contorted with agony. Like a picture returning to focus, regular white noise flooded the room. Felix rolled off her.

She went to sit up but the room started to spin. She lay back down. She was tired, as if she'd expended a large amount of energy in only a few seconds. She turned her head. It was about the only thing she could still do. Two bulking men in black flanked a thin, regal-looking woman with delicately waved hair.

She spotted Cali instantly, her grayish-blue eyes holding no emotion. "Get the girl."

Cali's jaw clenched. She was *not* a girl. She was twenty-four and lived on her own. Sort of.

Her temper was short-lived as the two men started into the living room. They lacked any sort of grace as they lumbered toward her.

And where the hell was her knight in shining armor?

Gone, she decided. She swallowed the sudden stab of disappointment. Fine. She didn't need that murderous bastard anyway.

The shorter one reached her first. He took hold of her right ankle, giving her an opportunity to gather her strength and kick out with her left leg. She nailed him in the face, but it was like hitting a brick wall for all the good it did.

My strength is obviously lacking today.

Now with a bloody nose and a pissed expression, the man nodded to his partner. "Take her arms."

Panic started to set in. If they took hold of her arms, there'd be no way she could squirm from their holds. She needed to get up. What had zapped her energy?

The taller of the thugs came at her with a grim determination. Cali balled her fists, prepared to go out fighting.

She never got a chance.

Felix sprang from the archway that connected the living room to another section of the kitchen. One of her father's bookends rested in his hand, and he slammed it down right at the base of the man's skull. The thug went down with a groan.

He didn't release the bookend, but eyed the man who was holding her ankle. Felix radiated protectiveness, and Cali tried not to stare. But it was damn hard not to. He was like some pissed guardian angel. Dark, slightly curled hair fell into those beautiful eyes that glittered against the bronze of his skin. His five o'clock shadow added an edge to his appearance, and he looked even taller from her vantage point on the couch, his wide shoulders and well-muscled frame taking up what felt like all the space in the room. Her body clenched in response.

"Felix?"

Cali's attention was ripped from Felix at the sound of the lilting feminine voice.

The woman stared transfixed at Felix. His face held the exact same confusion. "Collette?"

Too many expressions crossed his face for Cali to read any of them, so she summed it up to something like *motherfucker*.

There was history here between them. She could all but feel it. Her stomach lurched as if she'd swallowed something vile.

Felix's fingers tightened around her father's bookend. "What the hell are you doing here?" he demanded.

"I could ask you the very same question. You weren't scripted into this performance." Those blue-grey eyes speared Cali right through the chest before settling back to Felix. "I'm simply following orders. So tell me, Felix, what exactly are you doing here?" She looked positively eager to hear the answer.

Felix didn't budge an inch.

His silence only made the curl to Collette's lip grow. "Protecting your interests perhaps?"

His knuckles went white around her father's bookend but still he didn't answer.

Collette's second assessment of Cali was done with narrowed eyes. She was searching for something, but what that was, Cali had no clue. "No bother then. What the hell are you waiting for?" she snapped at the man holding Cali's ankle.

The thug's fingers tightened instantly.

Cali winced as he dug into her bone.

Felix took a step toward them, voice fierce. "Don't."

Collette turned on him like he was nothing more than an annoying gnat. "You never did learn your place." She gave a dismissive wave of her hand.

White cloth appeared out of nowhere like a nest of angry snakes. With a snap like thunder, Felix was encased and dropped to the floor.

Cali blinked.

What. The. Hell?

Fear gripped her. She searched desperately for Felix over the coffee table but the thug at her feet gave a pull on her ankle, causing her to slide halfway across the sofa toward him. A startled gasp escaped her. She grabbed blindly for the sides of the couch while at the same time she kept an eye trained on Collette. Her mind stuttered to try to make sense of what was going on around her. What the hell had Collette done? How could she possibly have done it?

Felix picked himself up off the floor, not a trace of the white cloth in sight. "And where exactly was my place, Collette? At your side like some lackey?" He paused. "Like Kevin?"

Rage flooded Collette's face, a truly terrifying expression that held a pinch of madness.

Her fingers turned to claws, and she lunged for Felix's throat.

His eyes widened in genuine surprise, and for a moment he looked at a loss for what to do.

Cali tried to call out to him, but another pull at her ankle had her collapsing back on the couch. She lost sight of them. Her focus turned to the man who was reeling her in like so much fish. He leered down at her with a sardonic smile, enjoying her poor attempts at rebellion. *Bastard.* She felt like kicking him in the face again. But she knew that wouldn't work. Instead she eyed the hand around her ankle. Taking a gamble that he wouldn't catch her intent and move his hand, she brought her left leg up and drove the heel of her foot as hard as she could toward her own ankle.

He didn't react fast enough, and the thick heel of her shoe smashed into the top of his hand. His fingers shot open like she'd pulled a release lever. Cali turned on her side to grab the large picture book of castles that her mother kept on the coffee table. With two hands, she swung for all she was worth and smacked her attacker across the side of his face. The hit disoriented him. His hands shot out as if to grab something but they met with nothing. The sudden shift in his weight caused him to overcompensate, and he went down. The side of his head met the edge of the sharp coffee table.

She stared down at him. "Shit," she breathed. She'd never knocked anyone out before.

A strangled cry of frustration had her rearing up. Collette stumbled back from Felix who was engaging three—four?—men.

Cali blinked, not quite able to follow what was happening. For every step the men around Felix took toward him, he took one back and waved his hand. *Poof!* They were gone. Stranger still was when he didn't react fast enough and the men that hadn't vanished yet threw a punch. A punch that never landed as their hands seemed to shimmer out of existence and pass right through him.

A few feet away Collette was breathing heavily.

Her eyes locked with Cali's.

"You." She threw an arm up and those twisted white strips of cloth came barreling at her.

She'd like to say that she jumped back in time, or that she put up a fight, but in reality her body froze. Froze like a fucking deer in the headlights.

The cloths brushed her face, the lightest of touches, before they shimmered and faded from view.

Collette snarled something but Felix was advancing on her. "You're too tired, Collette." He dodged a blow that wouldn't have landed anyway and waved his hand. "All this is pointless. Your Illusions are failing."

"Shut up." She threw her arm out. Blood bloomed on the side of Felix's arm. A dagger stuck out from the wall behind him, still vibrating. "You don't know anything, Felix." It was her turn to advance on him. "But I'm hoping soon you will."

Cali shuddered at the look Collette shot her way. But it was that look that undid whatever kept her frozen to the floor. She might have been caught unaware before, but she was damned if she was going to get carted off by this psycho bitch without putting up a fight.

"Is she important to you? Is that why you are here?" Collette's eyes didn't leave Cali, though her words were aimed at Felix. "There's something more to this scene. I can feel it."

The white binding cloth shot out again, and this time Cali was ready for it. She hurled herself over the back of the sofa. The impact of the cloth hitting reverberated down the back of the couch. Again Cali shuddered. How much force could Collette generate to have cloth hit with that much of an impact?

She wasn't going to wait around and find out. She eyed the archway that led into the kitchen. If she could make it in there without getting detected, she could slip out the back door.

Mom and Dad . . .

She couldn't leave them, but she couldn't very well help them in her position, either. Gritting her teeth, she got down on all fours and slowly crawled her way out from behind the couch.

The tingle at the back of her neck started again. Her vision blackened around the edges but she shook it back and exhaled, all the while willing her body to absolute silence.

Felix was keeping Collette occupied. Cali pulled her gaze away from them. Her headache was bad enough; she didn't need to make it worse by trying to make sense of the scene going on around her.

She made it into the kitchen without incident, but it wasn't until she was on the tile floor that she noticed it.

She wasn't making a sound.

Her mind had to be playing tricks on her. She placed her hand flat on the cold tile and pulled up. There was no sound of suction, no whisper of skin coming off a surface, only silence.

The tingling at the back of her neck intensified, and she rolled her head to try to ease the tension but it did little good.

O-kay . . .

She pushed any thoughts about what was happening out of her head and got to her feet.

Deal later. Right now you need to focus. Mom and Dad—
Were gone.

She cursed. And in her sudden haste to get to the area where they had last been, she couldn't remember if she'd heard the word come out of her mouth or not.

She took in the yellow kitchen, the white marble, and the flowery curtains, searching for any sign that her parents had regained consciousness and then left. But wouldn't they have heard what was going on in the living room? Wouldn't they have intervened if they'd seen her?

Her mind was a jumbled mess.

She raced to the back door, her hand on the handle when a pained grunt came from the front of the house.

Felix.

Her chest constricted. She couldn't leave him.

She flew to the kitchen sink, yanking open drawers.

Even if she had no idea who he was or how the hell he'd become entangled in this gigantic mess that was her life, he'd done nothing to warrant being injured.

Her dad had always wanted to keep a gun in the house for protection, but her mother was squeamish. She had insisted on a Taser instead, and Dad, ever dutiful, went out and got her one.

Cali found it in the very back of the kitchen junk drawer. It was fully loaded and ready. She ran through the kitchen, bypassing the hallway that led to the front, and went through the third entrance of the kitchen that connected with the dining room. The dining room opened up to the hallway and front door, the bottom floor of the house connecting in one large circle with a central hallway, putting her directly behind Collette. Her head kept darting to the sofa, no doubt thinking Cali was still hiding behind the couch.

Arrogant bitch.

Cali crept up on her, her body still disturbingly quiet. When she cleared the stairs she could see into the living room and saw that Felix was surrounded by even more guard-type men. Only this time they had no faces.

She faltered at the sight.

It was as if Felix were fighting a group of mannequins someone hadn't bothered taking the time to detail.

Collette hunched into herself, her shirt plastered to her back from sweat.

Felix was spinning around in a circle, his hands waving frantically. Only as each body vanished another one was already waiting.

Collette threw her hands wildly, and like the faceless men, the sharp shards that appeared had no detail or substance, almost resembling thin slices of mirror. The weapons went straight for Felix. He spun around just in time, his hand waving, the dagger-like pieces blipping out of existence inches away from him.

"We can do this all day, Collette," he said with an air that defied his heavy breathing.

"You haven't changed a bit, Felix. You're still playing the good guy, wearing his persona. You try to hide that darkness within you, but I see it. You might not use your gift to make people vanish, but you've erased others from this plane just the same."

His jaw ticked, and the next shard nicked him along the back of his hand.

Cali couldn't follow the conversation completely but she did agree with Collette on one thing. Why the hell didn't he make her vanish into thin air?

Raising the Taser, she stepped deeper into the room until she caught Felix's gaze. Disbelief was written all over his handsome face.

Collette caught sight of his hesitation before he could look away. "What are you—?"

Cali shot the Taser at her.

Collette's body convulsed before dropping. The guards that surrounded Felix turned to mist.

Cali dropped the Taser, a stab of unwanted guilt assailing her. She pushed it away.

Felix rushed to her. His arms came around her. They felt good. *Too* good.

The front door was thrown open. "Felix! Don't worry, I'm here. You're Shielded. You're—whoa." A blonde woman nearly collided right into the stairs. Her arms flailed until she caught the banister of the stairs. Readjusting herself, she found her footing and turned.

Her golden locks fell just past her shoulders. Her green eyes lit up with genuine joy. "You're all right!"

Felix unwound his arms from around Cali. She missed the sensation instantly and wrapped her own arms around her body as a poor substitute.

"Sydney? What are you doing here?" he asked.

Sydney glanced Cali's way and gave a welcoming wave before

returning her attention to Felix. Her bright expression darkened slightly.

"Niella told me what she Dreamed. Way to leave me in the dark. I went looking for you but you were gone. I came as soon as I could. What the hell do you think you were doing, anyway?" she scolded. "You could have gotten seriously injured, you dumbass. You have no idea who—" Her gaze caught on Collette, noticing her for the first time. Recognition flashed briefly. Her voice dropped, and Cali could just barely detect the fear behind it. "What is she doing here?"

Felix shook his head.

Sydney turned to Cali. "Was she the one that attacked you?"

Something tickled in the back of Cali's mind. "She said she was following orders."

Felix and Sydney both shared a look.

"She's a full-forced Illusionist, Felix. This wasn't the regular cookie cutter Dream from Niella."

Felix's face was solemn. "I know."

"How'd you take her out?" Sydney walked a small perimeter around Collette as if looking for signs of life.

Cali wanted to step forward. She wanted to boast that she'd taken a Taser to Collette and hadn't needed Felix's help. Only her vision started going black again. A sudden wave of exhaustion hit, and she reached out blindly.

Warm fingers grasped hers before everything went dark.

Chapter 3

Felix wrapped his arms around Cali as her body went limp. It lasted only a second. A dizzy spell? Had she fainted? Either way she was back on her feet shortly. She averted her eyes from his as she pushed away from him. He wished she wouldn't do that.

Put space between them.

He bit back a growl of frustration.

"I'm okay," she said before he or Sydney could ask.

Sydney, ever the doctor, came up and got right in Cali's face. Cali gave a start but she didn't back down.

Felix's lip curled.

"Too much, too soon," Sydney diagnosed.

"Huh?" Cali said articulately.

Sydney leaned back, arms crossed. "You used too much of your powers too soon. I take it you've never used them this much, if at all?"

"Power?"

"You're a Silencer. You know . . ." She wiggled her hands in a way that had Felix biting back a laugh. "You manipulate sound. I'm a Shielder." She thrust her hand out. "Sydney Spencer. I block everyone's powers around me."

Cali hesitated before shaking her hand. "Cali Crazar," she said carefully. "Nice to meet you." She turned on Felix. "And you're what? The Vanisher?"

He grinned at her sarcasm. "Eraser."

She rolled her eyes. "Of course."

"I don't know about you guys but I have a feeling we need to get out of here." Sydney kicked the unconscious Collette without remorse. "I'm sure there's going to be reinforcements when she doesn't report in."

Felix couldn't agree more.

Collette. Here.

Shit.

Shitshit*shit!*

The scar along his shoulder burned insistently. Every scenario he played out in his head ended poorly. Collette showing up here couldn't be coincidence. She had to know. The way she eyed Cali . . . it was as if she knew Cali was his missing half. His Mirror Mate.

Was this some kind of revenge gig then? An eye for an eye? The poetic and barbaric justice suited Collette to a T. He'd destroyed her Mirror Mate so she would get his?

Well, it wouldn't fucking work that way.

He reached for Cali's hand, wanting the contact, craving it like he'd never craved anything before in his life. His whole body was tuned into her, and it took all his control to stay his more intense impulses. "We should go out the back in case anyone was left in that van two houses down."

Cali swung her hand out from under his right before they touched. Their eyes locked. Felix grew hot and cold all at once.

Fuck, he wanted her.

Those insanely dark eyes left his quickly. Had she seen the carnal need raging within him? "I can't leave. All this"—she encompassed the whole house—"aren't we supposed to, I don't know, report it to the cops? We were attacked. What if my parents come back? They probably made a run for it."

"They didn't leave." He tried to say it gently. She needed to understand that her parents hadn't been real. "They were an Illusion. Like whatever it is you saw in the hallway. I'm guessing they were Collette's doing. They were planning this, Cali."

Her fisted hands came to rest on her hips. "Oh, yeah? And how the hell did they know I was going to be here? I don't live here anymore."

"A Dreamer," Sydney spoke up softly.

Cali spun on her. "A what?"

"Dreamer," Felix answered for her. "They have visions. Past, present, future. They usually don't have control over it unless they're a full-forced Dreamer." Was that how Collette had known to find Cali? But the only full-forced Dreamer he knew was Kevin, and he was in no position to help Collette.

"Look," Sydney said. "We'll explain everything to you, but we really need to get a move on. For whatever reason someone is after you." She stared pointedly at Collette. "That's bad news in my book."

"I can't just get up and leave," Cali persisted, stubbornly.

Sydney gave him an exasperated and somewhat expectant look. He gave her his own look. "What?"

"Can't you do something here?"

"What do you want me to do?"

"She's your Mirror Mate," she said. "Can't you, I don't know, control her or something?"

Felix gave her a wry smile. "I don't think it works that way, Syd."

"Well, it should," she huffed. "It'd definitely make this easier."

He grinned. "As entertaining as that thought might be, now is not the time to dwell on it." They needed to get out of here. Apart of him wanted to stay so he could question Collette when she awoke, but she was too unstable. Who knew how strong she'd be when she woke up? A full-forced Illusionist was nothing to mess around with. *Especially one you've scorned.* Ignoring his inner voice, he turned to his predicted Mirror Mate. She seemed to be handling everything relatively well, considering she hadn't flipped out and called him a freak yet.

He tried for logic. "Let's say your parents were real. If they left, then I'm sure they're getting the police as we speak."

That did it. Some of the edge left her shoulders and she rubbed at her temples. "That man . . ." She gestured down the hall to where it dead-ended into the kitchen. "He's gone, too. There isn't even a sign of his blood. How is that even possible?"

His eyes caught Sydney's.

They were both thinking the same thing. Someone was going to painstaking ends to set Cali up.

What the hell was Collette up to?

His confusion grew, as did his anger.

Cali started toward the kitchen, pausing to pick up a large, duffel-type purse and sling it over her shoulder. Her attention crept to where the first Illusion had been. She was trying to piece it together, to explain it to herself, and Felix kept quiet. She was strong, but even the strongest of people broke when their world was flipped too fast.

Hell, he'd locked himself in his room for two months when he'd first used his powers.

He understood all too well about the fear, the loneliness, that feeling of being lost.

"Are you guys some type of special military branch?" she finally spoke up.

Sydney held back a laugh.

"Not exactly," he hedged. What to tell her? They didn't even have a name for their little super squad. All he had was, "Hey, we go out and try to prevent disasters when Niella Dreams of them. And don't forget we even save cats from really high trees!"

The truth was that they were a small group. Very small. They had no idea if there was a military branch out there and personally he really didn't want to be some mad scientist's wet dream.

It was those types of thoughts that made secrecy so important to people like them.

"I know it's not a lot to go on," he began and then stopped. He cocked his head.

Cali's whole body tensed. "What?"

It came again. The slamming of car doors.

Sydney dashed to the front door and locked it. Cali jumped over Collette to pull back the curtains in the living room.

Her face froze. "Jared."

Felix couldn't help the white-hot jealousy that crashed through his body.

"Garnet." Cali spoke a second later.

Sydney hustled to pull Cali away from the window before she was spotted. "Who?"

"My brother and sister," said Cali.

The tension riding Felix's body eased.

"Right," said Sydney. "Time to move." She handed Cali off like a football, and Felix ushered her back toward the kitchen.

He heard Cali mumbling under her breath. "What are they doing here?"

A key jingled in the door.

Sydney drew up beside him. "Tell me again how this is going to work?"

He was supposed to have a plan? Didn't running in and saving the damn day count? "Uh, we run out the back and circle around to our cars?"

They'd reached the kitchen. The floor was clear of any bodies, though Cali kept searching the floor as if it held the missing answers.

As soon as they made it into the backyard they heard a male voice call out from the front door. "Cali?"

Felix cursed under his breath.

"Well, you can't blame them for searching for her," said Sydney. "They did, after all, park behind her car in the driveway." Something flashed across her face as soon as the words left her mouth, but Felix had no time to try and figure it out.

He wanted to run his hand through his hair but was too busy steering Cali. "Not now, Syd."

She strayed to one of the windows on the side of the house and peeked in. "They've found Collette." That didn't give them very much time before the police would be called. "Where'd you park?" Sydney asked him.

Hadn't she seen where he'd parked? "One house up," he told her. Then, with a sinking sensation, and a sudden understanding of her earlier expression, he asked, "Where'd *you* park?"

Sydney winced. "Don't go getting mad at me. You're the one that took off without telling anyone. I was just trying to help."

"Where did you park?" he repeated.

"In the driveway?"

"Dammit, Syd." This was not what he needed. Sure enough, as soon as they cleared the gate that led into the front yard, they saw Sydney's white Toyota Yaris trapped between a beat-up Nissan parked in front of it and a new Ford Ranger behind it.

New plan.

"We can't get to your car, Syd, so we'll pile into the Hummer. I hope you didn't leave anything valuable inside."

"I didn't know her brother and sister were going to come by," she defended.

Cali seemed to wake up from her shocked stupor. "Neither did I," she shot back.

Sydney ignored the comment. "Felix, the car's registered in my name. It has all my information inside the glove compartment. I have to move it."

"No time," he told her. He hated to do this to Sydney, but the less they were connected to whatever it was Collette was involved with, the better. He wasn't so much worried about the police finding them, but rather whoever Collette was working with finding them.

They stopped a few yards short of his Hummer, and he turned to Sydney's car.

Sydney eyed him up and down. Realization dawned. "Felix, don't you dare, I just bought that this spring."

The back of his neck began to prickle. He focused on her car. Fatigue beat at the edges of his awareness, warning him that he'd already used his powers a lot that day.

He waved his hand.

Her car blipped out of existence. There one second, gone the next.

"You bastard," Sydney hissed at him. "You owe me big." Her face was deadly. The expression was almost comical on her sun-tanned face. She'd get over it. Sydney couldn't stay mad at someone for longer than five minutes. Her incessant cheerfulness always overrode her anger.

When they reached his Hummer, he gave Cali a gentle nudge, signaling her to go around to the passenger seat. Sydney was already crawling into the back.

Once in the safety of his own car, he could breathe a little easier. Cali hesitated before getting in completely, a noise escaping her throat once she closed the door.

"Everything all right?" he asked.

Her eyes widened and a flush spread across her cheeks. "Fine." She stared out the window, arms crossed.

He wanted to press her for more details. Wanted to know if she had the same urge as he did to reach out and touch her. The setting sun flickered in through the car window, casting her in shadows. It exaggerated her dark hair and eyes. The mascara along her eyelashes seemed to glitter.

Sydney poked her head up between the two seats. "Hey Romeo," she burst into his thoughts quietly. "We going to get a move on or what?"

Cali turned.

He'd been caught but she didn't look away timidly. Her chin rose and her eyes narrowed.

Looks like she's finally breaking through the shock.

"You hustle me out of my parents' house to stare at me in a car?"

A smile split his lips.

Oh, yeah, he thought. *This is going to be fun.*

Chapter 4

Cali stared out the car window, trying to ignore her body's hypersensitivity to Felix and where he was in proximity to her. The scent of the ocean and freshly baked bread still lingered inside the Hummer, teasing her. The smell was positively intoxicating and she hadn't been able to help the moan of appreciation she'd let slip when she'd first entered the vehicle.

Felix had caught her red-handed, but she'd stared him down until he'd had to look away to start the car.

She'd let him think what he wanted. She was here for answers. She already knew they wouldn't hurt her, and she had to admit she was damn curious how Felix could make things disappear while that other woman, Collette, seemed able to make anything she wanted to *appear*. Not to mention her own inner turmoil as to what had been happening to her.

Did she believe them when they told her she could manipulate sound?

Yes.

No, she lied to herself.

She was going along to get answers. If she was in danger then it would seem idiotic to leave without any knowledge as to why. Someone was after her. Felix had come to help her. Felix had powers. Collette had powers. *She* had powers. What other explanation was there when she'd blacked out earlier? That prickling at the back of her neck . . . it hadn't been natural.

Questions consumed her, and she leaned her head back against the headrest to ease the ache that was starting.

There was only one way to get what you wanted. You had to chase after it.

Well, this was her, chasing it.

Buildings blurred past as they continued along the freeway. Their "getaway" was anything but fast-paced and exciting. Felix had pulled away from her parent's house as if he hadn't a care in the world. Now he kept his white H2 going at a steady five miles per hour above the speed limit as they headed westward, farther out toward the coast.

The freeway exit they took wasn't all that far from where Cali lived. The surprises kept on coming when they pulled into a small shopping plaza and parked outside a veterinary clinic.

Cali leaned forward to get a better look out the windshield. She tried to figure out the reason behind them stopping but none of the establishments popped out as offering getaway type necessities. There was the vet, a pizza place, laundry, groomers, and a dental office.

"Why are we stopping?"

"Welcome, Cali"—Sydney poked her head between the two front seats to say with much pride in her voice—"to our unofficial headquarters."

"This?" Cali couldn't help but blurt.

Felix shot her a cocky grin from behind Sydney. "Watch what you say about Sydney's baby."

"What's wrong with my clinic?"

Felix got out of the car, smothering a laugh.

Despite Sydney's petite size, she had a level stare that made Cali squirm. She didn't want to insult her.

Beneath those perfectly arched golden brows her eyes glittered with amusement as she waited for Cali's answer.

"Nothing's wrong with it. I was expecting something"—she floundered—"bigger."

The mirth behind Sydney's eyes faded.

Oops.

Felix saved her by opening the passenger door. Cali would have fallen out if she hadn't been belted in. She quickly undid the clasp and climbed out of the car, ignoring the hand Felix offered.

No touching, she told herself. *No matter how badly you want to.*

Felix dropped his hand and disguised his disappointment by leaning in to study Sydney. Both his eyebrows rose into his hairline. "Wow. What'd you say to her?"

Embarrassment flushed Cali's cheeks. "Nothing."

Sydney squeezed through the gap between the front seats to exit through the passenger side. "She called my clinic small," she said indignantly.

"Ouch." Felix bumped his shoulder against Cali's. "I told you to watch what you said to her."

Her shoulder tingled where he'd touched her. She glared at him.

Sydney didn't waste any more time on them as she went straight to the front door. She tried the handle but it was locked. She took out her keys, and still the door wouldn't open.

Cali tried to see through the glass. "Are you sure this is your clinic?" she asked skeptically.

Sydney narrowed her eyes and shook her head. "You're Felix's Mirror Mate all right," she mumbled. "Yes, this is my place," she spoke up, exasperated. "Joel must have Locked it." She pounded on the door.

A few seconds later a man appeared. For a moment Cali thought they really did have the wrong place, but a smile broke out on his face and he put his hand against the clear door. There was a faint click, though his hand never moved from the glass, and then Sydney was opening the door.

She rose onto her toes to kiss him. "Any trouble?"

"I should be asking you the same question." The man's navy blue eyes glittered with affection before they turned to Cali. "You must be the Silencer. I'm Joel Kegler, Locksmith."

She gave him the once over. He had at least three inches on her. He had thick, mahogany brown hair that looked a bit too long and in need of a haircut. His skin was a nice, golden brown from obvious sun exposure like Sydney's, but what caught Cali's eye were his hands. They were covered with scars, some going all the way up his forearms.

"Oh, these." He caught her staring. "I used to work on cars with my old man when I was little. Let me tell you, hot oil *burns*, and steel cuts mighty deeply."

"And now you're a locksmith?" That seemed like a rather strange transition.

He flashed a bright set of straight teeth. "Actually, I'm a computer technician. I was referring to my power." His brow furrowed at her expression.

Another person who claimed to have powers? If they weren't a military branch, then what the hell were they? Some kind of club? Super heroes anonymous?

"You have no idea what I'm talking about, do you?"

Felix came up behind her. She could feel the heat coming off him. Her skin felt too tight for her body. She wanted to step away but there was nowhere to retreat. Joel and Sydney blocked her path.

"We're here to explain things to her," said Felix.

"And keep her safe," said Sydney.

"You can explain things later. I want to know what the hell happened out there," a voice called from behind the counter on her right.

Seated at the reception desk, a woman shuffled through some papers. She had hazel eyes and oak-brown hair that was cut in a popular pixie fashion. There was a faint scar on the bottom left of her lip indicating that at one time she'd had her lip pierced. Her nametag read Niella Souveray. Their eyes met. "You look exactly as I Dreamed."

As far as introductions went, this had to be the strangest. This was the woman who'd had a vision about her? Cali had one question—why her?

Niella's interest in her was fleeting as she directed her attention to Felix. "Well? I take it you got there in time, but that tells me next to nothing. What are we up against?" There was something haunted behind her eyes, something that told Cali that Niella had an idea of what they were up against but didn't want to believe it.

A shudder ran through her.

Felix's hesitation was slight. "We ran into Collette." His voice was low, rough.

Niella pushed out from behind the desk, giving Cali a glimpse of her wheelchair.

She was paralyzed?

Niella wheeled herself into the middle of the lobby. Felix's answer wasn't what she had expected. Her face clouded and all she said was, "Huh."

"'Huh?' That's all you have to say? If this isn't coming to you as a shock then why the hell didn't you tell me there would be people with powers there? That Collette would be there?"

Joel stepped forward. "Easy, Felix. Niella didn't tell you because she didn't know."

Niella's jaw tensed. "I don't need defending because I'm a damn cripple," she bit out at Joel.

The retort was like a slap to the face, and for a moment Joel looked at a loss for what to say. His expression hardened, and he opened his mouth then shut it again. "My defense had nothing to do with the fact that you're in a wheelchair," he said at last. He turned from her to walk over to the far wall where a row of seats was assembled before large stacks of dog food.

Aren't they one big happy family? Cali thought.

Niella ignored Joel and the awkward silence that followed. "I didn't tell you, Felix, because I didn't Dream Collette." She closed her eyes, her brow wrinkling. "There was someone else."

Felix crossed his arms over his broad chest. "Who? 'Cause whoever they are, they'd have to be pretty desperate to stage a kidnapping in the middle of the damn day."

Niella shook her head and opened her eyes. "A man. That's all I've got. Who else was there besides Collette? A man?" The rest of them shuffled their way farther into the lobby so they were no longer clustered around the entrance.

Felix stayed by Cali's side and gave a shrug. "Two of them, but there was nothing special about them. Does this man that you've seen have powers?"

"I'm not sure. It's hard to tell." There was more to it. Cali could read it on Niella's face, but the Dreamer didn't say anything more. Cali didn't know if she was grateful that there was nothing else to discuss regarding her would-be captor, or if she should be worried.

"How'd you end up stopping Collette?" Niella asked.

Felix wrapped an arm casually around Cali's shoulders. She tensed on instinct. "Cali Tasered the hell out of her."

The corners of Niella's mouth curled into a quick smile before the smile faded. "Good to know at least one of you can handle yourself."

Cali found herself smiling. Despite Niella's strange moods, she could picture the two of them getting along.

Felix dropped his arm from around Cali to place his palm over his heart. "Your words wound me, Ell. But you know, for driving in there half blind, we didn't do too badly."

Whatever tension there was left in the room slipped away.

"All right," Sydney intervened, "you guys may have nothing else to do, but I still have to finish up for the day. Niella, were you able to reschedule the remaining appointments when I had to leave?"

"Every one."

Sydney started to move around the large main lobby. It was filled with bags and bags of dog food. Leashes hung on the wall to the left, flea treatments close by. Toys, treats, and everything Cali could think a new pet owner would need surrounded the perimeter. Sydney made her way toward a large bag of food that was already opened and badly resealed. "Good. The last appointments that I had to bail on, did you give them their complimentary food bag—Ah!" She screamed, jumping back to knock into Joel.

Niella quickly rolled out of the way as Felix rushed over, Cali right behind him.

"Gadget!" Felix cried scooping up a fat gray rat.

Sydney squealed.

Cali's brow rose. "Aren't you supposed to love animals?"

"I do. All animals except *rats*." She pointed to the cute plump rodent in Felix's hands. "I told you to keep him out of here."

"I swear, Syd, I try, but he's got a mind of his own. I have no idea how he got here." He brought the rat up to his face and brushed his cheek against it affectionately.

Sydney cringed at the display of affection.

An odd rush of warmth came over Cali before it was interrupted by her purse vibrating against her side. Startled, she started to dig through her things until she found her cell phone. Glancing at the ID, she stepped out of the clinic before anyone could say anything, answering the call.

"Hey, Jared." She tried for nonchalance.

"Cali!" Her brother's voice came barreling through the phone. "Are you okay? I've called you a million times. Where are you? Are you hurt?" Cali flinched at the concern laced through his voice. How was she supposed to tell him she was fine, never better?

Don't worry about me, bro. I came across this super group with powers. Oh by the way, apparently I'm one of them and someone is after me. Nothing to worry about.

Yeah, right.

The door to the clinic opened, and she felt more than saw Felix come out.

And did I forget to mention that I'm completely addicted to a strange man I've never met before?

Jared would love that. While she'd grown apart from her siblings over the years, her brother did have a surprisingly annoying protective streak when it came to her dating life.

Trying and failing to ignore Felix's presence, she turned her back to him to gaze out into the street. Night had fallen, the street lights revealing yellow blots of cracked pavement.

"Cali?" Jared asked, bringing her attention back to him. "Hello? Are you there?"

"Yeah, I'm here," she bit out.

Felix drew closer, her body hyperaware of his location.

"I'm fine," she forced out of her clenched teeth.

"Where are you?"

"I'm . . . with a friend."

"Cali . . . " He sounded conflicted. "Your car was parked outside Mom and Dad's. There were strange people inside when Garnet and I dropped by to pick up the mail for them—"

She cut him off. "Pick up the mail for them? Why'd you have to do that?"

A moment of silence. "Didn't you know? Mom and Dad went on vacation a week ago."

Her mouth gaped. "No. Why didn't anyone tell me?" She really shouldn't have been all that surprised. The distance between her and her family wasn't some small gap that could be bridged with a quick phone call. She'd gone months without speaking to them. She hadn't wanted to. She had to prove she could make it on her own first. She had to show them her passion wasn't a waste of time and effort. That she wasn't the screw up they thought she'd be.

"Cali, you haven't contacted any of us in months," Jared said, as if he were explaining something to a small child. "You moved out and then fell off the radar. We had no idea what you were up to or what you were getting involved with."

Getting involved with?

"What—?"

But he cut her off as if she hadn't even spoken. "If you were in trouble, why didn't you come to any of us? We thought you'd gotten over this, but apparently we were wrong. Now they know where Mom and Dad live. I guess we should count ourselves lucky they weren't home, but I mean *seriously,* Cali?"

She couldn't take it anymore. "Just what do you think happened?" He thought she'd planned this? Had known about it?

There was an exacerbated sigh from the other end of the phone. "Drugs, Cali. That's what I think happened. You got pulled into the wrong crowd again. By the looks of those guys I'd say they were after money." She could practically see his head shaking, "And you brought them to Mom and Dad's. Why? Were you going to ask for money? Were you going to steal from them?"

Cali's cheeks flushed with a combination of embarrassment, anger, and shame. She clamped her mouth shut, afraid of what she might yell at him. All those years ago, and that was still all they saw? A druggie? She'd never been one. She'd been a dumb seventeen year old who'd made the wrong choice in a boyfriend and had been left to the cops at an under-aged party when she'd been drunk, high, and given the date-rape drug.

She clutched her phone to try and stop the shaking in her hands. "I would never steal from them." She enunciated each word slowly, but the rage she felt still crept through.

Jared didn't even acknowledge her words. "The cops want you to come in for questioning."

Her entire body shook.

No!

She wanted to scream and rant. She'd done everything right from that moment on in her life. She didn't want to see those looks again. The ones people gave those beneath them when they pitied them and their poor existence. She didn't want to see the disappointment in her family's eyes. She'd done nothing wrong.

"Cali? Did you hear me?"

"I want to give my own statement of what happened."

She could feel his surprise through the phone. He and Garnet had already made their minds up about her. And it stung.

She inhaled deeply and caught the scent of fresh bread and sea salt. Felix.

Could he hear what her brother had said?

Why do you even care what he thinks about you?

She didn't know why. She just did.

There was shuffling on the other side of the line and then Jared came back on. "The police want you to come in tomorrow to give your statement."

"I didn't steal from Mom and Dad," she said again. "You're making assumptions you have no right to make, Jared." And based on his reaction and Garnet's, the police were sure to follow in their footsteps. Great. Tomorrow was going to be hell.

They hung up shortly after that.

Cali took some deep breaths. It didn't help.

Her back grew warm. Her heart sped up. "Are you okay?" Felix asked from behind her.

She turned around and dropped her head when she couldn't stand the compassion she saw in his gaze. She wanted so badly to rest her forehead against his chest, to feel those strong arms around her.

"My family thinks I'm a drug addict." She might as well get it out there in the open.

His hands slid along her arms comfortingly. Up and down, up and down. She shivered. He was really making her no touching rule difficult right about then. "Looks like they don't know you all that well," he said.

A harsh laugh escaped her. "And you do?" she couldn't help but retort. She knocked his hands away to stare him in the face. "I may not know the significance of the mirror part of your weird little 'mirror mate' word, but I sure as hell know what the word *mate* means. I also know I've been called that a couple of times today. Now, I don't know what you want from me, but I don't owe you anything. I saved your ass when I took out that woman,

Collette. You're indebted to me." She held up her hand, index finger extended. "That's one."

A smirked tugged at his lips. "We're keeping score now?"

"I don't like to owe anyone."

The smirk bloomed into a grin. "And my coming in and rescuing you from your parents' doesn't count as anything?"

"All you did was warn me. Not to mention it doesn't even give me much to go by. A man is after me—wow, that really narrows it down."

He shrugged. "Well, now all you have to do is stay away from men. I gotta say I'm not arguing with that."

The look he gave her sent a jolt right down to her toes. Her breasts tingled, the heat between her legs spreading.

Why did he have to look at her like that?

She stepped back from him. He stepped forward. "You do realize that would include you, right?"

She took a step back. He stepped forward. Back, forward, back, forward.

Her back hit a cement pillar.

His eyes sparked when she couldn't retreat. He leaned into her. "I'm the exception. That weird little phrase we like to use, Mirror Mate? It means exactly what it sounds like."

He was so close it was suffocating. Her body was on high alert as they stood there, at a standstill now, neither one moving.

She cleared her suddenly dry throat, trying to ignore the throbbing of her entire body. "You're really going to make this awkward for me, aren't you?"

The tension between them was palpable.

His grin was all rogue. "As awkward as I possibly can." He braced his weight on the palms of his hands, one on either side of her head, trapping her.

"You're certainly doing a good job of it," she said breathlessly.

Chapter 5

Felix's entire body was tense, his cock hard. Shit, but he'd never had this kind of reaction to a woman before. They both stood there, trapped, neither making the first move. Cali's onyx eyes watched him warily as if she didn't know whether to bolt or stay. Her chest rose and fell with her heavy breathing, her lips parted ever so slightly, as if inviting him to taste her.

He couldn't take it. He wanted her. *Needed* her.

He dipped his head to capture her mouth. She gasped but didn't pull away. Her hands grasped his hips, her grip like steel.

He kept his hands firmly planted against the cement behind her. He didn't trust himself to let them wander. Instead he surrendered himself to the tantalizing feel of her lips molding to his. They were soft and pliant and tasted like spearmint lip balm. His tongue snaked out to tease them. Her fingers dug into the flesh at his sides. Fire scorched his veins. He wanted to take her up against the wall, wanted to feel her sex clamping tight and hot around his aching cock.

He ran his tongue along the seam of her mouth again, coaxing her to open for him. He couldn't get enough of her. He wanted more. She hesitated, but when he nipped her with his teeth she drew in a ragged breath, and he slid his tongue inside.

She arched against him, her breasts just barely grazing his chest. He moaned, but the blood in his veins must have been roaring too loudly because he didn't even hear it.

Her tongue stole out to stroke against his, and his body went rock solid. He growled in animalistic desire. But again he heard nothing.

There was a gentle push on his hips, and Cali pulled her lips from his. Her eyes were fogged, her lips red, and she licked them as if to savor the flavor of his kiss.

His cock twitched as he imagined all the uses for those beautiful lips and tongue. He curled his fingers into the cement pillar. Lust clouded his mind and all he could think of was her. Her scent. Her taste. He dipped his head back in for another sample.

Her grip on his hips tightened to keep him away, though the effort was only half-hearted. But it was the sudden panic in her eyes that stopped him.

"*What is it?*" he tried to ask, but nothing came out.

Cold flooded his body.

He opened his mouth to speak. Again there was nothing. Understanding dawned. Cali was using her powers.

And by the looks of it, she had no idea how, and was terrified.

He knew that fear. Had felt it many times, only this time she wouldn't be alone as he'd been.

He gripped her shoulders as much to comfort her as to draw her attention back from where she was staring down at her own body as if it wasn't hers.

"*It's okay,*" he mouthed. "*I'm staying right here.*"

She nodded shakily.

He took a moment to think.

How the hell was he supposed to help her when they didn't have the same powers?

He kneaded her shoulders absently until something clicked. It was only a hunch but it was all he had.

He removed his hands from her shoulders and brought them to rest atop hers where they gripped his hips like a lifeline.

"*What are you doing?*" she mouthed.

Any other time he would have found her reluctance to release him amusing.

"*Trust me.*"

He pulled her hands from him and let them drop by her sides.

She gave him a funny look. "*What was the point of that?*"

Had it worked? He didn't feel any different, but then again, he never felt anything when Sydney used her powers either. "It was just a theory," he said.

His eyes widened.

"I made noise." He looked down at himself, amazed she was able to take all sound from him.

Her arms waved. *"Why am I still silent?"*

Panic was starting to set in. He reached out to grab her and stopped himself short. If he touched her again, her powers would leak over to him.

"Don't panic. Getting control of your powers is the hardest thing to deal with." He wracked his mind for some kind of instruction to give her, trying to remember back to those first cursed weeks when he'd discovered his power and had been abandoned and ridiculed by his "friends." When nothing helpful surfaced he went with his gut. "When your power first manifests, it's usually brought on by strong emotion." He bit back a smile at what must have triggered them. "Do you have a weird prickling at the back of your neck?" It was the only common symptom that he knew of.

Cali nodded.

Should he try what he'd done with Sydney all those years ago when they'd found out about her ability? It was worth a shot. "I need you to try and relax."

She gave him a dead stare. *Are you serious?* it said.

His lip twitched. "Close your eyes and picture yourself releasing all the tension in your body. Trust me. Just . . . let . . . go."

She eyed him balefully for a moment as if to convey that if he was pulling her leg she'd amputate his. Finally she closed her eyes.

He waited, watching as she inhaled, held it, and slowly let it out.

A few cars sped by and still she kept her eyes closed. "Did it work?" she whispered.

He threw his head back and laughed. "I can honestly say with some confidence that it did."

She punched him in the arm. "You jerk. That was not a laughing matter. I was terrified."

He rubbed his arm. "So does that count, then?" He held up a finger much like she had earlier. "That was one."

Her eyes flashed with the challenge. She raised her chin, not saying anything, and he took it to mean that he had indeed evened out her little scoreboard. But he was far from finished with it.

"How'd you know what to do?" she asked after a few more cars pass by.

He stepped back to give her some room, his shoulder rising in a careless half shrug. "That's the only thing that seemed to work for me."

"When did you first learn about your . . . " She faltered. "Your, uh, ability?"

It was not a time he liked to remember, but it looked as if she was opening up to the idea of having powers, so he'd do what he could to help her. "I was twenty-one. It was after finals. I went out with a bunch of my buddies and we got drunk. We were leaving when one of them made the offhand comment about my current girlfriend at the time being a whore. I got pissed, there were angry words exchanged. I wanted to fight." He shook his head at his idiocy. He should have left it. Maybe then he'd never have lost his friends. "Jeremy kept blowing me off. He went to get into his car, and I remember wishing his car would vanish so he couldn't leave without me knocking in a few of his teeth. There was this strange sensation at the back of my neck." He placed his hand there absently, as if he could still feel that first time. "I was too angry to notice it, and when I raged at Jeremy again, waving my arms at him . . . His car just disappeared."

"Did they know it was you?"

He exhaled. "Yeah, they were so freaked that they came after me. They ran me back into the bar we'd been drinking at calling me a freak, and when they couldn't get to me inside, they smashed my Jeep to bits."

"Fucking bastards," she whispered.

That about summed them up. He'd known those guys for years, and all it took was one night to ruin the very foundation of their friendship.

"Were you too new to your powers to bring that guy's car back?"

He gave a humorless laugh. The question was always inevitable when it came to his powers, and the answer always left a bitter taste in his mouth. "Once I Erase something, I can't bring it back."

He waited for the shock.

Check.

He waited for the horror.

Nothing.

He kept waiting.

It never came.

Cali leaned her head back against the cement column, exposing the long expanse of her neck. Felix's gut clenched.

"Well, shit," she said. "I guess there's no denying it, I really am a—what did you call me, a Silencer?" She shook her head in disbelief. "It makes me sound like some kind of deadly assassination weapon. That's gotta be a plus, right?"

Sydney poked her head out the front door. "Are you guys still alive out here?"

Felix frowned. "We'll be in shortly."

"All right, but you'd think that if someone was looking for Cali that keeping her on the side of the road where anyone driving by could see her would be a bad thing." Sydney dipped back into the clinic.

Felix groaned and ran a hand through his hair. He knew Sydney was right but damned if he didn't want to steal a few more moments alone with Cali. "Come on," he beckoned. "We better get inside before we get reprimanded again." He winked at her.

She gave him an amused expression and he took it as progress. At least she wasn't running away from him. He went to put his hand on the small of her back as she passed him and she jumped out of his reach.

He sighed. At least she wasn't running *far*, he amended.

Sydney had been busy cleaning while they'd been outside. The lobby was swept, the chairs put back into a neat order, and the lights inside the patient rooms were off.

Everyone was waiting for them.

"We need to figure out what we should do with Cali," Sydney said as soon as they were both inside. "It's not safe for her to go home. I'm guessing if they found her parent's house then they'll be able to find where she's living just as easily."

Cali walked over to the chairs on the opposite side of the lobby, no doubt trying to put space between them. He let her go. "She can stay with me," he said.

Cali stiffened in her seat. "No." The rest of the group eyed her at the immediate response. She shifted uncomfortably. "I mean, no . . . thank you. Can't I stay here?" She gave the lobby the once-over and barely managed to hide her revulsion.

Felix wanted to call her out on it, but he didn't have to. Joel beat him to it.

"You want to stay here?"

The comment earned him a hard elbow to the ribs.

"There's a futon in my office," Sydney said.

"She can't stay here alone." If she didn't want to stay at his house that was fine, but she couldn't remain at the vet's all by herself.

Cali crossed her arms. "No one followed us."

"It doesn't matter. If they have a Dreamer—"

"If they have a Dreamer," Niella cut Felix off, "then she's screwed no matter where she goes. But I doubt that they have a full-forced Dreamer, so let the woman stay where she wants and someone drive me home already. Syd?"

"I don't have a car," she said forlornly.

"What happened to your car?" Joel's hands tightened around her waist in concern.

Felix braced himself as Sydney pinned him with a look. "Felix Erased it."

Joel's jaw bulged. "He what?"

He held his hands out in peace. "Syd blocked herself in when she parked in the driveway. It was the only way to get rid of any evidence so whoever Collette was working for couldn't trace her."

Joel's anger eased at the mention of protecting Sydney, just like he knew it would. One obstacle avoided. Now he had bigger problems to overcome, like getting Cali to quit being so bull-headed.

"There's too much risk if you stay here alone, Cali. It's not safe."

She weighed his words, but all hope of her coming home with him was blown out of the water when Sydney decided to open her mouth. "If you're worried about Cali then I can always stay at your place, Felix. You live closest to the clinic, and if anything happens, she can call. As soon as I'm within range I can Shield the place."

"No." He and Joel spoke up at the same time.

Niella rolled her eyes and dropped her head back.

"What do you mean 'no'?" Sydney asked Joel.

He looked at her as if the answer should be obvious. "I don't want you staying the night there alone."

Felix cut short the retort he had ready. He and Sydney had been friends for years. Well before she met Joel. However, Joel was the over-protective type, and he couldn't begrudge the guy's not wanting his girlfriend to spend the night at another man's home, no matter how ridiculous the idea of him and Sydney getting together sounded. He checked his temper. "She's not staying at my house," he said, making sure to convey that to Sydney. She could be just as stubborn as Cali was turning out to be. "If Cali wants to stay here then I think Syd should too. That way she can Shield if anything happens."

"I don't need a babysitter," Cali spoke up from her seat in the corner.

"Agreed." Niella seconded the comment.

Felix didn't appreciate her interference.

Sydney instantly adopted the role of mediator. "How about I stay here until Cali gets settled, and then I'll crash at your place?" She turned to Joel. "We'll *all* crash at Felix's place."

"I'm sure as hell not crashing there," Niella muttered.

Felix ran his hand through his hair. He didn't want *any* of them crashing at his place. Yet, his fate was sealed when Cali gave a cross between a nod and a shrug in accordance.

Of course she'd agree. It wasn't her home that was about to be invaded.

Chapter 6

"You'll love it. Tom's pizza is the best." Sydney continued to gush as she led Cali out of the vet and two shops over to the little pizzeria. Felix, Joel, and Niella had left in the Hummer, leaving Cali alone with the very talkative and energetic Sydney.

"You really don't have to stay with me," Cali told her for what was perhaps the fifth time.

"Nonsense." Sydney brushed her comment off as she had all the others. "I promised Felix I'd get you settled, and I will."

She held the door to the pizzeria open as if this were part of getting Cali settled. Cali bit the inside of her cheek to keep from saying anything untoward. She didn't need to be coddled.

They're trying to help.

She had to constantly remind herself of that lest she go crazy from the constant hovering. With the rest of the group gone it was a little better, though she hated to admit that the sight of Felix leaving left an ache in her chest that refused to go away.

The pizzeria was a quaint little place. It was done up in a red, orange, and white color scheme that had Cali thinking only of pizza. The smell of fresh garlic bread and tomato sauce permeated the air. She tried not to drool on the floor.

"Hey, Sydney, what are you doing here so late? I'm about ready to close."

The man behind the counter could have passed for Sydney's older brother. A dirty blond mop of hair stuck out from under a visor that read: *Tom's Pizzeria.* He had laughing green eyes and a sun-tanned face, accentuated by the white uniform he wore that was dotted with red pizza sauce stains.

Sydney grinned at her male doppelganger. "The hunger calls,

Tom. It's not my fault you make the best pizza in the city. If I bother you so much, you should really look into lowering those standards of yours." She placed both hands on the counter and leaned forward until she could kick her legs out behind her like a little kid.

Tom placed the palm of his hand flat against Sydney's forehead and pushed her playfully off his counter. "I'm afraid I've built up quite the immunity to you and your flattery." His attention left Sydney and held on Cali. "Where's your manners, Sydney?" He wiped his flour-covered hand on his pants and held it out to her. "Thomas Larkin," he introduced himself.

Despite his attempt to clean the flour and dough from his hands they remained as if ingrained into his skin. "Cali Crazar." She took his hand.

"New to the city?" he asked.

"Uh . . ." Her gaze darted to Sydney before returning to Tom. "Kind of. I'm really only here visiting for a few days, hopefully."

Sydney's expression clouded but Cali didn't know what else to say. Was she supposed to tell Tom she was going to join their little group? Did Tom even know?

Hell, she hadn't known until a few hours ago that people with powers existed—that she was one of them.

She couldn't help but remember that feeling of terror and awe when she'd used her powers outside the clinic with Felix. One moment they were kissing and the next—

Her chest ached at the thought of Felix. Why did she want him near?

Her traitorous mind thought back to the moment before her powers had kicked in. The feel of his lips on hers, the taste of his tongue in her mouth . . .

" . . . so what do you like on your pizza?"

Cali blinked.

Tom and Sydney both stared at her with expectant expressions on their faces.

Shit.

"What was that?"

Sydney huffed. "What do you want on the pizza?"

She glowered right back at Sydney. "Pineapple and green peppers okay with you?"

Sydney bobbed her golden head and turned to Tom. "And can we have an order of those tasty chocolate, cinnamon, funnel cake stick thingies?"

"They have a name, Sydney."

She waved him off. "Yeah, but who wants to remember that? Funnel-ly cake thingies sound so much better."

With an exaggerated sigh Tom disappeared into the back to make their pizza. He called out, "Would you mind flipping the sign to 'Closed' so I don't get any more late nighters?"

Sydney dutifully went to do what he asked. "You know your life would be a bore without me," she called back.

Cali thought she heard a muttered, "If only," from Tom but couldn't be sure.

Sydney took the chair across from where Cali was now seated at one of the circular tables. "So?"

"So, what?"

Sydney leaned forward. "Come on, you have to have some kind of questions about all this." Her hands gestured around her as if to take in the pizzeria but Cali knew better.

And she did have questions about what had happened that day. The only problem was she didn't know how to phrase them, and those that she did know how to phrase she was more than a little apprehensive about hearing the answers to. There was also that small part of her that wanted to wait until Felix could answer her questions.

"How do you know Felix?" she asked. It was as good a place to start as any.

"Ah, you're going to go the old history route first, huh?" She got up and took a Vanilla Coke from the fridge. She tilted the bottle toward her like an offering.

"Don't you have to pay for that?"

Sydney took another bottle out despite Cali's lack of answer and handed it to her.

"Nah," she said as she sat back down. "I've been pilfering sodas from Tom since I was a teen. Why do you think he keeps the Vanilla stocked for me? Anyway." She cracked the plastic cap off and took a drink. "I met Felix when I was nineteen. We were in one of those combination first aid/CPR classes together. I stumbled across him when he looked like he could use some help. He was huddled into this ball in his chair, and I thought he might be injured. Turned out he was trying to control his powers."

"I take it that there's no destined age when we, uh . . . " She lowered her voice. " . . . come into our power?"

"Nope. My powers started manifesting when I was twenty, almost six months after I met Felix, though it took us close to four months to figure it out."

Cali took a sip of her own soda, the smooth vanilla flavor sliding down her throat. "And you're what, exactly? A shield?"

"Shielder," she corrected mildly. "Think of it as if I sent out a giant bubble that enveloped everyone around me, and while I'm actively using my powers no one else around can. Make sense?"

Tom came around the counter holding a large pizza box with a smaller one perched on top. He stopped short when he saw the soda in Sydney's hand. When his eyes fell on the one in her hand Cali felt an immediate flush of guilt. "I'll pay for this," she said instantly.

Tom gave her an easy grin. "No worries. I didn't expect Sydney to engage in her bad habits in front of guests." He gave Sydney a mock scowl.

She saluted him with the bottle before getting up to take their food off his hands. "Old habits die hard," she told him. "Thanks again for the pizza. You're the best."

"Yeah, yeah," he said, "now get out of here, I have to close up."

Back in the vet clinic Sydney directed Cali around the corner of the lobby to where a door was labeled "office." This way they were able to escape the smell of dog food that seemed to be rooted into the walls themselves.

The office itself was decorated with dark furniture and an aqua and white color scheme. The faint scent of vanilla drifted around the room, a nice change from the combination dog food, bleach, and animal smell of the lobby. There were pictures on the walls, most of them beautiful tropical beaches that hung on the wall right next to Sydney's doctorate diploma and certifications. A yellow futon was pressed to the wall on Cali's left. Though the room was filled with all sorts of furnishings and decorations, somehow Sydney had organized it in such a way that it didn't feel crowded. Instead, the office was warm and inviting.

Cali took a seat on the futon. "I take it I'll be sleeping here?"

Sydney followed her in, leaving the door partially open. She set the pizza down on her desk and pulled paper plates out from one of the cabinets above the mini fridge in the corner behind her desk.

She handed a plate to Cali. "It's a lot more comfortable than it looks. Trust me. I've spent a few nights on it myself."

They lapsed into silence as they tore through nearly the entire large pizza. Sydney passed out the funnel cake thingies and Cali took a bite of pure bliss. The dessert resembled a churro only with a more funnel cake-like consistency. The cinnamon sugar sprinkling had a touch of cocoa that only added to the flavor when combined with the fudge drizzle.

"Amazing, huh?" Sydney said around a mouthful.

"What are these called again?" She might just have to buy them once a week, if not daily.

"Technically they're called Tom's Incredible Twists, but Joel and Felix both got it into their heads to call them T.I.T's for short and I just can't say the name now without hearing one of them asking for a double order of tits to go along with their pizza."

Cali choked on her twist.

Her eyes began to water as she desperately reached for her Coke.

Sydney shot to her feet to give her a couple friendly pounds on the back. "Sorry, I probably should have warned you not to have any food in your mouth first."

Cali sucked in some much needed air. "Thanks," she gasped out.

"Don't mention it." Sydney moved around the room, cleaning up their mess.

Silence fell once more as Cali watched Sydney tidy up. She felt useless at that moment and wanted to volunteer her help but something told her Sydney would just tell her to stay seated.

Once everything was cleaned, Sydney took a seat on the opposite end of the futon and curled one of her legs under her like they were at a slumber party. "So did any other questions come up while you were eating? There has to be more on your mind than how Felix and I met."

Cali leaned back against the railing of the futon. "Look, I appreciate your friendliness and everything but you don't have to babysit me. Really. I'm fine."

"I'm not babysitting you. Why can't we just hang out?"

"And what? Paint each other's toenails? Thanks, but no thanks." Cali went to get off the futon but was blocked.

She hadn't even seen Sydney move.

"What's your problem?" Sydney snarled. She was bent over so that her green eyes blazed level with Cali's. "You look at me and all you see is the blonde hair and think I'm some stereotypical cheerleader who wants to do each other's toes?" Shame flooded Cali because that was exactly how she'd pegged Sydney. She opened her mouth to apologize but didn't get the chance as Sydney continued. "If you don't want to be my friend then that's fine, but Felix is one of my closest friends and you're his Mirror Mate, which means you're going to become a major fixture in his life, and I'm not going anywhere so you better damn well get used to the sight of me." Her green eyes widened, and she leaned back as if she'd never exploded at someone like that before.

Cali stared, transfixed, before she cleared her throat. Feeling like a real ass all she could think to say was, "Okay."

Sydney narrowed her eyes. "That's it? 'Okay'?"

"You were right. I was being a complete asshole thinking you were nothing more than a perky blonde with half a brain. Can we start over?"

Sydney exhaled in relief, a smile tugging at her lips. "I'd like—"

Her words cut off as the sound of shuffling reached them from the front of the vet.

Chapter 7

Cali and Sydney both froze.

The shock wore off Sydney first. Cali summed it up to being a part of a little super group longer than her. "Did you hear that?" She shot to her feet, Cali right behind her. The sound came again but it was too faint to make out.

Okay, Cali, you can do this. Your power is to manipulate sound, so . . . manipulate it. She shook out her hands to steady her nerves and shut her eyes. She tried to imagine all the sounds around her fading. After a moment of nothing happening she began to feel foolish.

Cali turned to Sydney. Her face was pinched in concentration.

"Are you using your powers?" Cali asked her.

Sydney nodded. "Why?"

How did she say that she'd tried to use her powers and was unsuccessful without sounding like she was whining?

Cali proceeded toward the door. "Just wondering," she said.

Sydney touched her arm. "Cali, wait. We have no idea what's out there. I promised Felix . . . " She let the sentence hang.

"You promised to get me settled," Cali pointed out. "He said nothing about what to do in the event of an attack." But damn, she had to admire Sydney's loyalty. She'd only ever dreamed of having a friend as loyal as that. Someone she didn't have to worry about going behind her back and taking her paintings, or sneaking drugs into her drinks. . .

She shook the thoughts away.

"What's our plan of action?"

Sydney nibbled at her bottom lip. "Well, I used my powers so if whoever is out there tries to use their own abilities they won't be able to and . . . that's all I'm basically used for."

"You mean you guys all don't know some crazy special kung-fu fighting technique?"

Sydney's gaze could have frozen water. "We've already told you, we're not a military branch."

More was the pity. How the hell were they supposed to defend themselves if all they had was a woman who could negate power and another who could manipulate sound? Where were the super strength and fire-wielding powers when you needed them?

The rustling came again.

Sydney grasped the door and gave her a nod. *We take this nice and slow,* it said.

Together they crept out into the large hallway. A faint light came in through the reception area caused by the streetlights outside. Sydney took the lead as they filed into the smaller hall that opened into the front lobby. Sydney stopped and took a deep breath before turning the corner.

She poked her head out just enough to see into the main room before she pulled back. "It's coming from behind the reception desk."

She leaned out to take another look. Cali was tall enough to lean over her and peer around the corner above her head.

The lobby was empty.

The faint rustling came from the far corner, right where Sydney had said. There was no light of any kind, which begged the question how the hell did whoever was over there see anything? Didn't they need a flashlight?

A small part of Cali had worried Collette had come after her, but with Sydney nullifying any and all powers, Collette would be useless. Plus, Collette didn't strike her as the type of woman who would hide out behind a reception desk.

Sydney's thoughts must have been following her own. She bravely made her way into the lobby, Cali right behind her. When they reached the desk, Sydney waved her back, signaling her to stay put.

Cali bit her tongue to keep from protesting but ultimately

stayed where she was.

Sydney stepped behind the reception desk.

And screamed.

Cali reacted instantly. She grabbed the first thing within reach. It turned out to be a dog leash hanging on the wall closest to her.

She rushed the reception desk and nearly got bowled over by Sydney. "What is it?" she demanded. There was nothing in sight.

Something moved past her foot and Cali yelped.

The fuzzy gray blob scuttled toward the dog food, giving Cali a moment to identify it. "Gadget?"

Felix's rat continued to make a break for the dog food. Sydney jumped out of the rodent's way with another screech.

Cali forced her laughter down. She hurried to scoop the fat rat up before it gave Sydney a heart attack. "Easy, Sydney, it's just Gadget."

Sydney's face was murderous. "I'm going to kill Felix."

Cali highly doubted it, but she kept her comments to herself as Gadget nuzzled into her palm. Sydney might hate the fact that Felix sometimes left his pet rat in her vet but he was important to her, special . . .

The dull ache in her chest throbbed. "Hey, Sydney?"

She was busy dusting herself off. "Hm?"

"What's a Mirror Mate?"

Her hands faltered before continuing to brush at her clothing. She looked up to give her a bright smile. "You are."

Cali wasn't buying it. "That doesn't tell me anything. Everyone keeps calling me Felix's Mirror Mate but no one's really told me what that means. How do you even know that I'm his or that he's mine? I don't get it."

Sydney held her hands out in surrender. "I understand, and I wish I had more information for you, but to be perfectly honest we're not even sure what it is. When I met Felix years ago, he thought he was the only one with powers. When we figured out I had them too, I freaked out thinking perhaps they were contagious. They're not. Felix eventually met Collette and found that she too had powers. Our little network of powered people was growing, but that still didn't give us any insight. All of us had different powers. Were there others out there with similar powers or was every person different? The questions continued to grow when Collette confided in Felix that she found work at a company that used people like us. Felix wasn't happy with this new discovery and exploitation. He stopped talking to Collette, and some months after that he received a call that she had discovered something amazing. It turns out Collette was the first one to discover Mirror Mates, though she didn't call them that. That's our own specialty term." Sydney grinned. "Anyway, from what Felix has told us, Mirror Mates are a sort of soul mate with the added benefit that, once a certain bond is formed between them, they increase each other's powers."

"Increase their powers how?"

Sydney shrugged. "Not sure. When Collette found her Mirror Mate, her Illusions became corporeal. So far she's the only one we know of who is what we term 'full-forced.'"

So that was it, the reason why Felix was so nice to her. He wanted to use her to increase his own power. Her heart sank, though she shouldn't have been surprised. She'd yet to meet anyone who didn't want her for some other purpose.

No one wants you for you.

"Are you okay?" Sydney peered up at her studiously.

Cali instantly pasted a false smile on her face. She didn't want Sydney to know how much Felix had inadvertently hurt her. And here she had started to actually like the bastard.

Her anger grew, something she welcomed as it burned away the betrayal and hurt she felt.

"I'm fine," she lied. "So I take it Felix and Collette dated back in the day?" The bitter words burst from her lips before she could even process what she'd said.

Sydney gave her a funny look. "No. Never. Felix refused to date her, which only added to Collette's anger toward him." She stopped abruptly as if there was more to the story but she didn't want to divulge it.

Fine.

Cali didn't want to hear it anyway.

"I think I'm going to turn in for the night," she said briskly. She started back toward the office.

Sydney huffed behind her as she tried to catch up to her long strides. "Hold on there Cali. Why do I get the feeling I said something to upset you?"

"I'm fine," she said through clenched teeth. "It's just a lot to take in."

"You don't believe us? Niella Dreamed it. I know to you that still doesn't make it a hard fact but I'm sure deep down you know it's true. There has to be some kind of connection you feel toward Felix that can support what we're telling you."

Her chest chose that moment to ache. Cali ignored it. "Goodnight, Sydney. Thanks. For everything."

Sydney came up short, unsure where she went wrong. She opened her mouth to speak but shut it just as quickly. She collected her things from around the office and made her way toward the exit. She paused at the door. "Goodnight. I'll lock you in. See you tomorrow."

Cali sat quietly as she listened for Sydney's retreating footsteps. A few moments after she heard the door close, a car started, no doubt Joel's truck. He'd left it for Sydney because she no longer had a car. Thanks to Felix.

Cali groaned and flopped back onto the futon.

Why did she keep thinking about him?

An annoyed squeak alerted Cali to the fact she was squeezing Gadget a little too tightly. She loosened her grip. "Sorry little buddy."

Lying there staring at the rodent did nothing to calm her

turbulent emotions. She cursed Felix anew and set Gadget on the floor. It was all his fault that she was lying there restless while he was no doubt calm as could be in his home, busy thinking up his next plan of action to try to trick her into trusting him.

She punched one of the futon pillows to try to mold it into a more comfortable shape. She wanted her own bed. She didn't want to have to be on the run or hiding from some group she'd never even heard about before just because, for some reason, they were after her. She didn't want any of this. She punched her pillow again, bad mouthing all the people involved in creating her current predicament. "I hate people," she grumbled.

*

Felix paced restlessly back and forth across his living room. "We shouldn't have left her there alone."

Joel rubbed at his temples. "She's fine," he repeated for the umpteenth time. "Sydney told you nothing was out of place when she left. Now can you please go to sleep so I can stop being a good friend and go to bed with my girlfriend?"

Felix spun on his heel to stride the length of his couch. He rubbed idly at his chest, the hollow ache continuing to gnaw at him. "I really don't think we should have left her alone."

Joel dropped his head back onto the couch. "You don't say." His sarcasm was lost on Felix.

Felix couldn't stop thinking about Cali. Alone. Somewhere Collette could easily find her. Felix had never told Collette about Sydney's clinic when they had been friends years ago, but she was clever and had resources at her fingertips. Resources that were becoming increasingly suspicious to Felix. He'd learned long ago that she'd sold her soul to the devil for a well-paying job, one with the shady prospect of paying people large amounts of money if they used their powers. As for what they used those people's powers for . . . he never asked Collette. He didn't want to know. It had been too much for him to take that she would give up her dreams, her hopes, everything, for money, for a chance to feel superior.

"It has to be more than revenge," he mused aloud.

Joel's eyes were closed. His head still rested back against the couch.

Felix kicked his shoe and Joel came awake with a curse.

His dark blue eyes searched for what had woken him before they focused on Felix. "What?"

"Revenge," Felix repeated. "It doesn't add up." He rubbed at his chest again.

Joel's eyes followed the movement. "What's wrong with you? You got a rash or something?"

Irritated that Joel wasn't listening to him he snapped, "No, I don't have a rash. My chest just feels . . . compressed. It's like I can't get a full lungful of air. It doesn't matter right now. What matters—"

"Is that you get some sleep. Felix, you look like hell. You've been up since what, three this morning working? You took on Collette and probably expended a lot of energy using your powers. You need sleep. Everything will fall into place after a full night's rest. And to be perfectly honest, if I don't get some sleep I'm going to be fucking miserable tomorrow at work. Cali is fine. Collette's not coming after her tonight. The most likely scenario is that she's locked up behind bars after being found at Cali's parent's house. No one will get to her tonight."

Before Felix could even protest, Joel got up from the couch and headed to the extra bedroom where Sydney was already fast asleep.

Felix stood alone in his living room only a few minutes longer. He was exhausted. But he couldn't explain the nervousness that coursed through him.

He ran a hand through his hair with a sigh.

Joel was right. He'd be no good to anyone tomorrow if his brain wasn't working right from lack of sleep.

Cali will be fine.

He tried to make himself believe it, but the cold that ran along his spine wouldn't cease. The others didn't know Collette like he did. The reason behind her ability to succeed at anything was her dedication. Some would call it obsession. And for whatever reason, Cali was that new target.

*

Cali awoke without having any idea as to why. Darkness engulfed her and she blinked furiously. It took a moment for her eyes to adjust and for her brain to catch up with her location. She wasn't in her apartment. She was at Sydney's vet clinic. The rest of the day's events caught up to her, and she was amazed that she'd even fallen asleep.

She must've been exhausted.

Exhausted from using your powers.

She shivered and reached for the blanket that had become entangled at her ankles.

A dark shadow shifted beyond the entrance to the office.

Cali's heart stopped.

Chapter 8

The black silhouette froze, as if it knew she'd caught sight of it. It was of average height and had the distinct build of a man.

Cali's limbs started to shake.

She blinked.

He was gone.

Cali jumped from the futon and grabbed a hefty picture frame off the small table next to her. It was well made and had sharp edges. She raced for the waiting room, uncaring of her rash behavior or lack of clothing. She'd much rather go with the element of surprise than wait helplessly for the danger to come to her.

There was no sound of retreat.

Faint light drifted into the front lobby from where the sun was starting to rise. Morning was approaching. She went over to the front door. Locked. The two patient rooms were open, both empty. She couldn't remember if the doors had been closed when Sydney left. But other than that everything seemed fine.

Was she simply losing her mind?

She knew she'd been exhausted and had gone through a lot of strange shit, but she'd never *seen* things before.

She checked the whole clinic to be safe before heading back to the office. Gadget had somehow made his way onto the futon. The sight of him made her feel a little better, but she still closed and locked the office door.

You can never be too careful.

She glanced down at her temporary weapon of choice. It was a high school photo, the title across the top identifying the group of teens as the hip-hop dance team. Sydney sat front and center, looking incredibly young with her giant smile and braces. Cali carefully put it back where she'd found it. The adrenaline was quickly fading from her system. She dropped to the futon and pulled her cell phone from her purse.

Sydney had left her number and the number to Felix's house. Should she call?

The idea was more than tempting. She wanted to hear Felix's voice. There was something about his deep baritone that calmed her, made her feel safe.

But he was using her.

She stuffed her cell back into her purse, along with the sticky note. There was no reason to call. What would she tell them?

That she'd seen a dark shape in the form of a man hovering outside the office doorway?

She gave a derisive snort.

*

A keening howl woke Cali from a dead sleep.

Her eyes shot open. She rolled to slam her alarm clock off, only to realize too late that she wasn't at home. She rolled straight off the futon.

Pain exploded all over her body and she cursed aloud only to be drowned out by that horrible howling.

She quickly cupped her hands over her ears. "What the fuck is that?"

She dug through her handbag to find her cell phone.

10:02 a.m.

She rolled onto her back with a groan, taking the blanket with her to cover her face.

A knock came at the door. The knob jiggled. "Cali? You awake yet? I really need to get into my office. I tried to wait as long as possible so you could sleep, but I thought by now—"

The rest of her sentence was cut off by another low wail.

"What the fuck is that?" Cali yelled.

"That's Yeller, my ten o'clock. He's in quite a bit of pain and I really need to treat him."

Cali groggily got to her feet. She wrapped the blanket around her as a makeshift skirt to hide her state of undress and opened the door. "Quick, come in and get whatever you need to get that thing to shut the hell up."

Another high-pitched yowl started. With the door open the sound was even worse. Cali cringed in pain. She started to close the door only to be knocked aside as Joel came barging into the room. He quickly shut it behind him with a curse.

He leaned against the door. "For fuck's sake, as if my morning headache wasn't bad enough."

Sydney cooed in sympathy. "My poor baby." She dug around in her desk and pitched a small container over to him. "Take two of those to help with the headache."

Joel popped four pills into his mouth. "I wouldn't have it at all if Felix had gone to bed at a decent hour. He kept pacing in his damn living room, restless, kept rubbing at his chest like it was hurting him." He glanced at the clock on Sydney's wall. Cali had gone stock-still. "And where the hell is he? I have to be in LA at eleven."

The dog howled from the front of the lobby. Joel cursed again. "I'm going to wait out front."

Sydney gave him a kiss. "Have a good day."

Joel's face gentled. "You too."

The emotion on his face hit Cali right in the gut. She shut the door after him, her mind spinning after what he'd said.

Felix had been restless too.

She had no idea if that meant anything. Was she making something out of nothing?

She stopped Sydney as she tried to follow after her boyfriend. "Cali, what—?"

"When you first met Joel, what did you feel?"

Sydney drew back. "What do you mean, what did I feel?"

"When you first touched, did it feel like you got shocked?"

Sydney gave her a blank look.

Cali tugged in frustration at the blanket wrapped around her. "You had to have felt something. He's your Mirror Mate. Didn't anything happen?"

Understanding slowly dawned on Sydney. "Cali, I told you last night that Collette is the only one who found her Mirror Mate."

"No, no." She shook her head. "You told me she was the only one who was full forced. I took that to mean that you and Joel haven't bonded, or connected, or whatever, yet."

Sydney's ever-present smile turned slightly bitter. "Joel and I aren't Mirror Mates."

"But . . ." Cali pointed uselessly behind her. "He. You. You're dating."

Yeller chose that moment to let rip one of his ear-piercing yowls.

Sydney didn't even seem to notice. "We don't have to be Mirror Mates to date. The thing with Mirror Mates is that we don't know if they're rare or commonplace. We only know that they exist. I'm all for a happily-ever-after ending, but I can't wait around for my soul mate to find me, or me him. What if he lives somewhere like Latvia? Or was killed in an accident when he was seven? There's no knowing."

"So what happens if you do find him?"

Her expression turned solemn. "I'm not sure. Sometimes I hope I never have to find out."

Sydney hastily left to treat her first patient, leaving Cali alone.

She pulled her hair back into a hasty ponytail and stepped into her shorts. She tried to fold the blanket as nicely as she could and left the office to join the others in the lobby.

Her feet froze as soon as she turned the corner and spotted Felix. He was talking to Niella over the desk. One of his hands held a white paper bag. That same hand was also pressed to his left ear.

The tenseness coiling within her chest gently eased.

As Felix stood there, smiling openly at Niella, she didn't know what to make of him. Was he playing her? Did she believe Joel? Was Felix feeling the same things as she was?

She didn't know what to think anymore.

She stepped more fully into the room. Felix noticed her instantly. He straightened to his full height, the shirt he wore straining against his broad chest. Cali swallowed.

"Morning," he said brightly. He held the white bag out to her. "I brought breakfast."

She smelled fresh pastries. Her stomach grumbled, and she snatched the bag from his hand.

"Aren't you cheery in the morning?"

She scowled at him and proceeded to dig through the bag.

Felix watched her with amusement. "Looking for anything in particular?"

"Anything with cherry filling?"

Felix made a thoughtful noise in the back of his throat and came up beside her to take a look into the bag.

He smelled of fresh bread.

Her heart skipped a beat.

He reached into the bag. His shoulder pressed against hers. It felt like heated steel. "There might be a cherry Danish in here somewhere. Ah, here it is." He held the pastry out to her. "I'll make sure to add them to my repertoire."

She eyed him carefully. "Thanks."

Yeller let loose a baleful howl. Cali jumped, her breakfast jumping with her, right out of her hand.

She stared at the splatter of cherry on the linoleum floor. "Seriously?" she mumbled.

"All right, I've had enough," Niella rolled out from behind the desk. "Take care of that, would you?"

Sydney stepped out of the patient room and closed the door on another howl. "I can't sedate him just because he's loud."

"Not you." Niella pointed at Cali. "Her."

"Me?"

"Yes, you. Zero out the sound. Take it away. Use your damn powers."

She could feel everyone's attention on her. Her eyes, unbidden, turned to Felix for help. He smiled at her. There was no hidden seduction behind it. It was all warmth and support. It set her nerves at ease.

Then he had to go and ruin it by raising two of his fingers and wiggling them. He mouthed, *"Two?"*

That scum-sucking jackass.

If he thought that she was going to ask for his help only to have to owe him one later, then he was sorely mistaken.

His smile took on a wicked glint at her expression. He lowered his hand back to his side.

"Sure thing," she told Niella with more confidence than she was feeling. Now she had to figure out how the hell to do it. "Could you open the door back up so I can see the dog?"

Sydney hesitated. "This isn't going to hurt Yeller, is it?"

Cali turned to Felix. "Does it hurt?"

"Not at all."

Sydney looked less than convinced, but she did as she was asked. Yeller was lying down on the patient table, his snout on his paws, his big brown eyes full of sorrow.

Sydney scratched him on the head affectionately. "I gave him something for the pain. Once it takes full effect, I'm going to check him over thoroughly for the cause. Maybe run some scans."

Yeller whined.

Cali inhaled deeply. She'd never done this before. The one time she'd knowingly taken sound from something was when she was with Felix and they had been touching. Now there was no physical connection, and her emotions were a lot more stable.

You can do this, she chanted to herself.

She focused on Yeller, the low whine coming from his throat, and the way it seemed to reverberate through the whole clinic. She imagined that sound as a physical presence, one she could suppress. She tried to do what Niella had said and cancel the sound out.

The back of her neck started to tingle.

Yeller's whine went in and out before the sound finally dropped off.

Cali held her breath, half expecting the sound to come back with a thunderous boom.

"Thank the lord," said Niella.

Sydney stared in amazement at Yeller, who now had his head tilted up as if that would help bring the sound of his howl back. It didn't.

"I have to admit," said Sydney, "that is a nice trick to possess. What I wouldn't give to be able to make all my animals shut up when I have a full holding room."

"I don't know how long it'll last," said Cali.

"That's fine. The medicine should kick in soon enough, so he should stop with the baying once the pain recedes."

"One can only hope," mumbled Niella.

*

"You ready?" asked Felix.

Cali's nerves were still a jumbled mess, but she wasn't about to tell him that. "Yeah." She buckled her seatbelt. Felix had "volunteered" to take her to the police station that day. She'd been prepared to call Jared to come and get her but Felix had protested the call, spouting something about blowing the location of their headquarters.

She would have protested more if Niella hadn't backed him up. She'd pointed out that they still didn't know what was going on with the people who were after her, and that it'd be plain stupidity to go out by herself.

Which left her to be chauffeured around. It was probably for the best that she didn't drive anyway. She had no time to focus on the road. She was too busy thinking of what she was going to tell the police. It'd been a good long while since she'd had to deal with governmental authority. And she wanted to keep it that way. She'd spent the last few years keeping her record as spotless as possible, but she doubted seven years would look as good to the authorities as it did to her.

She shifted in her seat.

The last thing she wanted to deal with was punishment for being pegged as an accomplice. Could they even do that to her? She'd fled for her own safety—surely they'd see that.

Not if Jared and Garnet already convinced them otherwise.

She wrung her hands together.

Beside her Felix chuckled. "What are you so nervous about?"

"A lot, actually."

"Like what?"

She stayed silent.

They came to a red light. Felix nudged her with his hand. "Come on, hit me with it."

She eyed him for a moment. "Fine." She punched him in the arm.

His eyebrows rose in challenge. "So you wanna go *there*?" He feinted for her knee and she jumped, a small laugh escaping her.

"Green." She pointed toward the street light.

Felix was forced to focus back on the road.

She scooted closer to the passenger door in a vain attempt to escape his long reach. Why did he have to be so damn playful? "You asked for it, you know," she pointed out.

"So you're saying I started it?"

"Absolutely."

He pretended to contemplate that. "Well, then, I should warn you I always finish what I start."

The look he sent her had heat rushing straight between her legs.

"So are you going to tell me what's got you so jacked up?"

She pulled her mind from the gutter.

What the hell, she thought. She'd already told him some of the story. The worst it could do was cause him to run from her. And wasn't that what she wanted anyway?

"I tend to try and avoid the police. I got enough of them when I was in high school. I earned myself a little record that I'm worried is going to creep up and bite me in the ass."

"It is a nice ass," he commented.

She wanted to punch him again but his humor helped ease the nervousness inside her.

They drove a few miles in silence before he broke it. "What happened in high school?"

"Two things happened, actually. Isaac Gregory and Tyson Miller."

Felix's jaw tensed. "I'm not going to like this story. I can already tell."

Cali smiled. "That makes two of us. Isaac wasn't so bad, it was Tyson who really screwed me." She stopped as old emotions welled up within her. "The short version is that Isaac and Tyson were both druggies. With Isaac I got caught with possession of marijuana and got fined for it. No big deal. I dumped him the next day. Tyson . . . Tyson was like a cancer. The trouble with him just kept growing. I was young and stupid, he was eighteen to my seventeen, and I thought he was the coolest thing on the planet. A couple months after we started dating he took me to a party. There was drinking, weed, you name it, they had it. I was pretty drunk and high by the time Tyson slipped some kind of benzodiazepine into my drink."

Felix's knuckles had gone white around the steering wheel.

"When I finally woke up I was in the hospital. I was really messed up but luckily the cops had been on their way when I was given the drug so Tyson didn't have time to do anything to me. But he sure as hell did enough. There was still marijuana in my jeans. I'm pretty sure he put it there, but it doesn't matter now.

I was fined, had my license suspended for a year, was sent to a detention facility, and had to do community service."

They were back at a red light.

"If I ever cross that guy, Tyson, I'll kill him." The serious protectiveness on Felix's face was as misplaced as his harsh words. It should have scared her. It didn't. In fact, it did the exact opposite. It made her feel worthwhile.

"Well, you can see why I have a problem with the police. My family never really believed that I'd quit drinking or smoking, so I can only imagine what the police must think."

"Fuck what they think. You're not that person anymore. You never were from what I've heard."

They pulled into the station parking lot.

Foreign emotions swirled inside her. Emotions she didn't know how to deal with. "Thanks." She reached for the door handle once they'd parked.

"I can go in with you if you want."

The offer caught her completely off guard. She'd never had such support. She suddenly wondered what it would be like to have a guy like Felix in her life. To always be there for her.

Don't even go there.

She got out of the Hummer. "I'll be fine."

As soon as she stepped into the police station she was anything but fine, which probably had a lot to do with the fact that she nearly ran face first into Collette.

Chapter 9

Cali's first instinct was to duck and cover.

Had it really only been less than twenty-four hours since Cali had seen her?

For her part, Collette looked like shit. It gave Cali a brief satisfaction to see the bags under her eyes.

But any satisfaction at seeing Collette's haggled appearance was wiped clean when Collette fixed Cali with a murderous expression.

For the tensest minute of her life, Cali did nothing but stare down her enemy. This was the woman who'd been sent to take her, the woman responsible for her being at the police station in the first place. But why did Collette want to take her? Who did she answer to? What did they want with her?

"Can we help you, miss?"

The voice broke the tension between them, and Cali stepped from around Collette to face down an officer sitting behind the front desk. She tried to walk over to the officer but was stopped when Collette grabbed her wrist painfully.

"I know what you are," she whispered. "I know what you mean to him, and I don't care what my *orders* are. I'm going to make him hurt like he hurt me."

Cali ripped her arm from Collette's grasp. She was taller than Collette by a couple of inches but what Collette lacked in height she made up for in presence. Still, Cali stared her down. "Don't ever touch me."

Collette grinned. "See you around."

The officer behind the desk watched everything with a careful eye, one hand held ready to go for his belt. "Is everything okay, miss?" he asked once Collette was gone.

"I'm here to give a statement. My name is Cali Crazar."

She waited patiently as the officer typed her name into whatever database they had. A few seconds later something flashed across his face. It was too quick for her to make any sense of it, but she had a good idea when he looked up and his expression was closed off.

So much for not pegging me based on my record.

"This way Miss Crazar." His tone lost all warmth, as if he were addressing a criminal.

Cali ground her teeth, but followed after him like a good little citizen.

The room she was to give her statement in looked a lot like an interrogation booth. Her escort dropped her off, instructing her to take a seat. The officers would be with her shortly.

Was being left alone supposed to intimidate her? Were they trying to wait her out and jumble her nerves so that she'd plead guilty?

The bastards could rot in hell for all she cared. Let them watch and analyze her all they wanted. She wasn't going to give them as much as a nervous tic.

After seven minutes of staring at the wall ahead of her, the door finally opened, admitting two officers.

"Miss Crazar?" the one on the left asked. He was short and stocky with blond hair and hard eyes. His partner looked a few years his junior with a short military cut and blue eyes.

"Yes." She kept her face devoid of any emotion. These assholes had lost all right to polite respect from her when they started treating her like a felon.

They each sat across the table from her. "I'm Officer Collins and this is my partner Officer Jacobs. Before we take your statement, there are a few questions we'd like to ask you."

"Of course." She pasted on a pleasant expression. "Anything I can do to clear up this mess." Her mind wandered to Collette. How the hell had she been released? She was found at the scene. Cali wanted to demand answers of her own, but she didn't want to make them think she was involved more than she really was.

"We're happy to hear that." Collins' voice could have been discussing the weather for all the emotion it held. "Are you familiar with a woman by the name of Collette Lizeroux?"

The opportunity to broach the subject was too much to pass up. "Was that the woman I ran into in the lobby? Shouldn't she be behind bars? She attacked me."

The two officers exchanged glances but didn't answer her question. "So you don't know her or why she was in your parents' home yesterday afternoon?"

Cali went for dumb innocence. "No, I have no idea why she came after me." Unfortunately, that statement was true. All she knew was that Collette had orders to collect her, and not even Felix and his super friends had any leads as to why.

Or maybe they did and just hadn't told her.

She stiffened her spine.

Officer Collins looked through some of his paperwork. "And you've had no problems . . . *socially* since this little incident in high school?" He turned the folder around so she could see her record. She wished for all the world that she'd bitten the bullet and paid the money to have it sealed. He gave the papers a quick tap. "No dealings with those that might hold something against you for not paying on time?"

Cali's temper spiked. "Do I look like a druggie to you?"

Collins leaned back in his chair and exchanged another look with the still silent Jacobs. "Why don't you tell us, Miss Crazar?"

Underneath the table, her hands balled into tight fists. "I'm not a druggie." She enunciated slowly through clenched teeth.

"So what were you doing at your parents' house yesterday?" Jacobs spoke up for the first time. His voice was a startling contrast to his appearance. It was a deep rumble that rolled through the whole room. "Looking for some quick money?"

Cali bit the inside of her cheek to keep from snarling at him. The truth was she *had* gone there for money. Dammit. But it wasn't what they were thinking. She'd needed the money for her rent. "I'd never steal from my parents."

"Of course not, Miss Crazar," Collins soothed. His patronizing tone grated on her. "But we're curious as to why you would be at your parents' when they were conveniently on vacation."

The hairs on the back of her neck started to prickle. "I didn't know they were on vacation." *Asshole*, she added silently.

Jacobs opened his mouth to speak, and Cali already knew she wasn't going to like what came out of it. "You know what I think, Miss Crazar?"

Don't give a shit.

"I think you're still a little lost, that you haven't quite got your feet under you yet. I think you panicked and sought out the only safety you knew."

She'd had enough. The whole back of her neck was tingling, her anger raging inside her. "I'm not a druggie. I'm not a dealer, or a user. I don't care what misconceptions my siblings might have given you, but I'm clean. Have been ever since . . ." She tapped the folder perhaps a little too forcefully for emphasis. But screw them. If they thought she would just go along silently with their accusations then they could go fuck themselves.

The silence in the room was deafening, a deep, rhythmic *lub-dub*, the only sound to be heard.

Cali's whole body turned to ice. *Oh, no.*

She tried to reel in her emotions. It didn't work. In fact, the sudden anxiety made it worse. The *thumping* grew louder.

Collins' and Jacobs' eyes both grew wide.

Jacobs put both hands on the table as if to shoot up from his seat. "What the hell is that?"

The *lub-dub* increased as Collins and Jacobs began to lose their cool. At this point it sounded like a cacophony of drums.

Collins was trying to keep his resolve. "Easy, Andy." He put a hand on his partner's shoulders. "I'm sure it's jus—iss—azar's—ell—one."

Cali sat in stunned horror as his words went in and out.

Holy shit, holy shit. Calm the fuck down, Cali!

She shut her eyes and exhaled. She desperately drew on what Felix had told her to do the other day. Damn, how she wished Felix were here with her.

Jacobs shot to his feet, the chair smashing to the floor behind him as he started to yell. Half his sentence was not even audible as his voice went in and out like Collins'. His sudden outburst did little to help Cali relax, but she pushed through it.

Stay focused.

Collins was now on his feet, attempting to calm the young cadet.

Come on, Cali. Think serene forests, calm beaches . . .

It didn't work.

Felix's arms around you . . .

The prickling receded.

The pounding of the officers' hearts faded. Cali sagged in relief, but it was short-lived.

She needed to get out of there.

She got to her feet. Collins and Jacobs both took a step back from her, their faces pale. "I wanted to give my statement and here it is: I went to visit my parents. I had no idea they were on vacation. While I was there, I was attacked, I believe the people were robbers, I fled for my own safety. Now, if there is no sufficient evidence to detain me, I'm leaving."

Collins looked like he wanted to say something but he stopped. "Very well," he said finally. "Good day."

Cali nodded and got the hell out of there.

Chapter 10

Felix could tell Cali was upset. Hurt, angry, and underneath it all, sad. She tried to hide it. Did a pretty good job of it. But he knew better.

He was supposed to be taking her back to the clinic or even her own place if she asked him. But she'd said nothing since she had stomped out of the station with her chin high and her eyes haunted. He wanted to ask what had happened. He wanted to chase away the fears he saw in her eyes but she wouldn't let him, dammit.

So instead he decided to take matters into his own hands and help her deal with her anger another way. He maneuvered the Hummer in the opposite direction of the clinic, and it wasn't until they were almost to their new destination that Cali even noticed the change in scenery.

"Where are we going?"

"My place."

That knocked her straight out of whatever slump she'd been in. "Why?"

He pulled into his driveway. "For some anger management."

"I don't need anger management."

"Fine, for stress relief."

"I don't need stress relief."

He turned in his seat to face her. "Is that so? So you always clutch your hands like that until they're white and shaky?"

She instantly unclasped her hands.

"Look, you obviously don't want to share with me what happened in there, but I'm still going to try and help you. It's not good to keep all that locked inside. Now come on."

He led her into his house and left her in the main living room to go retrieve his gloves and mitts from the guest room. The place was more like a storage unit. A really unorganized storage unit.

How did Sydney stand sleeping in here, he wondered as he shoved an old pile of clothes out of his way to get to the closet.

"Boxing gloves?" Cali asked once he was back in the living room with her. He threw his pair of mitts onto the couch.

"Best therapy there is," he told her. "Now give me your hand."

She held her arm out to him.

Her arms were long and smooth. Her hands slim and elegant. He imagined she could deliver the most teasing of caresses with those babies if she wanted to. He wanted those hands on him again. Though they looked gentle, he knew firsthand the power behind them. Like when they'd gripped his hips that time he had her pushed up against the cement pillar, his lips on hers. He remembered all too clearly the taste of those lips. Instantly he was hard for her.

Shit.

He swallowed as he guided her hand into the glove and strapped it on. "Next." His voice was gruff, and he hoped she didn't notice the bulge in his pants.

She held her other arm out to him, and he strapped her in. He quickly turned his back on her to readjust his jeans and slide his hands into the punching mitts he'd brought out for himself.

"Okay." He turned around to face her. He held up his hands, palms out so she could aim for the little white circles in the center. "Hit me."

She looked skeptical. "I don't want to hurt you."

He grinned. "Trust me, you can't hurt me."

Instead of putting her at ease, the words put her on the defensive. "Oh, yeah? How's that shin treating you?"

He winced as he remembered the killer bruise he'd woken up with that morning. She definitely wasn't a fragile little thing. But he had a feeling the strong, independent front she presented to everyone took its toll on her.

You can't keep your shields up forever.

Yet he had the feeling Cali never let anyone close to her. Her distrust bordered on paranoia. He couldn't imagine living like that. Everyone needed someone to trust, to accept them for who they were.

"Come on," he goaded her, wiggling his hands for emphasis. "Punch me."

She barely hesitated before her glove came flying at him. She hit the mitt hard enough to have his palm stinging.

"Good," he said. "Again."

And she did, over and over and over again, until she was breathing heavily and her eyes were distant. He could see her pain in their onyx depths. She'd given him a glimpse of her betrayal. That bastard Tyson had left his scar on her, and Felix wanted nothing better than to pound that asshole's face into the dirt until he bled. The pain she had experienced there had only gotten worse when her parents refused to see the real woman their daughter had become. His heart went out to her. She had a lot of problems to work out, and he would be there for her. Even if the only way to stay close to her was by operating as her own personal punching bag.

He knew what she was going through. He knew that sting of betrayal, could still taste the disappointment of losing those closest to him. He'd been cast out by his best friends on the cusp of his own power discovery. Hell, he'd been screwed over thrice by Collette. He could still remember the shocked stupor he'd been in the last time he'd seen her, years ago. He'd run from her apartment bleeding, with no idea if he'd killed Kevin or not, and the sight of Jasmine's corpse forever burned into his memory. His world had been turned on its side. Much the same way he imagined Cali's had been.

He reined in his wandering thoughts and focused on the woman in front of him. Her punches were getting sloppy. Sweat glistened at her temples. Her body shook from fatigue, and her eyes were brimming with unshed tears.

"I think that's enough," Felix said gently.

She threw another punch. "No." Her voice cracked and she

punched again. "Bastards thought I was nothing but trash, like I was worth nothing!" Each word was emphasized with the slap of her glove meeting his mitt.

Felix lowered his arms before she really hurt herself. "Cali . . . "

With no target to set her anger upon, she deflated. She shook her hands. "Ow," she said weakly.

Felix dropped his mitts and went to take hers off. Her knuckles were red and slightly swollen. One was starting to sport a little purple coloring while another was cracked and bleeding.

"Shit." He went for his first aid kit.

He guided Cali to the sofa and knelt before her. He took one of her hands and studied the handiwork. "Well, I'll give you this, you're a better boxer than Joel."

The comment pulled a small smile from her, one that disappeared as soon as he applied the peroxide. They lapsed into silence.

"They think I broke into my parents' to steal money to pay off a dealer."

Her words came out of the blue.

"They wouldn't listen to me, already had me pegged from the beginning. As soon as they looked up that fucking record. I tried to stay calm but it didn't help. My powers came all the same. The officers freaked out. I think they knew it was me but they were too afraid to say or do anything. Maybe I'll luck out and they'll explain the weird occurrence away."

Felix didn't interrupt in case there was more she needed to say. He continued to carefully wrap her knuckles. When nothing else followed, he brushed his thumb over the backs of her hands. "The first time I went to confront my best friend after accidentally using my powers in front of him, he called me a freak and slammed the door in my face. I got so angry at what he'd said and done that what little control I'd gained of my powers at the time slipped. I Erased his entire front door. My friend screamed. Slid down a whole set of stairs, he was so scared. I'll never forget the look on his face though. He didn't know who I was anymore, he was terrified of me."

When he looked up from her hands, he found she was watching him intently. Those deep brown orbs were as unguarded as he'd ever seen them.

He cleared his throat. "We all lose control of our powers, especially in the beginning. We'll help you work through it. Work through *this*."

"Is this going to cost me?" she teased.

"Absolutely." Those beautiful lips kicked up at the corners, sending a jolt straight through him. His blood pounded through his veins. His hands itched to touch her. He wanted his mouth on hers, his skin against hers, his body inside hers.

He wanted her with such force it shook him to his very soul.

He needed to pull away.

He couldn't.

And when her lips sought his, what little control he thought he might have had was obliterated. He fell on her like an antediluvian beast.

He couldn't touch enough of her. Her face, her neck—he trailed his hands down the sides of her body, just barely grazing her breasts. She arched into the touch. It was all the invitation he needed.

He flicked his thumbs over her hardened nipples. Her breasts were small and tight. They were perfect. With a growl he pushed her deeper into the couch. His tongue sought hers, and she responded with equal force.

This was no delicate flower beneath him. Cali was all wild, raw energy. Her fingers raked him, set his blood boiling. One of her hands dove into his hair, pulling his head closer so that their teeth nearly scraped. She drew his tongue seductively into her mouth and sucked him till he moaned.

Oxygen was an annoying necessity.

They broke apart, inhaling lungfuls of air. Their gazes locked.

Shit, he'd never felt this strong a pull to a woman before. She stared up at him with surprisingly naked eyes.

I'd never hurt you, he wanted to promise her. But Cali was beginning to look more and more like the type who would believe actions over words.

That was fine by him. He'd protect her, guard her with his life if he had to. This explosive attraction he felt toward her was more than he'd ever felt before. He was drawn to her and not just physically. He wanted to know her, to learn her hopes and fears, to take her in his arms and comfort her whenever she needed it.

Cali reached up and traced her finger along his jaw. "I don't even know you," she said as if she were mirroring his thoughts.

"That can easily be fixed," he drawled.

Cali inhaled sharply. Felix frowned, not understanding her reaction until he replayed his comment. What he'd meant to come out as innocent and genuine took on a totally different context when he took in their compromising position. Especially when his erection was so clearly pressed against her.

Well, shit.

He went to backpedal but something caught his eye outside of his sliding glass door. It was a person. A man in his backyard.

Felix shot to his feet. One minute the guy was there, the next he was gone. "What the hell?" he mumbled. He raced for his back door and ripped it open.

Nothing.

"Felix?" Cali called from behind.

"Stay here." He closed the sliding glass door on her, but not before he heard her say, "Like hell."

He ran around the side of the house and out the gate. He scanned his neighborhood. No new cars. No strange people running from his house.

What the fuck?

Had he imagined that guy?

The tickling at the back of his neck wasn't something from his imagination. He knew he'd seen something. The only question was how the hell had it escaped so fast?

An Illusion, perhaps?

Cali plowed through the gate, nearly knocking them both over. Felix righted her without thought. "What gives? What'd you see?"

He continued to search but found nothing out of the ordinary. *No one can move that fast.*

"What's out there?" Cali spoke softly.

Felix watched a car drive past. The sun was already starting to wane in the west. The salty ocean breeze rustled through the nearby trees. "I don't know. I saw a man standing in my backyard, near the sliding glass door. One second he was there. The next . . . he was gone."

Cali made a small noise in the back of her throat.

Felix turned to her. "What is it?"

She shook her head as if in disbelief. "Last night. At the clinic. I woke up and there was this shadow lurking in the doorway to the office. As soon as I blinked, it was gone. I searched the entire vet but couldn't find anything. All the doors were locked too. I figured I'd imagined the whole thing."

A bolt of dread went straight through him. Someone had gotten inside the clinic, and he hadn't been there. "Are you hurt?"

She didn't shake off his grasp like she usually did. "I'm fine. Nothing happened. I woke up and saw the outline of this guy but it was like he vanished. And it couldn't have been Collette because I saw her today at the station. She was being released."

This was news to him. "What?"

A bitter note crept into her voice. "She must have only been detained for the night. I didn't get the whole story. It was pretty anticlimactic. She tried to intimidate me but she can suck it, for all I care."

Her words brought a faint smile to his lips, but it didn't last.

"Did she admit to anything when you saw her? If it was her Illusions being sent after us she would've said something. She enjoys the feeling of power she gets when others fear her abilities."

She shook her head, her ponytail swaying with the motion. "She didn't say anything. So I'm guessing it wasn't her. Who else could it be?"

He pulled out his cell phone. "Shit if I know, but we're not safe here. We need Sydney. I'll let the others know we're on our way over." He ushered Cali back through the side gate, making sure to lock it behind him. *Like that's going to do a lot of good.* If only Joel's Locks lasted without him being near, Felix would have him Lock his whole damn house.

Who knew, maybe they'd luck out and Niella would get a Dream of whatever the hell was going on. They could sure do with some answers.

Chapter 11

"I need clothes," Cali spoke up from beside him as they got in the Hummer. "I can't keep wearing this." She picked up the T-shirt, gave it a distasteful look, and let it drop. "I need to stop by my apartment . . . before I'm evicted from it."

He started the car. "I don't think your apartment is going to be the safest place to go right now."

"Well, I'm sure as hell not wearing any of *your* clothes."

The thought of Cali in his clothes had him gripping the steering wheel and clenching his teeth.

Down, boy.

When he was more in control of himself he shot her a wicked grin. "You're welcome to go naked. I sure as hell won't mind."

He caught the flare of desire in her eyes before she looked away. "You're hopeless, you know that? I'll only be a second. I really need to get some clothes. And talk to my landlady."

"Why's that?"

She turned back to face him, "Because I'm not going to go walking around naked."

He tried to keep a straight face. "That's not what I meant." Her expression turned mortified. A flush made its way into her cheeks. He laughed. "I meant why do you need to talk to your landlady?"

"So I can straighten up the mess with my roommate. She stiffed me. Up and took my most recent painting so I was left high and dry. It was my turn to pay the rent, and now I'm not going to be able to. Hopefully, she'll cut me some slack, but she doesn't like me very much so I doubt it."

"Let me guess, your charming personality didn't work on her?"

"I hate you."

There was no real bite to the words, and that made Felix laugh all the harder because it told him just what he wanted to know. She most definitely did *not* hate him. In fact, he'd wager she actually kind of liked him.

"You don't have the best luck with people, do you?"

"Don't have the best luck, period. I'm stuck with you, aren't I?"

He put his hand over his heart. "Ouch. You almost said that like you meant it."

She shook her head, and he caught her smile out of the corner of his eye.

If only they hadn't been interrupted earlier . . .

*

"You really don't have to look so on edge," Cali told Felix as she jimmied her key in the lock.

Felix pushed the door open for her and went in first.

"Hey! I'm not defenseless."

"No," he agreed, "but you can't Erase things coming at you either. Let's say, for example, like if some crazy Illusionist was hiding out in your apartment ready to gut you with a knife."

When it was obvious no one was going to gut her, she pushed him aside to turn on the light. Everything was as she'd left it. Half empty. It looked like Jessica really had left her. Off to the side of the main living room sat her easel, naked. The oil painting that had been sitting there for two months was now in the hands of God only knew who. It was probably propped against a wall somewhere, unseen. The idea made her hands fist.

Felix bumped his shoulder against hers. "You okay?" The man could read her *way* too easily. And just like that, she remembered his powerful body atop hers, pressing into her in all the right places. It made her throb all over with sexual frustration. She wanted Felix with a carnal need that was only getting stronger the

95

longer she spent in his presence.

Hell, if Felix hadn't seen that man in his backyard, she probably would have let him take her right there on the sofa.

Get to know him better, indeed . . .

She looked up at him. He was still waiting for her answer, his brilliant blue-green eyes regarding her with nothing but openness. His five o'clock shadow was a little fainter today, he must've shaved that morning, but she remembered all too well the tantalizing feel of his face scraping against her neck.

She swallowed thickly and turned from him. "I'm just upset because, for some stupid reason, I thought Jessica might have come back. That she would bring my painting back." She pointed to her easel, amazed she'd admitted that much to him. "I worked so hard on it," she added quietly.

She felt the heat from Felix's body as he came up behind her. His arms wrapped around her waist, putting her back flush with his firm chest. His breath tickled her neck, and when his lips brushed the skin there she wanted to moan from the pleasure of it.

She could feel his erection pressing into her from behind.

He didn't try to comfort her with false words, he simply held her. She didn't step away. Not yet. She wanted to memorize the way his body fit against hers.

He kissed her neck again. Heat flooded her body and without conscious thought she pushed back against him, rubbing against the obvious bulge in his pants. The growl in her ear was such a turn on that she was afraid her knees would buckle. But he would never let her fall. Somehow she knew that. His arms tightened around her, and she arched into him as he gently thrust against her. Together they started an agonizing rhythm that had Cali wishing she were naked and he were inside her.

His tongue trailed along her neck, leaving a warm, wet path that had her shivering in need.

Step away, some conscious part of herself yelled. *You can't have sex with a man without getting attached.*

She knew the voice was right but just as she was getting ready to break from him, one of Felix's hands drifted down from her waist to cup her sex. White-hot pleasure ripped a gasp from her throat.

He nuzzled his cheek against the side of her face. "I can't stop myself when I'm around you." His voice was ragged, as if he'd been running a marathon.

"I—" Her throat had suddenly gone dry. "I don't want—" *you to stop.* She never wanted him to stop touching her.

The doorbell to her apartment rang, followed swiftly by three harsh knocks.

Cali jumped from Felix's arms, her face scalding, as if she'd been caught, like that time her father had walked in on her first make-out session.

"Who is it?" Felix's voice, and the pinched look on his face told her how much distress he was in. The bulge in his pants looked down-right painful.

Her chest was heaving. "My landlady." She quickly smoothed out her clothes.

Felix nodded. "I'll leave you two alone, then. Where's the bathroom? I need to fix myself."

She tried to avoid staring at his pants. "The room on the left just before the kitchen is mine. When you enter, the first door on your left is the bathroom."

Her heart was still pounding even after he was gone.

She tried on a smile and opened the door. "Mrs. Deder."

The crotchety old woman was eye level with her chest. She sneered at Cali's breasts, as if she were wantonly jiggling them in front of her. Naked.

Mrs. Deder held her ever-present walking stick in her left hand, though everyone in the building knew she never used it unless it was to pound at someone's door. Usually Cali heard it on her door the day her rent was due.

When she was done giving her chest the evil eye, Mrs. Deder looked up to meet Cali's stare. Her eyes were a washed-out blue, her face only marred by a few wrinkles, and when she spoke, it was with a voice raspy from years of smoking. "Rent's due tomorrow, Crazar. I've got a doctor's appointment to take care of my cough so I won't be here to hound your lazy, criminal ass."

Cali's jaw ached from how hard she was clenching it. Ever since she moved in, Mrs. Deder had taken one look at her dark hair and dark nail polish and instantly tagged her as a criminal. And on the days she didn't call her a criminal, usually the words "street corner" or "whore" weren't far from her vocabulary.

She cleared her throat. *Stay professional,* she chanted to herself. "I actually wanted to talk to you about this month's rent, Mrs. Deder. You see . . . " She glanced over her shoulder at the half-empty apartment. "Jessica broke her contract and left, so I don't think I'm going to be able to make the full payment tomorrow. If I could pay you—"

Mrs. Deder's face twisted. "I know all about poor Jessica, criminal. She said she left because you stole money from her, and she couldn't stand to live in fear anymore."

She what?

"That bitch. She stole from *me*!"

So much for professionalism.

"I don't care who stole from who, but you have two weeks to get me my money." She turned her back and made her way down the staircase.

Cali stood stupefied. That had gone better than she'd imagined. Only now she had two weeks to make twelve hundred dollars.

She was so screwed.

If she emptied out her entire savings, she'd only need two hundred dollars or so. But then she'd have no money for food. Or clothes. Or her art supplies.

She tried not to think about that and closed the door so she could start packing her things.

Maybe Sydney would let her live out of the clinic.

I'm sure Felix would let you stay with him . . .

The stray thoughts had her stopping dead in her tracks. Since when had she started thinking about the super squad like they were her BFFs?

She was getting too comfortable with the idea of them being in her life. She'd been fine on her own up until now. Hadn't she?

"How'd it go with the landlady? She let you off the hook for the month?"

She sidestepped Felix to get into her room, being extra careful not to touch him. "She gave me two more weeks."

He followed her and took a seat at the foot of her bed.

He looked good there, like he belonged in her room, his bronze skin offset by the white-and-purple sheets.

She could just imagine walking over to him, pushing him flat on his back and riding him till she screamed.

"—ali?"

"Huh?"

Her whole body shook with need, the burning between her thighs incessant.

"I asked why you don't sell any of these." He motioned to the wall covered with license plate holders.

She grabbed a duffle out of her closet and avoided looking at Felix, lest she do something really stupid. Like throw herself at him. "Those are more like a creative assignment. They force me to paint according to whatever is written there. I use it to make sure I don't get sucked into painting the same old pictures over and over again." She grabbed a handful of T-shirts and thrust them into her bag.

She methodically made her way around her room. By the time she got to her underwear drawer, Felix was standing to examine her art close up. She hesitated.

"Afraid I might see something?"

He'd snuck up on her. She glared at him over her shoulder and shoved him away. "Don't flatter yourself."

Her shove moved him about two inches. The man was like a mountain of muscle. She could still feel the heat from his chest on her hand, as well as how firm he was to the touch.

"Are you just going to stand there?" He hadn't moved, which meant he would still be able to see into her drawer. For some reason the idea of Felix seeing her lingerie made her skin hot.

That roguish grin was back. "Are you asking me to help?"

Not dropping his challenging stare, she ripped open her drawer and purposely went to the side with the lace. She grabbed the first thing her fingers grazed. Whatever she ended up pulling out wiped that grin right off of Felix's face.

"I-is that . . . edible?"

Her head whipped around in alarm. Sure enough, she held up the gag gift Garnet had sent her on Valentine's Day. "Shit." She shoved them back in her drawer and slammed it shut. She stormed over to Felix, who still looked as if he'd been bashed over the head, and practically dragged him from her room. "Get out. Now."

Once alone, she packed in humiliated silence.

Chapter 12

Edible underwear.

Edible. Underwear.

Edible fucking underwear.

Felix ran a hand through his hair. "Fucking hell," he breathed. As if his cock wasn't hurting bad enough already. Now he had the image of Cali in . . . edible underwear. He slapped a hand to his forehead and groaned. "Stop thinking about it."

He forced his feet to move him over to the kitchen and sat his ass at one of the barstools. He continued to stare at the door, as if he'd develop x-ray vision and be able to see through it. It was useless of course. He could hear Cali moving around in there, knew he should be on high alert in case anything came in through the front door, but he couldn't get himself to focus.

It doesn't matter what's in her underwear drawer, you're never going to see it anyway.

The harsh reality was like a face full of cold water. No matter how much he'd like to think he was making progress with her, Cali's words from ten minutes ago kept repeating over and over in his mind.

"I don't want—"

There were a million different ways that sentence could have ended. The one that bothered him the most, and what she had probably been going to say was: *I don't want you. Ever. End of story.*

He slammed his fist down on the counter. The connection between them was not a figment of his imagination. He knew she had to feel something. Chemistry like they had wasn't an everyday occurrence. She had pushed back against him. She'd been the one to kiss him in his home. Which meant she had to feel something.

Anything.

It didn't fucking matter. He wasn't about to give her up. He'd waited a long time for his Mirror Mate to come along. He could wait a little longer.

*

It turned out Sydney's clinic had some overnighters scheduled for surgery the next morning. Ergo, Cali was not staying the night there.

Sydney had been alarmed to find out that someone had been inside her clinic the previous night, but like Felix, Cali had no explanation of what had happened. There was nothing for them to do. Sydney couldn't Shield everyone 24/7, no matter how much she might've wanted to try. The best course of action they all decided on was for her to stay with Felix.

And so it was that she found herself back in his Hummer on her way to his house.

At least you won't be alone.

The thought was comforting, but Cali didn't want to have to rely on the others constantly. She needed to learn to take care of herself. She needed to learn control of her powers.

Who knew? Maybe there was more to her power than she thought.

She looked around the Hummer for anything to Silence when an idea struck her. Silence the entire car. The task was a daunting one, but Cali was determined. It was just like her license plate painting exercises. If the plate read "I'd rather be snowboarding," she painted a mountain range. If the plate read "I'd rather be surfing," she painted the ocean. "Daddy's little girl?" No problem. She sketched a fictitious little girl growing into a beautiful woman.

She could do this.

She settled back into the passenger seat and focused her body. She imagined herself like a black hole. A vacuum for sound. The back of her neck tingled. She branched out, pulling the sound from beneath her feet. She imagined going into the flooring, into the wheels, and noticed with some satisfaction that the radio grew louder without the outside noise from the wheels rolling across the pavement.

A dull ache started behind her eyes, but the adrenaline coursing through her veins pushed her to go farther. She reached out with her powers for the engine of the car, traveling up the middle console into the radio. The light-up display still showed the radio station but the music disappeared.

Felix reached for the volume knob.

She watched the volume rise but nothing came from the speakers. Cali switched her focus to Felix himself, seeing him in her mind, trying to keep him from going Silent. It was the most difficult task—keeping someone *in* sound when she was taking away everything else, but she did it. Or so she hoped.

Felix continued to toy with the volume. She wanted to laugh but didn't want to break her concentration. After a moment his head turned ever so slightly from side to side, no doubt noticing all the volume changes.

Finally his eyes fell on her. "Did you—?" Felix slammed on his brakes.

Cali threw her arms out in front of her. Her scream lodged in her throat as an ambulance raced past, centimeters in front of Felix's car. They were in the middle of an intersection, the light for them glowing green.

Instantly, her sound bubble popped.

The ambulance's siren wailed out into the distance. Inside the Hummer, the radio blasted the latest dance song. Felix fumbled for the volume while simultaneously turning down the nearest street. From what Cali could tell, they were only a few blocks from his house.

They came to an abrupt stop, her seatbelt cutting into her chest and neck.

Felix shoved his car into park. "What the hell was that?" he snarled.

He was white as a sheet. His pulse pounded in his neck. His grip on the steering wheel was so intense Cali feared he'd snap it. She'd never seen him so shaken.

"Sorry. Wanted to keep you on your toes is all." She tried to laugh it off.

Felix's lips didn't even twitch. "That's not funny, Cali. Do you know how close I was to Erasing that ambulance?"

Cali winced as his voice rose with every word. "But you didn't." She tried for the silver lining. It didn't work.

"That's not the point. The point is that I nearly slipped up. I could feel my powers kicking in. I felt my body act out of self defense. All I would've had to do was finish that final thought—move my hand just a millimeter, and all those people would have been gone." He gently peeled his hands from the steering wheel and stared at them as if he didn't understand what they were doing attached to his body.

"Hey," she said gently and reached out for him. He jerked away from her touch. It was like a punch to the gut. She covered up the hurt the only way she knew how. With anger. "Look, you were telling me earlier that it was okay to fuck up every once in a while. No one's perfect. You can't be prepared for everything."

He quit staring at his hands to pin her with his eyes. "I meant that it's okay for *you* to mess up. You manipulate sound, Cali. I fucking Erase things. Gone. Never to be seen again. I don't even fucking know where they go. Bottom of the ocean?" He shrugged. "Inside a volcano? How the hell am I supposed to know, huh? They could be trapped in some kind of limbo, starving or suffocating to death, and I would have no idea. I could be responsible for *killing* people with nothing more than a flick of my wrist. I've never Erased someone before. I couldn't live with myself if I did."

That was when it hit her. Somewhere deep down, under all the humor and charm, Felix was afraid of himself.

Without even thinking about it, she leaned over and pressed her lips to his. He tried to pull away. Did he think he was going to Erase her? She grasped his shoulders and held firm. "You're not going to Erase anyone. Especially me. Could you imagine how pitiful your life would be without me?"

Something flashed in his eyes too fast for her to read. "Does that mean you're sticking around for a while?"

Her breath caught in her throat. Did it?

She eased back into her own seat and gave him a nonchalant look that was at complete odds with what she felt inside. "Don't push your luck."

The tension riding Felix's broad shoulders seemed to have lessened. He started the Hummer and drove them the few blocks back to his place.

By the time they got into his house he was starting to act more like himself.

"What the hell do you have in here?" He lifted her duffle for emphasis.

She bee-lined for his kitchen and a cool glass of water. "You're the one that wanted to carry it for me," she pointed out. "And be careful, some of my art supplies are in there."

He disappeared down the hallway and came back empty handed. "I put it in the guest room."

They lapsed into silence as Felix took down his own glass for water.

"You know that's two, right?" Cali broke the quiet. Felix raised a brow in question. "Calming your ass down." She held up two fingers and wiggled them playfully. "That's two."

Felix took a slow sip from his glass. His eyes glittered.

Cali's body instantly went hot. "Well, goodnight."

She went to escape but Felix caught her in two easy strides of his long legs. His hand clasped her upper arm loosely, letting her know he'd let go if she wished it. Which made it all the harder. If he'd hold her in place against her will, she could simply explain that she'd had no choice but to let him touch her, but when he left her the option of pulling away and she didn't. . .

She didn't want to admit to craving his touch.

"In the Hummer you were trying to practice. If you want to practice, we'll practice. Tomorrow. When I get off work. Deal?" The clipped way he spoke told Cali he was holding his own temptations in check.

She shouldn't have stayed with him. She needed to get away from him, not spend more time with him.

Her mouth betrayed her. "Deal."

*

Living with Felix turned out to be everything Cali could have wanted when she'd moved out on her own. The added benefit of Felix being a baker who brought her fresh pastries was just the cherry on top. Literally.

There was a companionship between them that she never would have thought possible. And when it came to her powers, despite his wicked and playful attitude, Felix was actually a great teacher. He was patient with her when she was sure others would have quit on her. He was supportive when she wanted to quit on herself.

The only drawback?

Felix's ungodly morning schedule. He even worked weekends. He woke up way before the sun rose and was finished with his day before lunch, usually around the time Cali was getting up to start her day. And on the days she was still sleeping when he got home, Felix took it upon himself to be her personal wake-up call.

She'd only bloodied his nose once.

And it was by accident.

Either way, Felix loved scaring her ass out of bed.

But as the days ticked by, Cali could feel the unspoken tension between them building. It was there in every glance. Every touch. In every unsaid freaking word.

And on top of that tension was the anxiety that came from sitting and waiting as everyone anticipated Collette's next move. There hadn't been any sight of her or the mystery shadow in nearly a week. It was beginning to wear on everyone. The signs were there for all to see. Sydney was more jumpy, Joel constantly looked tired, and Niella was more snappish than usual.

Felix was better at hiding it. He held his tension in his posture. Everywhere they went his shoulders were stiff, as if he expected an ambush attack at any moment. A few days ago the doorbell had rang. He'd been taking a nap on the couch while she'd been sketching. The sound had him shooting up over the couch and colliding with the side table so hard he sent a lamp careening into the wall, shattering it. When he'd wrenched open the front door the young boy selling magazine subscriptions had been terrified.

"A little FYI," she had called from her sketch spot in the kitchen. "I don't think Collette would ring the doorbell before an attack."

As for herself, she tried to stay relaxed but it was difficult when everyone else was so on edge.

Even now, as she sat sketching at Felix's small round table in the kitchen, her body was on high alert. Felix had gone out to get them fixings for a late lunch. She'd stayed behind to finish her sketch. The clock was ticking when it came to her two-week deadline for Mrs. Deder, and she hadn't even started painting yet. She only hoped this piece of work would make enough to reach her rent without dipping too much into her savings.

When her phone went off she nearly jumped out of her skin.

She fumbled in her bag, spilling makeup and other contents across the table.

She didn't recognize the number.

Could it be Collette? Or was she being paranoid?

"H-hello?"

"May I speak to Miss Cali Crazar, please?" a pleasant feminine voice asked. This was most definitely not Collette.

"This is she."

"Hello, Cali. I'm calling on behalf of Mr. Vander Donahughe in regards to the Kratos Corporation."

Cali stomach nearly dropped right out of her.

Vander. The job offer he'd proposed three months ago. After all those sporadic check-ins he was finally getting back to her, for real. Excitement bubbled. She'd be able to make her rent after all.

She wiped her suddenly sweaty palm on her shorts. "I'm so glad to hear from you. What can I do for you?"

"Mr. Donahughe would like to schedule an interview with you for a position that has recently opened."

The interior design-like position. Vander had briefly explained it to her when he'd approached her with the job. They'd give her the layout of all the different room designs before they started construction on a new building, and it would be her job to match her painting to the decor of the room.

It sounded too good to be true, but she'd done some research on the Kratos Corporation. They'd gotten their start a few years ago designing active wear. Their mission was to create "clothing that empowers." No doubt they would expand to empower lots of new items, not just clothing.

She flipped her sketchpad to a blank page. "An interview? Of course. Uh, what time?"

There was the faint clicking of a keyboard on the other end of the line. "Does tomorrow at nine a.m. suit you?"

Cali blanched at the hour. "Nothing in the afternoon?" she blurted before she could stop herself.

There was a long pause.

Cali dropped her head to the tabletop.

Way to go, Cali. You just ruined any chance you had. You really couldn't have woken your ass up at nine?

"Miss Crazar," the secretary spoke up. "There is an opening at two o'clock tomorrow afternoon. Shall I pencil you in?"

Cali sat up so fast she nearly toppled backwards. "Yes!" She winced and lowered her voice. "I mean, yes, that works out perfectly. Thank you."

"We'll see you tomorrow, Miss Crazar." The secretary rattled off the time again and an address that Cali quickly jotted down onto her sketchpad.

She sat for a few moments, letting the reality of it all sink in.

The sound of Felix's Hummer pulled her from her thoughts, and she stared at the table she'd made a mess of. "Crap." Felix might use his guest bedroom like a messy storage unit, but he kept the rest of his house pretty neat.

She quickly started throwing her spilled make-up back into her bag. Her eyes landed on one of her shiny lip-glosses.

Felix's keys jiggled in the lock.

Cali swiped the gloss over her lips, checked her hair, and closed her purse.

*

Felix knew something had changed the second he entered his house. For one thing, Cali looked flustered. She stood by the table in the kitchen, face flushed.

His first instinct was to think something was wrong, but nothing screamed *threat* to him.

He placed the groceries onto the counter. "Everything okay?" he asked, continuing to scan for anything unusual.

Cali instantly went for the bags of food when he stepped away to put the milk in the fridge. "I have a job interview tomorrow," she said brightly. Some of the cheerfulness left her voice. "Where's the bread? I thought we were making sandwiches later. How are we supposed to make them without bread?"

He closed the fridge and leaned against it, arms crossed. He gave her a droll stare. "Cali, I'm a baker. I don't buy bread at the grocery store. I make it. Fresh. At home."

He went to the oven and set the temperature.

"Get out the flour, the salt, and one of those yeast packages, would you?" he called over his shoulder.

"Are we really doing this?" Cali questioned, though she did as he asked without complaint.

"Yes. Honey."

Cali's footsteps came to a halt. "What did you call me?"

He looked up from where he was retrieving his mixing bowls. "I didn't call you anything. I said honey, as in 'take out the honey.' We're making honey wheat bread."

Red dotted her cheeks.

He couldn't resist. "I didn't think you were the type to want cutesy nicknames, Cali, but if you want, I'll call you honey. Honey." He added a wink because the temptation was too great.

Her hand disappeared into the flour container. "Like hell," she said playfully. Flour shot out of her hand, hitting him square in the face. "Don't you ever call me that."

He wiped flour from his eyes.

Cali was grinning.

He got to his feet. When he stood at his full height her smile waned. Her expression turned into something like *Oh, shit*.

Now it was his turn to grin. He lunged for her. Cali screamed and raced around the counter that acted as an island separating the kitchen from the living room. Her hand disappeared into the flour, and she blindly threw it over her shoulder. She missed. By a mile. He was gaining on her as they ran in circles. Or he was, until his sock hit a patch of flour on the kitchen floor and his foot went out from under him. He slid like an ungraceful baseball player into his cabinets.

Pain flared in his knees. "Fuck."

Cali was at his side in an instant. "Are you all right?" An idea formed in his mind. He hid his smile of victory.

"I think I broke something," he added a pained edge to his voice that should have won him an Oscar.

"Shit. Don't move. I'll call the paramedics."

He waited till her back was turned and took a large scoop out of the flour she'd abandoned. He got to his feet. "Hold on, Cali, I think I'm all right."

As soon as she turned, he plucked her up with one arm and set her on the counter next to the sink where he got a close up view of her face as he rubbed the flour onto the top of her head.

Her expression was priceless.

"You jerk." She shoved at him, but he leaned closer so she couldn't get away. "I thought you'd seriously been hurt."

"Serves you right for wasting my flour like that."

She tried to get away again but with a leg on either side of his hips and his body so close she couldn't get enough room to maneuver away. It didn't take her long to figure that out. Or to figure out how close they were. Their eyes locked, and all that tension he'd been feeling between them started coming to a head.

Her pupils dilated, the black bleeding into the dark of her iris to make it look like one solid color. Her chest rose and fell with shallow gasps. Her lips parted and . . . was that . . . lip gloss?

Felix didn't think he'd ever seen her wear it before.

Was it for him?

Images flared to life.

Those shiny lips on him, around his cock, sucking, sliding up and down his—

He went hard as a rock and groaned mentally, cutting off his train of thought.

He didn't close the space between them. He wanted her to do it. He wouldn't force her. He'd like to think he'd been upfront about how he felt about her. If she didn't want him, then she needed to say something. And soon.

*

Cali sat frozen, Felix pinned between her legs. The heat of his body seeped into hers, making her dizzy and achy.

His body was rigid, his eyes blue and green fire. He swallowed. "I can't stay like this forever, Cali." His rough voice made her shiver. "I need you to make a decision here."

Her heart sped up even more. Her mouth had long since gone dry. She licked her lips, tasting the flavor of her lip gloss. But she didn't want to taste it. She wanted to taste Felix. She leaned forward, her decision made.

He came alive the moment her lips touched his. His strong arms crushed her to him. He tasted like flour. She wrapped her legs around him. His tongue slipped between her lips, demanding invitation to her mouth. She opened wider for him. He growled, his hands sliding to cup her bottom and pull her against his erection.

Her brain fogged. Her body undulated against his. She felt the shudder run straight through him. The feeling of power she got from being able to make a man like Felix shudder was downright intoxicating. His lips broke from hers to trail down the side of her neck. His hands snaked up her shirt to cup her breasts beneath her bra. Her head fell back on a moan as he rolled her nipples. A dull ache started between her legs. She tried to squeeze her legs shut to ease it, but Felix was pressed too hard against her.

Her hands skimmed along his torso, tracing every ridge and groove. He was built like a football player—hard muscle everywhere she touched. And she wanted to touch more of it. She grasped the hem of his graphic tee and tugged insistently. Felix got the message and pulled back enough for her to drag it over his head.

Holy fuck.

What she felt beneath his shirt was nothing compared to what it looked like up close.

"I had no idea bakers were in such good shape," she mumbled.

A deep chuckle rumbled from his chest. "It's all the kneading we do." He spoke against her ear. His tongue flicked against her skin, causing her to jump. "We're also very good with our hands." As if to emphasize his point, he squeezed her breasts.

The air left her lungs. "Show me."

His lips were back on hers. Hot. Demanding.

There was a tug on her jean shorts. Suddenly they loosened. Anticipation spiked. She wrapped her arms firmly around Felix's neck, lifting herself off the counter so he could pull her shorts down.

The cold on her ass made her yelp.

After a few more seconds of kissing Felix she didn't care. His fingers skimmed the inside of her leg, making their way to where she burned.

His fingers skimmed the center of her. Felix hissed. "You're so wet."

She slid her tongue into his mouth, her hands grasping the hard muscle of his shoulder. She arched into his hand, wanting his touch. Craving it.

She'd spent so much time resisting him.

Stupid.

All thought stopped when he pushed a finger inside her. Her body clenched. He added another finger, and she gasped. When he started to thrust her vision blacked out. All she could do was feel. It'd been so long and it felt so good.

His thumb rubbed against her clit, building that sweet pressure higher and higher.

He pulled back from her mouth to growl into her ear. "Come for me."

That was all it took.

Her climax hit hard. She strained against him, her fingers digging deep into his shoulders as he rode her through it.

As she came back down, his fingers were still thrusting but they were slowing, easing her to a stop.

She was all but panting as she tried to suck in lungful after lungful of air.

Felix nuzzled her neck. The gesture was both intimate and possessive. It made her heart flip.

"I told you I was good with my hands," he whispered, his tongue trailing down the side of her neck. He was positively radiating smugness.

"You want to know a secret?" she purred.

"Mm?"

She went to the front of his jeans and slipped her hand inside. Felix's whole body jerked, a curse exploding from his lips.

She leaned forward to kiss the underside of his jaw. "Artists are good with their hands too." She pumped her hand as best she could while she went to work on the front of his pants with the other. His jeans were too constricting. A man of his size—and good God, he was huge— needed more room.

When she got his jeans undone, she released him and pushed them down as far as she could reach from her position. Her eyes went wide at the sight. The burn Felix had eased between her legs pulsed to life. She cupped him again and worked him with her hands.

He braced a hand on either side of her, as if it were a labor just to keep himself upright, which she guessed it was considering how tight his body was and how hard he was breathing.

She could feel his tension rising.

"Are you going to come for me, Felix?" She slanted her lips over his and swallowed his cry as his body slammed forward with his orgasm. Warmth covered her hands, but she continued to pump, wanting every last drop.

"Fuck." Felix dropped his head into the crook of her neck.

Nothing could have satisfied her more.

Chapter 13

The next day Cali practically skipped into the kitchen for her brunch. Technically it was her breakfast, but Felix called it brunch because she usually had it around noon.

She went straight for the white paper bag on the counter. Cali blushed when she realized what counter Felix had placed the bag on.

He's never going to let you forget yesterday.

Her body hummed just thinking about it. And there was a lot to think about. Or more likely a lot to remember and fantasize about.

And she was determined not to over-think the whole situation. What she and Felix did had been done between two adults. She damn well wasn't going to start getting attached. No sir.

She took a bite out of her cherry pastry and walked over to where she'd left her purse on the table. She dug around for her apartment keys and left them out. She needed to go back to her apartment and pick out some clothes fitting for an interview. She doubted her jean shorts and T-shirt combos would be very impressive to someone like Vander Donahughe. The only problem was that she'd left her car at her parents' house. She could always ask Felix to take her or ask to borrow the Hummer.

She sat at the table and finished her breakfast in quiet contemplation as she weighed her options. As she got her glass of milk out of the fridge, she decided to risk asking Felix to borrow the Hummer. Sure, she'd never driven a huge SUV, but how hard could it be?

"Do you even know how to drive one of these?" Felix gave her a skeptical look as he held the keys out to her fifteen minutes later.

She went to grab for them, and like every other time, he pulled them out of reach at the last minute. "Sure. I'll be fine."

"I want you to call as soon as you get there."

"Who are you, my dad?" She lived twenty minutes away.

The heated look he gave her had her eating her words. Felix was most definitely *not* her dad.

"Fine, I'll call you when I get there. Now give me the damn keys. I can't be late for this interview."

He handed them over and she opened the driver's side.

"Oh, Cali?"

She paused, one leg in, one leg out.

He held up two fingers, grinning. "Borrowing my Hummer, that's two."

Her mouth slacked open. *The nerve!* She slammed the Hummer door and grumbled angrily all the way to her apartment.

She had to sneak past Mrs. Deder's office. The last thing she wanted was for her landlady to see her and want to talk. Cali really didn't feel like talking to her. In fact, she never felt like talking to the woman. Though maybe if she told Mrs. Deder had a job interview, the landlady would prolong her missed month of rent.

She threw the idea out as soon as it crossed her mind.

If she told Mrs. Deder she had a job interview, the woman would probably think she was going to be involved with drug cartel.

She took the stairs two at a time and jimmied her key to get her front door open. With all the drapes pulled shut the place was nearly pitch black. She put her arms out in front of her as she made her way inside and felt for the light switch on the left.

Once she made it to her room she threw open her closet to scout for anything she might own that would look interview worthy. There wasn't much. She found an old black skirt she'd worn to Garnet's college graduation a few years ago, as well as a dark purple pencil skirt she'd bought on the spur of the moment.

She laid both pieces out on her bed and fumbled around for a shirt that wouldn't show her bra straps. She came across a reasonable cute shirt. It was black. Of course. And had delicate lace trimmings. She paired it with the purple skirt.

She studied the ensemble and shrugged. "Good enough."

Her only pair of black heels completed the outfit. Now it was time to really impress. She took out a manila folder from her stack of supplies and gently took down her best work from her wall of license plates.

A knock at her door stopped her halfway through.

Mrs. Deder?

Cali put the folder down with a curse. How the hell had she known she was up here?

She looked through her peephole. Her heart stopped. It wasn't Mrs. Deder. It was Officer Jacobs.

Her first instinct was to shut off the lights and run. What the hell was he doing here? Did he still think she was responsible for the break-in at her parents'?

What if he's here because of what you did at the station?

Would he be able to arrest her for that?

Of course not. Stay cool. If he asks about it, act confused.

With trembling hands she opened the door.

"Officer Jacobs." She tried for pleasant but her voice came out squeaky. "What can I do for you?"

"You can extend some common courtesy and invite me into your trash hole of a home."

Her fingers tightened around the doorknob. She was this close to slamming the door in his fucking face but at the last minute he seemed to pull a warrant out of nowhere.

He waved the slip of paper in front of her face before tucking it back into his pocket. "Now," he said.

She forced herself to step back and held her arm out for him to pass through.

Behind his back she mouthed, *"Asshole."*

"With all due *respect*," she said after she shut the door. "I'm kind of in a hurry. So you want to tell me what it is you have a warrant for?" *Please nothing serious.* And where was Officer Collins? She'd assumed the two were partners. Didn't cops always travel in twos? At least when they were going to a house with a warrant?

Jacobs stopped a scant foot in front of her and grinned. Cali frowned when his whole body seemed to shimmer. "I came for a little girl-on-girl time."

His voice turned feminine, sounding very familiar. "Wha—?"

Faster than she could blink, his hand shot out. Pain exploded on the side of her face. She didn't even remember moving. One second she was standing in the middle of her living area, the next, she was propped up against the wall for support.

She blinked away the stars dancing in front of her eyes and tried to focus on Jacobs. He wasn't there. Standing where he'd been seconds ago was Collette. Her cheeks were more pronounced, her eyes sunken. Wherever she'd been for the past week, it hadn't been Hawaii.

She'd finally made her move, and she'd caught Cali all alone.

"What the hell do you want?" Maybe if she kept Collette talking she'd think of some way to get out of this. The door was to her back—she could make a run for it, but that left her wide open for an attack. Besides, Cali didn't run. Especially from perfectly dressed little bitches.

Collette gave a polite smile, taking in Cali's poorly furnished home. "No Felix to come and save the day?"

"Leave Felix the hell alone," she growled.

Cali knew there was a history between them, but she'd never been brave enough to ask Felix about it. A part of her didn't want to know it.

Collette rested her hands on her hips. "Aren't you a defensive one? Don't tell me he's gotten to you already."

Cali ground her teeth and kept her mouth shut. She would not fall for the bait.

"He's good like that," Collette said in a breathy voice. Cali's blood roared in her ears. "But I should warn you, he'll reel you in and then leave you in the dust like so much parchment."

Her eyes grew distant, glazed, as if she weren't quite all there. Then just like that, she was focused again. The clarity in her eyes belied the insanity Cali had witnessed seconds ago. She didn't want to believe a word Collette said. This was the enemy, dammit! But she couldn't help herself. When she'd dated Tyson, she'd ignored the warnings and look how that had turned out.

Felix is nothing like Tyson.

"He'll use you, Cali," Collette continued. "He'll get your hopes up and then walk away without so much as a backward glance." Her face darkened in remembrance.

Cali's stomach sank, a chill creeping down her spine. Her words played on the one fear Cali'd been unable to overcome. To care for someone and then have them stab her in the back. Or worse, to have them use her and then leave.

"Leave Felix out of it," she bit out. "They told me you've found your Mirror Mate so why the hell are you so fixated on him?"

The darkness in her face grew at the mention of her Mirror Mate. "I take it your defensive tone of voice is because you believe Felix to be your soul mate? Did they tell you he was? That you two would fall desperately in love with each other with just one glance, like star-crossed lovers?" She sighed in dramatic effect. "Did they make you believe you have to *love* your 'Mirror Mate?'" She sneered at the word. "You see Cali, love is a fickle thing—always has been, always will be. To love or not to love is up to the person. I don't believe in destiny. The man meant for me wasn't the one that would unlock my powers." She looked genuinely disappointed by that fact, and jealousy reared its ugly head. Collette obvious was not over Felix or their relationship. Whatever it had been. "You'll always *feel* for them, but there doesn't have to be love. Did they tell you that? Did they get you to believe there is a single love for you out there? Waiting?" She scoffed. "Only fools wait for their destiny to unfold. I waited. For a long time I waited, and you want to know something, Cali? I was never good enough. I never felt good enough until I met Felix." A warm smile bloomed across her face.

Cali felt sick. She didn't want to hear this.

"Look—"

Collette cut her off. "But even after everything I tried to do for him, you know what ended up happening? I wasn't good enough for him either. Not only did he take away my dreams, he took away my Mirror Mate."

Cali's stomach dropped.

Collette smiled as if she knew the path Cali's thoughts were taking. "They didn't tell you what he did to him, did they? He's not as innocent as you paint him to be. He took my soul mate away from me."

"So this is a revenge gig?" She straightened her spine, hoping Collette couldn't detect the fear squirming within her.

Collette's grin grew. "I wish it were that simple, but I came here to find out why you're so special to everyone." She drew closer and Cali instinctively took a step back. "Why are you good enough, but I'm not? They all want you, and it makes no sense to me. Why you? What makes you so different?"

That crazed glint was back in her eye. Her arm shot out. Cali hissed as pain sliced across her cheek followed by the hot flow of blood.

Collette watched the blood drip down her face, detached, curious. It freaked Cali the fuck out. "I wonder if what they're after is inside you? If I cut you up into little pieces, take away your beauty, would they still want you?"

Terror threatened to take control of Cali's whole body. The curious way Collette spoke shook her down to her very bones. Yet at the same time, Collette asked the very same question that had plagued her since she was attacked. Why her? And still she only had part of the answer. Apparently she was important to someone. Important how? Was there some kind of strange prophecy she was supposed to help come to pass? Were her powers stronger than others' and she just didn't know it?

With a sickening sensation she wondered if Felix had lied to her. Did he play up the whole Mirror Mate bit so they could keep her for themselves? Did they want whatever it was Collette's employer wanted?

She remembered Felix telling her Niella had Dreamed about her. Had she seen something more, something she hadn't told Cali?

If she got out of this, she vowed to get her answers. She was sick of being in the dark, especially if she was the only one.

She'd been foolish to start relying on the others. Foolish to let them in when they could have been holding back from her and laughing behind her back about it.

That familiar sting of betrayal settled in her chest. She pushed it aside as best she could. She had a mental Illusionist to deal with. The only good news was that Collette seemed to be under orders not to kill her. Though maiming still seemed to be on the menu.

Way to find that silver lining, Cali.

The only way out of this was if she used her powers. She'd been practicing with Felix, honing her skill to try to use it as an offensive weapon. She'd been able to move a pepper shaker by gathering her power and launching a concentrated sonic wave. She'd have to go from moving something four inches tall to moving an entire person.

Fuck it, she thought, she could do this. It was do or die.

If she knocked Collette off her feet, she could make a break for the door. Or she could risk going deeper into her apartment to grab a more substantial weapon to try and knock Collette out. With all the rage boiling under the surface, Cali really wanted to go with the second option.

The skin on the back of her neck started to tingle. She gathered all her energy, focusing it all into one ball of unheard sound.

Pain slid along her arms.

"What the hell are you doing?"

Cali didn't answer. She ignored the blood dripping from the

fresh wounds on her arms and face.

"Are you going to attack me?" Collette sounded delighted. "Please, show me this power that has made you coveted by all."

The cut on her face stung as sweat slid into the open wound. With no warning, she threw her arms out. A deep *whomp* echoed in the room like a subwoofer set on high.

Collette staggered back.

Cali dove for her easel. The long wooden legs would make a perfect bat.

Collette laughed, the grin on her face stretching the white skin over her skull. She slowly got to her feet. "Was that it?"

Cali held her collapsed easel in front of her like an elongated sword. "Get the fuck out of my apartment."

Collette rubbed her chest where she'd been hit. "Make me, sound manipulator. Show me why you're so important. How are you better than me?"

Though she hated to admit it, she should have gone with her first option and made a run for it when she'd had the chance. Now Collette stood between her and the door. Cali had let her anger cloud her judgment.

In the blink of an eye, shards of glass came hurling at her. She used the easel as a shield, but the sides of her arms and her legs were left exposed. Glass bit into her skin again and again. She bit her lip as pain flared, white-hot. Strong arms grasped her from behind. One of Collette's freakish, faceless mannequins stood behind her, a knife raised in one of its hands.

"Mar her face," ordered Collette.

Adrenaline scorched Cali's veins. She jerked from the grip and swung her easel for all she was worth. The thick wooden legs knocked the Illusion back into the barstools by her kitchen. The faceless man blinked out of existence right as something wrapped tightly around her ankles.

Her feet were pulled from behind. Tears sprang to her eyes as she landed heavily on her knees.

That strange white cloth Collette was so fond of was wound tight around her ankles and part of her leg. She couldn't move, but that didn't stop Cali from swinging the easel and missing Collette by a few feet. The attack was enough to startle her, and she stepped back. The Illusion at her feet flickered. The fabric loosened and Cali ripped it away from her. It dissolved in her hand.

Collette was breathing heavily, and the fact she wasn't holding her Illusions for prolonged periods of time meant she was exhausted. Cali scented the weakness like a threatened predator. For the first time, Cali felt she could win this. She needed more of an advantage.

Come on. Think. You control sound. How can you use that?

She scanned her apartment and spotted the lone light fixture above her head. She hadn't bothered to open the drapes, which meant if she took out the light they'd be in near darkness. For Collette to harm her she needed to be able to tell where she was. Right?

It was worth a shot. She concentrated her power and flung out another sound wave. Black danced at the edges of her vision, but it was worth it when the bulb shattered. Her apartment fell into darkness. She had to move fast.

The back of her neck felt like ice but she kept going, sucking the sound from the apartment, throwing false noise away from where she stood to redirect Collette's attention. She heard something break to her right.

"Stop hiding in the dark, Cali," said Collette.

It gave away her position and Cali crept up behind her. When she was relatively sure she was within range she swung her easel. Collette never heard it coming. There wasn't even a sound of impact. The only indicator Cali had hit her mark was the vibration traveling up her arms.

Collette screamed.

Cali lithely stepped away, feeling invigorated.

The sensation didn't last. Something in the center of her

apartment flickered. It looked like the tiniest of candle flames.

Was Collette so exhausted she couldn't even create light?

No. It appeared again, this time flickering faster, and each time it flickered it grew in size. It started the size of a golf ball, growing in diameter until it was larger than her fist. The brilliant orange and yellow coloring was blinding in the semi-darkness. Cali held her hand up against the light as it started to pulse as if alive.

Her stomach sank as it pulsed faster and faster.

The floor beneath her feet vibrated as Collette ran toward the door. Cali tried to follow but it was too late.

The ball erupted like a mini explosion. White light blinded her. Her feet left the ground. Her easel was ripped from her grasp as heat enveloped her.

Pain spiked through her back, and belatedly she knew it was because she had slammed into the wall. Again. Cali had no idea how long she sat there slumped against it, her chin on her chest, her whole body stinging. Hours? Days?

One of the drapes had been pulled back. The bright afternoon sun hurt her eyes. Footsteps came closer, and Collette appeared in her spotted vision.

She leaned over Cali. "There's nothing special about you. You can't even best me. You never will. Felix will have his fun and then he'll leave you. Just like he left me." A baton shimmered into existence in her outstretched hand, like the kind cops wore on their belts. Cali braced for the pain as Collette swung.

Blackness engulfed her.

Chapter 14

"Cali? Cali!"

Sensation slowly started coming back to her. Her body felt as if she'd been hit by a semi truck and then boiled in acid. Her apartment smelled of sulfur, and underneath she could just catch the scent of baked goods. She knew it was Felix even before she smelled him. Her body just seemed to know when he was near. That coiling tension she felt in her chest whenever she was apart from him was gone. She felt safe. Calm.

Felix continued to call her name, interchanged with some cursing.

She cracked open an eye and shut it instantly as the sunlight blinded her.

Felix caught the movement. "Cali?"

"I'm alive," she muttered. "Wish I wasn't, but I am. Son of a bitch." If this is what it felt like to be struck by a bomb, she never wanted to experience it again. She was disoriented, achy, and when she moved in certain ways pain flared like a motherfucker.

"What happened?" He helped ease her up, and she hissed when one of his hands touched a piece of sensitive skin on her shoulder. "Shit, I'm sorry. Let me get something to bandage you up, okay? Don't move."

That wasn't going to be a hard order to follow.

As Felix got a bucket full of cool water, ointment, and bandages, Cali surveyed her surroundings. She was in her room on her bed. A chair was pulled up next to it. When he returned, Felix started to gently wipe her face clean. When he reached the cut on her cheek, she jerked away.

His jaw bulged and he strangled the rag in his hand. "Collette did this, didn't she?"

She didn't feel like talking about Collette quite yet. "What are you doing here?"

How had he known she needed him?

He carefully applied ointment to the side of her face. "You didn't call. I waited forty minutes after you left before I raced over here." He cursed under his breath. "I knew something like this was going to happen. I should have left sooner. I fucking knew it. Was it Collette?"

She couldn't avoid the question a second time without looking guilty. "Yes."

He continued to clean and bandage the small burns along her arms. His face hardened every time he came across one of her cuts. "How were you able to get away from her this time? Are you keeping a Taser on your person at all times now?"

"I didn't get away from her. She left me." Collette had beaten the shit out of her and that defeat burned worse than any of her wounds. She had been useless against her.

Felix's hands stilled against her forearm. His hands were so warm. "She left you?"

"Like so much garbage," she said bitterly.

His fingers grasped her chin, careful to avoid her burns. "You're not garbage," he growled fiercely.

His blue-green eyes glittered with protectiveness and, if she admitted it to herself, a little bit of fear.

He was worried about you.

Her heart flipped.

She pulled her face from his grip. "Doesn't matter. She came to try and understand why her employer wanted me so badly. After she wiped the floor with me, I don't think she found her answer."

A low growl sounded from Felix's throat. "I'll fucking kill her."

The deadly intent in his face gave her pause. *He's not as innocent as you paint him to be.* Collette's words echoed. She didn't want to believe them but she couldn't help herself. Could Felix really be capable of killing someone?

She inhaled deeply. "Did you kill Collette's Mirror Mate?"

He didn't flinch from her question. Didn't even bat an eye. He leveled a steady stare at her that she had trouble holding.

Oh, my God, he really killed him.

She didn't know how she felt about that. She should be terrified, but she wasn't. She knew from experience that there was more to a story than what someone else said. Was she really going to label Felix like others had labeled her?

Fuck, no.

"D-did he deserve it?" she asked. Did that excuse murder? In Cali's mind . . . yes. She didn't care how that made her look. That was what she believed. Some fuckers deserved to be put down.

Felix put down the rag he'd used to clean her wounds and pulled off his black tee. All that bronze muscle rippled as he moved to bare his left shoulder to her.

She was momentarily stunned by Felix's near nakedness until she caught sight of the scar. It stood out like a rotting corpse in a field of dandelions. The puckered, twisted tissue made her cringe. She traced the wound with her finger. It was a little wider than her thumb and at least six inches long.

Rage burned within her. "He shot you?"

His expression was grim. "For Collette, he tried to kill me. His name was Kevin Bauer. He adored her, worshipped her like the girls here do the sun."

"But she never loved him."

Her comment caught him off guard. "She told you that?"

She shrugged, glad the movement didn't cause her any pain. "She told me Mirror Mates didn't have to love one another." She avoided his eyes and studied a point beyond his shoulder.

"She lied."

Her gaze shot back to his.

"I don't think Collette even knew what the meaning of love was. I think she was too busy wanting me that she didn't open herself up to Kevin. She didn't know what she had until it was taken from her."

"If she was so head over heels for you, why'd she want you dead?"

His smile was bittersweet. "You know that mentality that if you can't have something, then no one can? Yeah, I think that's Collette's life motto. I befriended her back in college. I wasn't looking for a girlfriend. My powers were still too new. Either way, Collette sort of attached herself to me. She turned more hostile as time progressed. She was also a very jealous person. Our friendship started to crumble when we found out about each other's powers. You'd think it would have brought us closer together, but all it did was make Collette believe that she was entitled to use them. She tried to break up one of my relationships back in the day by sending an Illusion of myself to my girlfriend's dorm. I stupidly forgave her for that, but she crossed the line when she disclosed my powers without my permission. I stopped talking to her for a long time after that, until I got a call from her explaining she'd found something amazing. She invited me over for dinner, told me to bring my girlfriend." Grief lined his eyes. "Her name was Jasmine. Collette decided to make an example out of her. She wanted to show me how finding her soul mate had increased her powers. Collette was a theater major. She always had a taste for the dramatic. She materialized a dagger at the dinner table and threw it right into Jasmine's chest."

He stopped for a few seconds as if to gather his thoughts. Cali didn't dare speak. "She was dying right next to me, and all Collette did was invite me to be back at her side. Right there in front of Kevin. I freaked out. My powers went haywire. I screamed at her, told her she was a murderous bitch that needed to be locked away. She didn't like that at all. Next thing I know, Kevin is leveling a gun at my chest for breaking Collette's heart. Kevin was a full-forced Dreamer, so naturally I thought I was fucked, but he still had to close his eyes and drift to see the future. He did it to try to find where I'd hide for cover so he could shoot me before I got there. I didn't bother hiding. I knew I was going to die so I picked up the chair I'd been in and swung as hard as I could at his head. I didn't kill him." He stared deep into her eyes as if to convey the truthfulness behind his words. "He was knocked out, unconscious. Still is. He's on life support last I checked."

Cali reached for his shoulder again. "And the scar?"

"He managed to pull off a couple of shots. I was lucky this one didn't take me in the heart like it was supposed to."

"How'd you escape Collette?"

He ran a hand through his hair. "When I knocked Kevin out, it did something to her. I think I somehow damaged the bond that forms between two Mirror Mates. I remember hearing her scream as if she'd been the one I'd hit. I was too busy running for my life to see what had happened to her, but after seeing her last week. . ." He let the sentence fall away.

He didn't need to continue. The madness was there for all to see when they looked into Collette's gaze. She was constantly missing her other half. That kind of wound didn't heal—it simply played on the mind, twisting it. Festering.

Cali didn't want to feel sympathy for Collette, but she remembered all too clearly the other pain-filled memories the woman had disclosed to her. "She was damaged long before you came along."

Felix's head tilted.

"When she was here she kept rambling on about how she was never good enough. How she never measured up to what others wanted."

"Her parents," Felix said with a nod. "They pressured her from a very young age to become a world-class actress. They treated her like a princess until she blew an audition when she was twelve. They were filthy rich and as punishment cut off her trust fund. She spent her whole life trying to get back on their good side." He shook his head. "I'm not going to pity her. Been there, done that. She had a shitty life, but it was her choice to follow the path she's on."

It was frightening how much of herself Cali found in Collette's story. If Felix hadn't been the one to find her first, would she have followed Collette willingly? Was her endless need to prove her independence to her family nothing but a cry for power?

"I think it'd be better if you took your shirt off."

Cali blinked. "What?"

Felix picked up the rag again and motioned to her body. "I can't get to the other wounds with that tattered piece of cloth hanging on you."

It was stupid to feel embarrassed about taking her shirt off, especially after what had happened yesterday, but Cali still hesitated. The worst was when she couldn't do it by herself and Felix had to help her. Just having his hands so close to her exposed skin made her heart trip all over itself.

Her shirt was beyond ruined but at least it had saved the skin underneath. There were a few red spots along her sides, and she sighed in relief when Felix pressed the cool rag to them.

He inhaled sharply through his nose. The muscles of his torso looked tense. Cali couldn't stop staring at him. All that bronze skin. She wanted to lick every square inch of it.

She dropped her gaze out of curiosity. Felix's erection strained against his jeans. She remembered how large he'd been in her hands, how soft and responsive. Her sex pulsed. She cleared her throat and looked away.

"How'd she do this?" Felix's voice was husky. She pretended not to notice.

"She made some kind of bomb right in the middle of my living room. Bitch probably took out a lot of my belongings too."

"We'll get them back," he promised as he fingered her bra. "This needs to come off. There's a burn right on the side of your body."

"Is playing doctor the only way you know how to get a woman naked?" she teased him. His eyes flashed.

She reached to undo the clasp at her back and paused. "Close your eyes."

Both his eyebrows rose in amusement. Heat crept up her neck.

"It's nothing I haven't *felt* before," he murmured.

"Eyes. Closed."

He gave an over-exaggerated sigh and shut his eyes.

Cali pulled off her bra and flung it into the closet. What was left of it anyway.

"Can I look yet?"

"Not yet." She drew her arm across her chest.

Felix continued conversationally. "By the way. . ." He held up three fingers and drummed them against his chin. "I do believe I've taken the lead with three."

She wanted to punch that smirk clean off his face.

"You know I can feel your glower from here." He cracked open an eye then shut it. "Yup, definitely felt the glower."

"Shut up and open your eyes already."

Grinning, he continued his nurse-like duties. He pressed the rag to her side and she clamped her mouth shut at the stinging.

"Do you want me to get you anything for the pain?"

"I'm fine. Really."

His other hand came up to press against the opposite side of her rib cage to keep her steady. He ran the rag along the small burns, and the fingers resting on her side twitched. His thumb brushed the underside of her breast, causing her to gasp.

Felix froze.

His voice was low, throaty as he said, "Sorry," though his eyes told Cali a different story entirely. His gaze lingered on her chest. He trailed his thumb against her breast purposefully.

Cali inhaled sharply.

He watched her, waiting for any kind of negative reaction. *Yeah, right.* She could do nothing but stare at him, his hand continuing to tease her skin. His fingers brushed against the hand she was using to cover herself and, in an act of pure insanity, she removed it.

The greens and blues in his eyes churned. His fingers danced along her exposed nipple, light as a feather. Cali shivered, a deep ache starting between her thighs.

"I could stare at you for hours." He cupped her breast and squeezed.

Her lips parted on a sigh. All her aches and pains evaporated.

He kissed her.

She could feel all that coiled power within him, but he held back. Most likely he didn't want to hurt her.

Screw that.

Cali leaned into him, sliding her tongue deep into his mouth. She ignored the twinge in her arms as she reached for him. She wanted to feel all that hard, warm skin beneath her hands.

His chest rumbled beneath her palms and she pressed more fully against him, nearly tipping off the edge of her bed.

The rag he'd been using against her burns dropped forgotten onto the floor with a wet splat.

Both his hands grasped her breasts, rolling her nipples between his thumb and forefinger. Pleasure streaked through her, the ache between her legs growing.

Felix broke far enough away from her mouth to speak four words. "Fuck, I want you."

Her arousal spiked, her body shaking with the need to have him inside her.

She spoke against his lips. "Take me." She was sick of waiting. She wanted him with such longing it was nearly burning her from the inside out.

"You're . . ." His tongue stole into her mouth. Retreated. "Hurt."

Her hands slid down the hard planes of his body. She followed the trail below his navel and started to undo his pants. "Then be gentle with me." She planted an open-mouthed kiss right against his heart. It beat wildly under her tongue. He groaned his surrender, his hands making fast work of the button and zipper on her shorts.

He pulled them and her panties down in one hard swipe.

Cali pushed off from her bed to straddle his legs, the cool air tickling the sensitive skin between her legs.

She worked the material of his jeans down. Then his boxers. It was difficult with him sitting, but eventually she cleared enough room to free his cock. It was thick and swollen, the tip glistening. Her heart stuttered. Moisture flooded her sex.

He was so big.

The muscles in his neck strained. "Everything. Okay?" he gritted as she palmed his shaft.

More than okay, she wanted to say, but her brain was too fogged to connect the words to her mouth. Instead she slid further up his lap and eased herself down onto him.

Felix threw his head back with a shout.

His hands gripped her hips, but still he held back, not wanting to hurt her. She didn't think she'd ever been with a man who thought about her before himself. It made her want to please him more.

She worked herself down farther onto him. She had to go slow. He was so big, and it had been so long for her.

But God, he felt good.

"*Cali*." His voice was like a plea. She grinned wickedly and squeezed her inner muscles around him. He moaned helplessly. Once he was fully sheathed within her, she did nothing but sit there to allow herself to get accustomed to him. She licked his neck, tasting the salt from his skin before working herself back up to his mouth.

One of his hands snaked up to grab the nape of her neck. He pulled her close, putting all his pent-up emotion into his kiss. Cali's head spun. She wound an arm around his neck and rocked herself against him.

Pleasure sparked. She started moving faster, but their position suddenly grew very limited. She needed more friction. Her already weakened body couldn't keep up with the pace she wanted.

"Felix," she all but sobbed against his neck. "I need more."

As if they shared one mind, he wrapped his arms under her and stood, keeping himself pushed as deep as he'd go.

Cali had no idea how he managed what he did, but somehow he got them both down on her bed without jarring her injuries. His pants were no longer around his thighs but hanging half off his ankles. Then nothing mattered anymore because Felix started thrusting. Deep, powerful strokes. All she could do was hang on.

Her hands slid along his sweat-drenched back, gripped his hips, trying to draw him in closer to her body. "Faster," she all but whimpered.

His breathing was heavy in her ear. The sound of slapping flesh filled her room. Pleasure built inside her. Higher and higher still. Felix worked a hand between their bodies and pressed on her clit.

Cali screamed.

Her climax hit hard. She wrapped her legs tight around his waist and squeezed around his still-thrusting cock. He gave a strangled growl, his body jerking. He stiffened inside her as he came.

Chapter 15

Cali had no idea how long they lay there, his heavy, warm body atop hers. And she didn't care. She never wanted to move again. She was drained and not just from mind-blowing sex. The fatigue from using too much of her powers had a headache knocking at the edge of her conscious. She wanted to tell it to fuck off, but that wasn't likely to happen.

Felix kissed along her jaw. "Did I hurt you?"

She ran her finger up his spine, loving the way he shivered against her. "Never."

Her body was positively glowing. She wanted Felix in her bed every night. She'd never felt this way about anyone before.

Briefly she wondered if it was even her feeling this. Or was it that Mirror Mate bond everyone kept telling her about?

Some of the lust-filled fog left her brain, her mind returning back to her encounter with Collette.

People were after her because there was something they wanted from her. Her stomach plummeted as she remembering thinking Felix and his group could have been some of those people.

Felix propped himself up, instantly aware of her stiffening muscles. "What's wrong?"

She'd made a huge mistake.

She stared into his eyes, wanting her heart to lay dead in her chest, but it pounded with traitorous fervor. It was already too late. Her feelings for Felix had already grown roots that dug into her very soul. She could lie to any number of people, but the one person she couldn't lie to was herself. And she was falling for Felix. Hard.

Fuck. What if he has some kind of hidden agenda?

She needed to find out what Niella had Dreamed. She had to

know if she was being played for the biggest fool. She didn't think she could survive the experience twice.

"Cali?" His fingers trailed down her face.

She couldn't stand being so close to him when she didn't know his intentions. Fuck Collette. Fuck her and her manipulative comments!

"I—"

Her phone went off.

Cali shot up from her bed. Felix barely moved away in time to avoid a bloody nose.

Her body protested the movement. Her skin stretched, her wounds stung, and her vision went black for a few seconds. She fumbled with her cell and nearly dropped it when she figured out the number on the ID.

The Kratos Corporation. Her interview!

She ran her free hand down her body as if to smooth out her clothes only to realize that she was still completely naked. "Hello?" she answered hesitantly.

"Miss Crazar?" That same pleasant female voice came from the other end. Cali wanted to sob in frustration. She hadn't forgotten her interview, honest. She'd been attacked by a psycho bitch.

Somehow she doubted they'd find that excuse acceptable.

"Is everything all right? You had an appointment with Mr. Vander Donahughe at two p.m. We were wondering if perhaps you were having car trouble? Were you still planning on attending the interview?"

Cali couldn't speak. This was too surreal. No company was this amazing.

"You mean I can still come in for the interview even though I'm late by over a half hour?"

"Yes, Miss Crazar. Mr. Donahughe was most concerned that something ill had happened to you."

Something ill *had* happened to her.

She stared down at all her battle scars. Fuck it, she thought.

"I'll be right there. Thank you so much."

"My pleasure, Miss Crazar. We'll see you soon."

Warmth covered her whole backside. "What was that all about?"

She turned and nearly collided head first into Felix's chest. Her heart tore as mixed emotions bombarded her. With all that taunt muscle in front of her, she wanted to push him back onto her bed and ride him till her body collapsed. She wanted to hear him call her name as he came. She wanted to take him over and over again until her heart was so full it burst.

But she couldn't.

She wouldn't.

She wouldn't be that girl again, that girl that was used then discarded, who was set up and left behind to pick up the pieces of her ruined life and heart.

He reached for her and she jumped out of range. "They called about my job interview. I missed it—" *Because we were having amazing sex.* "—because of Collette. They're still letting me come in late. I have to leave. Now."

Felix pulled his pants on. She missed the sight of all that naked flesh. "I'll drive you."

"That won't be necessary. I'll go on my own." She slid into her purple pencil skirt with a wince as it scraped her tender legs. As she pulled on her top she asked, "How'd you get here in the first place? I have your car."

"Joel came over after you left and I took his truck. He's probably still waiting at my house. I should call him."

Cali ran to her bathroom. "That sounds like a good idea."

*

Felix watched as Cali raced out her front door without even sparing him a backward glance. He had no idea what the hell had just happened. His body was still stirring after being with her.

He'd never experienced anything like when he'd been inside Cali. He could have sworn something had formed between them, but then why was she pulling away from him?

He ran his hand through his hair with a curse.

There had to be something more to her paranoia. She'd been fine when they'd been having sex. Even afterward, she'd run her hands along his body like he was hers. He'd wanted to take her again right there, to push himself to the hilt as her warm body clenched around him, her small injuries be damned.

His cock hardened.

He growled in frustration and readjusted himself.

They'd been fine. More than fine. And then it was like some stray thought had worked its way into her head and frightened her off. She'd jumped from his touch when only moments ago she'd been clinging to him, begging him to give her what she wanted.

Every instinct told him to go after her. To drag her back here and demand to know what the hell had just happened. He knew she was afraid of trusting people. He knew she was wary of every action someone took, thinking it was against her. But Cali wasn't the type to have sex with someone she didn't trust or didn't have feelings for.

She must have heard something.

Or been told something. By someone.

Felix slammed his fist into the closest doorjamb. Pain exploded across his knuckles but it helped focus his thoughts.

"Collette," he growled. That bitch had manipulated the women in his life enough. He should have known she'd divulge traitorous suspicions along with her truths. It explained why Cali knew so much about her and why she'd asked him about Kevin.

The fact she even believed him capable of killing someone settled like a stone in his chest.

You are *capable of killing*.

He clenched his hands into fists. It was true. Who was he to think he was some sort of saint? When pushed to his limit, he could kill. It was only through fate that Kevin hadn't been killed when he'd hit him across the head. And at that moment the idea of silencing Collette permanently was starting to sound more and more appealing.

He was never going to fully bond with Cali if Collette continued to get in his way. The worst part was that Collette was the only one that knew anything about Mirror Mates. Niella had only gleaned information to offer support to Collette's claims. Sometimes he cursed himself for not getting more information out of her all those years ago. He still had no idea how the bonding process was completed, or if it would give him the control he sought with his powers. He never again wanted to fear making someone vanish.

Mirror Mates don't have to love one another.

The comment haunted him more than he liked to admit. He'd told Cali what she'd been told was a lie, but what if he was the one lying? He couldn't believe there could be a soul-deep connection between two people and no love. He refused to believe it. Sydney called him a hopeless romantic on occasion, and he guessed she was right.

But deep down he just *knew* love had to be part of the equation. Soul mates couldn't bond to become full forced without some intimate connection.

He wished he'd asked how Collette had bonded with Kevin, but that ship had long since sailed. He was going to have to flounder around on his own. And the idea of feeling his way around in the dark with Cali was fine by him as long as she was by his side.

He pulled his phone out, his fingers itching to call Cali, but he refrained. If he pushed too hard he'd only frighten her. Instead he called Joel.

"Felix." Joel sounded relieved. "Where the fuck have you been? Is everything all right?"

"Cali was attacked."

"What?"

"Collette made her move, but not the one we were expecting.

According to Cali she was doing some kind of recon work. She left Cali behind after blowing up half her apartment."

Joel cursed. "Is Cali okay?"

Felix forced his muscles to relax. "Just peachy," he gritted out. "She's already gone to some job interview covered in minor cuts and bruises."

There was a short pause. "She left? You let her go somewhere on her own after being attacked?"

Felix pressed his already bruising knuckles back into the doorjamb to clear his mind. "She didn't want me to go with her."

"Well, fuck that. She's in danger. I would have told her to suck it up and gone with her."

Joel's overprotective forwardness was going to bite him in the ass one of these days. "You didn't see her, Joel. Something Collette said spooked her. If I had pressed, she would have distanced herself from us even more."

"How much farther can she get from us? She's come around the clinic a couple times with you, but she hasn't exactly extended her friendship. She's quite the loner, isn't she?"

That was his Cali, all right. An isolated island for one.

He walked to the kitchen to shove his aching hand into the icemaker.

"Look, I called to let you know everything's all right. I'll be home in a bit. Thanks for letting me steal your car."

"No problem. As long as you don't Erase it, we're golden."

*

By the time Cali arrived at the Kratos building off Laguna Canyon Road in Irvine, it was after three. The wind had started to pick up, the salty ocean breeze a cooling balm on her burns.

Cali strapped her heels on after she got out of the Hummer. She'd left her portfolio of art at her apartment so all she had to bring in with her was her purse. She didn't even have a resume on her. She felt like such a screw up, but at least she was here.

No one can say that you didn't try.

With her shoulders back and her chin held high she made her way for the entrance, only twisting her ankle in her heels once.

A small victory.

"Wow." The glass door closed behind her with a hiss. Soft music played from well-hidden speakers, the instrument either a violin or a cello. The entire lobby was constructed of marble. The large Kratos name mounted to the wall in gold script looked as if it was made out of real gold. Cali was tempted to go over and check, but the lady behind the desk on her left stopped her short.

"Good afternoon. Do you have an appointment?"

She made her way over, her eye catching on the short hall off to the side of the desk. Cali tried to gaze around the corner but she couldn't lean over that far.

The woman eyed her suspiciously. "I'm sorry, do you have an appointment?" she repeated.

Cali straightened, realizing that, in her attempt to see around the corner, she'd been giving the receptionist a pretty good view down her shirt. "I'm sorry." She gave the woman her best smile. "My name is Cali Crazar. I have a job interview with Mr. Donahughe."

The woman's eyes widened, as if she couldn't believe that Cali would even know who Mr. Donahughe was, much less have an appointment with him. Her gaze paused at the bandage on her cheek.

Cali tapped the white gauze. "Shaving accident."

The woman frowned. She didn't get the joke.

Stop harassing the staff, Cali's voice of reason chided.

After a few seconds the woman typed Cali's name into her computer. Her eyebrows disappeared into her hairline when she saw that Cali did indeed have an interview and that it was in fact with the CEO of the company.

"Y-you're expected right away." She pointed over her shoulder to the mysterious hallway around the corner that Cali was itching to see. "Take the elevators up to the twenty-third floor. Someone will be up there waiting to direct you. Have a good day." That last sentence was tacked on like an afterthought.

"You too," Cali said with just as much dispassion.

She eagerly made her way toward the elevators. The marble continued to dominate every square inch of the place. There were six elevators waiting around the corner for her, along with a couple of locked doors. Not that she tried the handles or anything.

The elevators were mahogany lined and had more of that soft instrumental music playing. There were twenty-six floors total. She hit the twenty-third button and was a little surprised when she arrived with no interruption. No one had gotten on with her.

I guess when you have six elevators it doesn't get very crowded.

The first thing she noticed as she stepped out was the amount of greenery. Someone *really* liked plant life.

A variety of potted plants stood between every elevator. The hallway only opened one way, and Cali followed the plants along the windows to a reception desk that had more red and orange blooms set on the desk. The secretary caught her gawking and gave an inviting smile.

"Mr. Donahughe loves plants, though I'm told he doesn't have much of a green thumb."

"That's . . . interesting," Cali said for lack of a better word.

"You're Miss Crazar?"

"That's me."

She looked behind her, "And did you travel alone? Mr. Donahughe is still attending a meeting, and he didn't want your party to have to wait for you."

"I came alone."

The secretary typed something into her computer. "Very good. You're going to take this path here and take the first right followed by the third left. Mr. Donahughe's office is on the left. You can't miss it."

Cali smiled nervously. "Thanks."

The floor was eerily deserted but she didn't know what to expect when she was on the floor that the CEO occupied. If she were the president of some huge company she'd keep an entire floor to herself too. Once or twice her curiosity had her wanting to venture down some of the different hallways, but she stayed on her path. She could always feign getting lost, but she didn't want to make Mr. Donahughe wait any longer. She was already getting a second shot at this.

Finally she came to a set of thick, wide, mahogany doors. Two purple-blossomed plants sat on either side, and again Cali wondered at the authenticity of the gold plate with Vander Donahughe's name on it.

She knocked. There was no answer.

She looked around for any kind of worker to ask if Mr. Donahughe was still in his meeting, but the floor was vacant. She was tempted to go back to the secretary but didn't want to go through the maze of hallways again.

She knocked again and when there was still no answer, she tried the handle.

The door was unlocked.

Was she supposed to wait in his office for him?

It sure as hell beat standing around like an idiot. Not to mention she was still exhausted from earlier. There was almost guaranteed to be a couch inside or at least plushy chairs.

The large doors swung inward soundlessly. The office was huge and dark. The blinds were all pulled shut, the decorative sconces on the walls dimmed as if to conserve energy.

There was a faint, repugnant smell Cali couldn't quite identify. It was emanating from the left side of the room where the entire wall appeared to be made of large cabinets. Finely detailed cabinets. Vander's desk was straight ahead with two overstuffed chairs sitting opposite. She made her way forward although she wanted to veer right where a leather couch and a mini bar resided.

She took a chair and sat for a good minute before she started fidgeting. She studied the ceiling but couldn't find any of those black-domed cameras. She scanned Vander's desk and picked up a business card displayed in a holder.

Join the Guild of Kratos and help empower the world.

It was quite the motivational business card. She tucked it away and continued to studiously examine her surroundings.

The smell came again. Cali wrinkled her nose, a strange sensation creeping its way down her spine.

She double-checked the ceiling and, deeming it safe, she went over to investigate the smell. It was coming from one of the larger cabinets. The double doors were as tall as she was and three times as wide. She grasped the handles and heaved.

The smell was stronger now.

She covered her nose and mouth with her hand and pushed the cabinet doors as far back as she could to let in what little light there was.

More plants.

Only this time they were dead. Really dead.

Who the hell kept dead plants? That was just . . . weird.

She shook off the sudden chill.

So Mr. Donahughe kept dead plants in his office. No big deal. Maybe they'd died that morning and he hadn't had time to clean them up. The secretary had said he didn't have much of a green thumb.

She closed the doors right before the sound of footsteps approaching reached her.

Shit.

She threw herself into the plush chair and smoothed down her hair, ignoring the brief flare of pain in her arms and legs.

The footsteps grew louder and instantly she became nervous. Was she supposed to stand when he walked in or stay seated? Maybe curtsey?

Dammit, she wasn't cut out for this sort of stuff.

The person was just outside the door.

Cali held her breath.

The footsteps receded.

What the hell?

She dropped her purse into the other chair and scampered to open the office doors and peer out. Through the corner of her eye, she saw someone disappear around one of the mysterious corners she'd been unable to explore.

She ducked back into the office but kept her hand on the knob as she debated what to do. The smell of dead plant tickled her nose, bringing with it that eerie sensation again.

She stepped out into the hall.

She didn't realize how creeped out she'd been in that office until she got out of it. Closing the door behind her, she followed the path of the person she'd caught a glimpse of. The only problem with that plan of action was that once she made it down the corner she'd seen them disappear into, she had no idea where they'd gone from there.

"Perfect." She turned her head left then right. Which way, which way?

Voices drifted from her right. Two of them.

She slipped her heels off and followed her ears. She entered a large work area with a maze of empty cubicles. She ducked down so no one would see her head peeking over the top and continued forward.

The two voices belonged to one male and one female. The male was currently talking, and she took advantage of the noise to slink closer.

They were almost in sight.

Just then the woman's voice cut in.

The blood in Cali's veins froze.

She knew that voice.

She leaned out to make sure and there was Collette.

Cali ducked back behind the cubicle, her body shaking with rage and fear. Mostly rage. What the fuck was she doing here?

"—there is nothing special about her!" Collette was seething. "His obsession is pointless. Misguided."

"Do you forget who guided him to her in the first place?" That male voice was aloof. Bored. And young.

Cali braced herself and eased out again for another look.

"Don't test me, Jente." Collette shook her hand menacingly in front of his face. The window behind him faced west, and the sunlight streaming in cast him in shadow. Cali felt a strange sense of déjà vu.

Jente shoved her hand out of his way and took his own menacing step forward. As he moved out of his shadowed cover, Cali got her first good look at him. He was a handsome kid with bronze skin and jet-black hair. If she had to guess his background, she'd go with a mix of Asian and Egyptian. He barely looked old enough to drink, but what really drew her attention were his eyes. Bright gray, the right one with a splash of green in it.

"I'm not testing you. I'm reminding you of your place, because you seem to be forgetting it a lot lately. You fucked up royally. Getting arrested?" He tsked at her. Collette turned purple. "That little stunt cost us big. You had a fight that night, remember? You're drawing unwanted attention to us. You're too emotionally involved in this one." He eyed her up and down as if he could glean her activities by looking at her. "And where the hell have you been?"

"Around," she said coolly.

Quick as lightning Jente had hold of her wrist and wrenched her close. "Where were you?"

Collette tugged on her hand. Jente didn't even budge. Kid was strong.

"Let me go or I'll show you exactly why you should fear me."

Jente smiled and held on just long enough to convey that he wasn't intimidated by her. Then he released her. "If anything happens to her, you're going to be the one to pay, and trust me when I tell you it will be a lot worse than being Tasered."

His smile deepened at the outraged expression on Collette's face. "You were there? You saw her coming up behind me and didn't apprehend her?"

Jente crossed his arms over his chest. "Apprehending her wasn't my job. I'm surveillance, remember? I did my job. It wasn't my fault you were distracted by your boy toy."

Cali felt an answering growl to Jente's comment about Felix. He wasn't Collette's anything.

Collette straightened her shoulders. "You forget your place, *Mitchell*." Jente's jaw tensed at the name but Cali couldn't fathom why. "I could crush you and you wouldn't even know it."

Jente's hand shot out again. This time around her neck. His upper body remained motionless. "Save it for the arena."

A thin line appeared around his neck. It dripped red. Blood.

Cali squinted and could just barely make out the thin wiring tight around his throat.

"Get rid of it, Lizeroux," Jente hissed. He looked pissed but could do nothing about it. Cali didn't realize until that moment how lucky Felix was to have his power when pitted against someone like Collette. She was rendered useless against an Eraser.

So then what were Jente's powers?

"If you keep this up you're going to tire yourself out," said Jente. "How are you going to make fighters then? You have a match at two a.m. or have you forgotten? You'll be in no condition to create anything that will last. We'll end up losing, or worse, you'll drop the act and expose us."

"You're more likely to expose us than I am," Collette snarled. "One wrongly anticipated move and someone could bump into you. Then what are you going to do?"

"That's not going to happen. The cage has enough room for me to move around freely. Besides, if I were you I'd be watching my own ass. Stop trying to figure out where I can fuck up and maybe you'll be paying enough attention to catch your own fuck up before it happens this time. You look like shit, you'll probably perform like shit, and Mr. Donahughe sure as hell doesn't want shit in his arena."

The wire around his neck vanished. He rubbed the tender area, his fingers coming away bloodied. He glared at Collette.

She paid it no attention. "Do you know why he's after her?" she asked in a low voice.

He continued to rub his throat. "So now you're going to treat me like an equal?"

Collette shrugged. "You didn't plead for your life, cry, or piss yourself. That earns some respect from me."

Jente shook his head. "You're strange as fuck, you know that, Lizeroux? And no, I don't know. I'm not privy to that information but—"

Another pair of footsteps was coming up behind Cali.

Her heart leapt into her throat. How long had she been hunkered down here?

She quickly backtracked, tears threatening to fall from her eyes. She'd been worried all this time about being played by Felix when really she should have been looking a lot closer. Disappointment settled in the pit of her stomach. She felt humiliated. She'd been such a fool to think that for once something was going well in her life.

She made it back to Vander's office to collect her purse. No one was there. At least Fate wasn't kicking her when she was down. She knew she should be scared. She'd found the one who was searching for her. But at that moment she was too exhausted, too beat down to really care.

She almost wanted to find Vander Donahughe and confront him. *What the hell do you want with me?* She wanted to scream at his face. Why was she so special? Obviously it wasn't her artwork or her powers. From where she was standing there wasn't a damn thing going for her. She really was useless. Her parents had been right—

she should have majored in accounting. At least then she'd have a steady job, respect from those around her. No one would look at her and think "criminal." No one would peg her as a drug user.

Her vision blurred with tears, and she kicked the plush chair she'd been sitting in earlier when she'd waited for her "interview."

Her self-pity turned to anger. Fuck this.

*

"M-miss Crazar?"

She hadn't even realized she'd made it back to the secretary.

"I'm leaving." She still held her high heels in her hand. She wanted to chuck them across the room but she couldn't because they were her only pair and she couldn't afford another.

The secretary looked downright terrified. "B-but your interview . . . you can't leave. You . . . can't."

For the first time since she'd left Collette and Jente she felt a real spark of fear.

They weren't going to let her leave.

She thought quickly, her eyes landing on her bandaged arms. She hastily ducked her arm so the receptionist wouldn't see it. Then, gritting her teeth, she dug her finger deep into one of her cuts, reopening the wound. When the blood started to pool along her arm she held it up for the secretary to see.

She lurched back with a squeak.

"I reopened one of my wounds. Please tell Mr. Donahughe I'll call to reschedule." *Yeah, right.*

She made her way to the elevators and at the last minute took the stairs. Twenty-three flights of stairs. The only thing fueling her aching muscles was the adrenaline coursing through her veins. It increased ten-fold when she made it to the lobby and found the elevators locked down. The main entrance was deserted.

Fear had truly taken root now, and Cali ran for the glass doors.

They wouldn't budge. She smashed her high heel into the glass but it was double paned. "Fuck." She went back the way she'd come and searched for the emergency exit.

One of the elevators dinged.

Cali ran for the front desk, tearing open drawers left and right. There had to be a key for the front door. There had to be. Fate wouldn't do this to her. She was already crawling in the gutter. "Please," she whispered.

She found a key ring in the very back of the second drawer. She sprinted for the front door, fumbling with the lock for a good minute before she found the right key. She didn't bother removing the key from the lock, she simply shoved her hands through the double doors and wrenched them open with all her strength. Footsteps echoed on the marble floor behind her. The gap in the door could barely fit a person but Cali jammed herself through.

Jente came around the corner.

He stopped dead when he saw her. She didn't wait around to see what he did. She ran blindly, her heart beating a mile a minute.

Chapter 16

Cali's body was still trembling when she arrived at Felix's house. She hadn't even realized where she'd been going until she arrived. It was strange to think that instead of driving to her apartment she'd come here; that she felt safer here than at her own home.

The driveway was empty, which was to be expected. What wasn't expected was that no one answered the door.

"Felix?" she called hopelessly. She knocked then rang the doorbell again.

Still no answer. Her phone had died in the car. Leaving her stranded.

When it was obvious no one was going to come to the door she sat down on the front step.

Dusk was settling in. What was a cool ocean breeze in Irvine was a lot stronger out here, and she hugged herself tight.

She felt so alone.

A dog howled in the distance, the sound reminding her of Yeller.

Yeller . . . Sydney's clinic. Duh! That's where Felix must be.

Hope flared as she hopped in his Hummer. His scent lingered in the car and Cali inhaled greedily. Her whole body ached, but not as much as her heart seemed to. She just wanted to be near him. Was a little comfort too much to ask?

"Apparently so," Cali mumbled dejectedly as she stared at the *Closed* sign in the window of Sydney's clinic. The lights were off. Nobody home.

Better luck next time, Crazar.

Something wet fell from her eye and she wiped it away furiously. Stupid wind was making her eyes water.

"Cali?"

She turned and found Tom standing outside his pizzeria. A small bucket and rag were resting on the table he had set up outside.

"What are you doing out here?" He gave her a warm smile that disappeared when he caught sight of her injuries. He rushed over, gingerly taking her bandaged appendages into his hands. "What happened to you?"

His genuine concern was almost too much for her to handle. She cleared her suddenly raw throat. "There was an accident at my apartment."

It didn't look like he was listening. His green eyes were fixed on her cuts, his hands warm against her forearms. Her skin started to tingle. From the wind?

No.

She stared at Tom. His visor was pushed up at an odd angle, messing up his dirty blond hair. His face was pinched in concentration.

Was that tingling coming from him?

She opened her mouth to ask but he dropped his hands from her. The tingling sensation disappeared.

She shook her head, dismissing whatever thoughts were trying to form in her mind.

"Is everything okay?" he asked.

I think I'm losing my mind.

"Fine. Do you happen to know where Sydney is?" She wanted to ask about Felix but didn't know if Tom had even met him before.

Tom rubbed his jaw. "I think I saw her getting picked up about fifteen minutes ago."

"Was Niella with her?" She needed to confront the Dreamer and get her answers.

Tom's brow furrowed. "Her assistant? I'm not sure. I've never really seen her before. She's never there when I'm around. I can try Sydney on my cell if you'd like though."

"That'd be perfect."

Tom dug his phone out and dialed Sydney. "Hey, Sydney, it's Tom."

There was a muffled reply. Cali was too far away to hear it, but she could make out the bubbly tone of voice easy enough.

"I'm great. Listen, your friend Cali is here looking for you." Again he paused as Sydney said something. "Does she know where that is? All right, great. I'll send her over."

He hung up.

"She told me to tell you to meet her at Felix's house? You know where that is? They're in the backyard."

She must've just missed them.

"I do. Thanks a bunch, Tom." She impulsively gave him a hug. Something she never did. But she was feeling so much better. Her burns didn't even sting anymore.

He gave her a friendly pat on the back. "Anytime." She released him, unable to believe what her body had just felt. Underneath all that pizzeria uniform was a wall of muscle. There must have been some kind of secret gym society out here that men who were involved in culinary arts attended. What other explanation was there for a baker and a pizza cook to be so ripped?

*

Joel's truck was parked in Felix's driveway.

Cali went around the back like she'd been instructed. The side gate was open, and she could hear Joel and Felix along with Sydney's laughter. No Niella though.

She came around the corner of the house and stopped. Felix's backyard wasn't all that big. There was the porch, connected to the sliding glass backdoor and then a section of grass that had a few flowers rimming the fence.

Sydney was seated at the only wood bench by the fence, clearly enjoying the view. The view that had Cali's feet frozen to the grass. Both Felix and Joel were shirtless, playing some type of two-player football.

"Come on, Joel, you have to make a play for the ball sometime," Felix was goading him. The ball was fitted snugly into the crook of his arm. He feigned left then right. Joel tried to mirror his moves but was slower by a few seconds, obviously lacking Felix's quick reflexes and grace.

Joel made a play for the ball. Felix spun out, easily avoiding him and strutted to the far end of his backyard where Cali guessed the touchdown zone was.

"That's five to one, Kegler." He threw Joel the ball.

Joel caught it with a grunt. "Hey, not all of us were All-American athletes."

Felix grinned, the waning sun reflecting off his bronzed chest and shoulders.

Cali could hardly breathe. She longed to fall into his arms.

His gaze flicked to her, his face brightening further. He jogged over. "Hey." He bumped into her affectionately but didn't touch her more than that. She didn't know whether to be grateful or disappointed. "How'd the interview go?"

Cali held onto her self-control by a thread. "I think it'd be better if we went inside." She looked to Joel and Sydney, then back to Felix. "All of us."

He frowned. "What's wrong?"

"Where's Niella?"

"At home." Sydney came over. "Why?"

How much to tell them?

She wanted to tell them everything. She really did. But she couldn't be betrayed again. She somehow needed to get herself alone with Niella.

"I need to talk to her. Where does she live? I'll go pick her up."

Sydney exchanged glances with both Joel and Felix.

"Are you sure everything's okay, Cali?" asked Felix.

"I'm fine. Please, I just need to figure things out right now. The drive will do me good." Not necessarily a lie.

"I'll get you the directions and tell Niella you're coming to get her." Sydney ran back into the house.

Felix continued to study her. She avoided his eyes. He had an uncanny ability to read her better than anyone, and she didn't want to give anything away.

"How are you feeling?" Joel's question caught her off guard.

"What?"

He pointed to her arms and bandages. "You don't look too bad. Felix made it seem like you were seriously injured. Guess Collette doesn't know how to construct a very good bomb. You're lucky. Are you feeling better?"

Cali looked down at her arms and noticed they were nearly healed. Completely.

What the. . .?

"I feel . . . great actually."

Felix looked just as puzzled as she felt. "How'd you heal that fast? These were all open cuts earlier."

"She's Wolverine, man." Joel was truly impressed.

Felix shot him a look and took one of her arms to remove the bandage. Underneath was nothing but slightly tender, smooth, pink skin. He went to the bandage on her face.

Cali held her breath. "Well?"

Felix took a step back. "The same thing. You're . . . healed."

Sydney came over waving a piece of paper. "Got your directions right here. Want me to come with?"

Cali pocketed the paper. "I got it."

Sydney's face flashed with something like hurt before she covered it up. "Are you sure? You're going to have to help Niella into the car, fold up her wheelchair, and heft it into the back of Felix's Hummer."

"Like I said, I got it."

She only made one wrong turn the entire journey and that was because Sydney's bubbly script made her p's look like r's.

Cali's first reaction to Niella's home was, *I need to get a job working for Sydney*. She had no idea how Niella afforded the place. She never in her wildest dreams would have thought a vet clinic secretary would be making enough to afford a house like that, but the proof stood right in front of her.

Unless she'd done something before working for Sydney.

She'd have to remember to ask but first she had bigger questions to breach.

Niella was outside waiting as Cali parked in the driveway. When she got out of the Hummer, Niella had already wheeled herself over to the passenger door. Cali hastened to her side to help. Wrong move.

Niella shoved her hands away. "I got it," she snapped. She continued to struggle. Felix's Hummer was just a tad too tall for her to get the right leverage to pull herself up.

Cali braced herself and grabbed Niella around the waist. "What the hell did I tell you?" Niella barked instantly. But Cali wasn't listening. She only lifted her high enough to grab the "oh shit" bar then unceremoniously let her body drop.

Niella clamped her mouth shut on what Cali was sure would have been a good cursing. Instead Niella glared at her. Evilly.

You're welcome.

Niella pulled herself in, one of her legs twitching.

Cali jumped back.

"What?"

"Your leg. It moved."

Niella gave her one of the bitterest smiles she'd ever seen. "I'm not paralyzed. My legs are just mangled." With that she shut the car door in Cali's face.

Cali wheeled her chair around to the back of the Hummer where, after much cursing, she was able to collapse it and shove it inside.

"Look," she said as she climbed back into the driver's seat. "There's a reason I'm here to pick you up."

"You mean besides wanting to spend time in my charming presence?" Niella asked sarcastically.

Cali held her own attitude in check. *Don't piss off the Dreamer. She's the only one with answers.* "There's something I want to ask you."

Niella quit fiddling with the radio. "Of course there is. Don't insult my intelligence, Cali. I knew there had to be a reason why you wanted to come pick me up. No one seeks me out for social events."

Cali's mouth opened before she could stop herself. "Well, maybe if you weren't such a punk ass you'd get invited to the party a little more."

Niella stared at her for a long moment, her face impassive. Had Cali pissed her off? Hurt her feelings? She highly doubted that last one.

"Sydney told me over the phone that you were acting strange. At least you're not one to dawdle. What the hell do you want? And if all you want from me is to answer a damn question then why am I being forced to leave my home?"

Cali backed out of the driveway, collecting her thoughts. Why *was* she bringing her to Felix's? Was it to save face? Did she want the group to trust her when in fact she didn't trust them in return?

Why did she care so much what they thought of her?

She had planned to tell them what she'd learned. She wasn't going to leave them defenseless. But she had to know first and foremost if she could trust them.

She pulled out onto the main road. "I learned some information I think you all have the right to hear, but before I give you anything I want to know what you Dreamed that day. About me. I didn't want the others around when I asked."

Niella arched one perfectly plucked brow. "Why do you want to know now when for the past week you've been nothing but placid?"

Her grip tightened around the steering wheel. *Don't read too much into her diversion. It's an honest question.*

That didn't stop the niggling inside of her. Had she been right? Was Niella holding out on her? Were they trying to keep her for themselves for whatever reason?

"Let's just say I'm curious now. I've been through a lot in the past week." *More like the past twenty-four hours.* "I'm sick of not understanding. If you don't want to tell me, that's fine, but don't expect me to tell you anything when I can't—"

"Yeah, yeah," Niella cut in. "When you can trust us. Right? Look, I know all about your little suspicion of us, okay? We're not the bad guys. We aren't using you, we're not going to use you, and we're never going to use you."

"How did you know what I was going to say?"

She shrugged and continued to toy with the radio until she found a fast-paced dance song. "I know quite a bit about you. Not by choice, mind you, but if I constantly think about someone or something I can almost direct how I Dream. There's been a lot of mistrust on our end too, about you."

The comment stung more than Cali liked to admit, but what the hell had she expected?

"We're constantly wondering about you," Niella continued, "and that leads to me catching glimpses of you and your history. I get why you don't trust us. I really can't blame you for that. That asshole Tyson did a number on you. If that happened to me, I'd probably be just as paranoid as you."

That was a little disconcerting.

They drove a few more blocks in silence.

"And you expect me to just go along with that?" said Cali. "To believe everything you're telling me?"

"I know you won't, but I'm just saying we're not the one attacking you in your apartment or trying to kidnap you. I Dreamed about you being taken by a man in your parents' house. Dark hair, dark eyes. His appearance has slowly come into focus, though not by much."

Dark hair? Dark eyes?

Cali's stomach clenched.

Vander Donahughe had dark hair and eyes.

"But Collette was the one who came after me that day."

"Only because I sent Felix to go get you. The future is in constant motion. By altering one piece, it's only fair to assume the future as a whole would change."

"And you saw that we were . . . were . . ."

Niella's face softened. She really was beautiful when she didn't have that angry scowl on her face. "Soul mates?" she supplied helpfully.

Cali stared straight ahead. "He's not using me to further his power, is he?"

The question had nagged at her until she was sick from it.

"As much as Felix can annoy the hell out of me, he's really a good guy. But I don't need to defend him against you. You've seen it better than any of us. If you have any grievances with him, then you're going to have to take them up with him."

Fair enough.

They were almost back to Felix's when Cali realized she hadn't gotten all the information she wanted. "What else did you see in your Dream of me?"

She was met with silence.

"Niella?"

She glanced over.

Niella's head was propped against the window, eyes closed, face peaceful.

No one falls asleep that fast.

She shook Niella's shoulder. Nothing. Most people she knew jerked awake when she moved them in their sleep.

Unless . . .

Cali's foot slipped from the gas.

Niella was Dreaming.

"Holy fuck." She gripped the wheel like a life-line. She didn't know the Dreams could take her whenever they wanted. She'd thought she Dreamed when she went to bed or took a nap.

Her eyes dropped down to Niella's mangled legs. Oh, God, had she been driving when she'd had a Dream? Was that how her legs had gotten like that?

Cali felt sick to her stomach.

She focused on the road, forcing her eyes to stare straight ahead. Her gaze wandered.

She pulled them back but that didn't stop the questions. What was Niella Dreaming? Were they in danger? Was Felix in danger?

When Niella moved Cali nearly screamed.

Just like that Niella was awake. Cali spared a glance her way and almost wished she hadn't.

She was crying.

Chapter 17

Felix.

Cali's first thought was that something horrible had happened to him. "What'd you see?" Her first instinct was to stomp on the gas but the cars ahead of her were blocking her path.

When Niella didn't answer she gritted her teeth. "Well?" she pressed.

"Nothing." Niella wiped at her face.

"Bullshit," Cali spat. "Is it Felix? Is he hurt, going to be hurt?"

She turned the wheel sharply to cut across the street. Horns blared. Niella screamed, her hands shooting out in front of her to brace herself on the dashboard.

Cali nearly took the Hummer up a curb. She threw the huge vehicle into park and got up in Niella's face, sick of being left in the dark. "What did you see?"

Niella's eyes were shut tight, fresh tears leaking through her shut eyelids. When she finally cracked them open, Cali got a good look at the stark terror before anger burned it away. Niella shoved her back in her seat. "What the fuck is wrong with you?" she yelled. "Are you trying to scare me into answering you? Traumatize the woman who was in a car crash even more? Huh? Is that your plan?"

So she had been in an accident.

Cali pushed her pity aside. Something told her Niella wouldn't want it anyway. "I'm sick of being in the dark, Niella. I really am. I'm going out on a limb here and trusting you guys. If you know so much about me then you know how much this blind trust is costing me. I need to know what you saw that day. I need to know that I'm not just being played by anyone and everyone around me. Please."

After a few seconds of silence Niella finally spoke. "I saw a cage. I felt pain, both from you and Felix. I got flashes of your powers, of you and Felix, something connecting you two together. There were others there, more pain, more blood." She sighed as if weary. "It's really not much help, and I still don't know when this is supposed to happen. You may have already avoided it, but that's all I can tell you."

She'd take it. "And what about what you saw a few minutes ago?"

"That doesn't concern you."

Cali temper flared. "The hell it doesn't. Stop alienating yourself. Whatever the hell it is you saw had to be something powerful to make someone like you cry."

"Someone like me?" She gave a humorless laugh.

Cali didn't let it faze her. "Yes, someone like you. Someone strong. You're a hard-ass, Niella. I know them when I see them. You can stop acting like the whole world is against you. Trust me, it gets old very quickly. You may not think the others care for you, but they do. I can tell. You're little group dynamic is something I've craved my entire life. And you better not fucking tell anyone I said that to you." That pulled a small smile out of the Dreamer. "If you expect me to trust you then you're going to have to trust me too. I won't judge you. What did you see?"

Niella inhaled deeply and stared her dead in the face. "Myself."

Oh.

That was the last thing she'd expected to hear. Had she seen herself killed? Cali didn't even want to think about that. But what else could have been so bad as to make her cry?

She swallowed the lump in her throat and forced herself to speak. "What happened?"

Niella's hands rubbed absently along her thighs, as if they were paining her. She caught what she'd been doing and stopped. She opened her mouth and shut it. Cali didn't push. She'd speak when she was ready.

"I was walking."

Cali was momentarily stumped. "And that's a bad thing?"

Niella jerked the waistband of her pants down. Her whole lower half was covered with scars, some big, some small. Some puckered and thick, others white and thin. It was like a road map on her skin. "I'm never going to walk again," she seethed. "They did everything they could to try to put me back together again."

"Maybe the doctors were wrong," Cali ventured.

Niella rubbed her forehead. "I doubt it."

Cali wanted to push the issue but Niella's cell phone went off before she got a chance.

"Yeah?" Niella answered, her voice defeated.

Sydney's bubbly voice was muffled on the other end.

Cali started up the Hummer and pulled back out into traffic. There was no way Niella would broach the subject of her walking again. That window of opportunity was now closed. She didn't blame Niella, not really. She could understand the need to forgo hope. After what Niella had been through, holding out for the dream to walk again was probably exhausting. No wonder she was so bitter all the time.

"We're almost there. Don't worry. See you soon."

Niella hung up and tucked her phone away.

"They think I kidnapped you?" Cali couldn't help but ask.

Niella shrugged. "You didn't. I highly doubt you could."

They exchanged knowing smiles.

The rest of the drive Cali felt lighter. Niella didn't seem to be in too much of a bad mood either. She didn't complain when Felix helped her out of his Hummer or when Joel wheeled her inside.

Sydney was already waiting for them as they entered the sitting room. She was leaning over the counter in the kitchen. She came around the island to take a seat on one of the couches with Joel. Felix took a seat opposite them with Niella positioned as if at the head of a table.

Cali sat next to Felix, dropping down onto the couch so she was pressed against him. She craved contact with him, wanted to sink into his skin.

He'd donned a shirt since she left but she remembered all too clearly the look and feel of all those muscles. She pushed deeper against him. Felix gave her a questioning look but she ignored him, giving no outward appearance that she knew what she was doing.

His hand slid lazily over to her thigh where he absently started to trace random symbols on her leg.

She suppressed a shiver.

"Why are we all here?" Felix asked.

She forced her mind to concentrate on things other than Felix's hand on her leg, his body pressed against hers.

Just the thought of Vander Donahughe was like a bucket of cold water. She leaned into Felix again, only this time for comfort.

"I went in for my job interview today. I was supposed to meet with Vander Donahughe of the Kratos Corporation." She dug out the business card and handed it over. "But it turned out the interview was a fake." It hurt to say the words. Again she felt humiliated, as if everyone else would have realized what was really going on except her. "Collette was there." Felix's body went stock-still. "I overheard her talking with this other guy named Jente."

"It was a ruse?" asked Sydney.

Cali nodded. "Apparently one three months in the making. Vander approached me back in April during one of the festivals I attended in the Inland Empire."

"Shit," said Joel. "If he's spent that much time and effort on obtaining you, he's not going to sit by and let it all fall apart."

Cali's stomach clenched. Felix's hand tightened around her knee protectively. "That wasn't everything." She locked eyes with Niella and continued. "Collette and Jente kept talking about matches and a cage." Niella's eyes grew wide. She'd had her own sneaking suspicions after Niella told her about her Dream but now she was certain. The cage Niella had seen was tied in with the Kratos Corporation. "I know Vander Donahughe was the one responsible for trying to kidnap me, but I also think he's holding some kind of underground fighting arena using people with powers." Which meant that even though Cali had avoided him, there was still a huge possibility she'd find herself back in his possession. Niella's Dream could still come true.

Sydney was horrified. "Is that why he's after you? So he can pit you against someone in a fight?"

If only. "I don't think so. If that was all he wanted, he would have had Collette take me out and bring me to him. But for some reason he doesn't want me harmed. He must think there's something special about me."

"Could there be something we haven't been made aware of?" Felix asked Niella.

She shook her head. "I think I would have seen it or at least have felt it. Cali's the same as any of us. I don't know why he wants her."

"I could try to find out," Cali volunteered.

Joel, Sydney, and Niella gave her looks of disbelief. Felix said quite firmly, "No."

"Felix is right," said Sydney. "You can't go barging in there, Cali. You manipulate sound, you can't go invisible."

"But aren't you the least bit—" Something clicked in her head. "Are you using your powers?"

Sydney drew back. "No, why?"

Cali waved her hand frantically. "Put them on. Now." A few seconds passed. "Well?"

"I'm using them, now are you going to tell me why?"

She turned to Felix. "That man, the one I thought I saw in Sydney's clinic, the one you thought you saw outside your house? I bet you anything it was him. That's Jente's power, he can turn invisible."

"Hold on a second," Joel interrupted. "There's someone who can turn invisible? Someone who was inside Syd's clinic and you didn't tell anyone?"

Note to self: if you ever endanger Sydney, Joel will kill you.

"She wasn't there and I thought I was hallucinating."

"I don't know about you guys but I'm a little more concerned about some huge conglomerate using our own kind for his entertainment," said Niella.

"I'm with Ell," said Felix. "We can't sit here and do nothing."

"Wait a minute," said Sydney. "Since when did we become a vigilante group?"

Felix looked at her as if she'd suffered from some sudden onslaught of amnesia. "Since we've operated out of your clinic to help anyone Ell's ever seen? Come on, Syd, we're not new to this."

"Yes, we are," she countered. "You're talking about going after a huge conglomerate based on—no offense, Cali—nothing but her word."

Joel leaned over. "Sydney's very by-the-book."

Sydney slugged Joel in the arm. "I'm serious. You guys think this is nothing but some video game you can try and beat."

"No, we don't, Syd," said Felix. "We know how serious this situation is, and we also know that right now we're probably the only ones who know about it and can do anything."

"And what are we going to do, huh? Storm the castle? Are you even thinking this through?"

"What's there to think through?" Felix shot right back. "People like us are being collected like rare sports cards and we have a chance to stop it. I say we go for it."

Sydney turned to Niella. "Will you please voice some reason for me?"

Everyone seemed to hold their breath as they waited for Niella's verdict. Cali didn't know what to expect from the Dreamer. She could understand Sydney's perspective, but sometimes action needed to be taken against those that believed they were untouchable.

"I felt the pain, Sydney," Niella started. "I can't begin to describe it to you, but I know it's unfair. These people, whoever they are, are helpless." She stared down at her legs. "I know what it's like to be helpless," she said softly. "It's really all up to you guys. I'm not much help in my wheelchair but if I could help them, I would. No one should have to feel what I've felt. Not if it can be helped."

Sydney fell silent. There was no arguing with that. Cali wondered if Niella realized the weight she carried in their little group. The others, without even meaning to, seemed to look to her in times of disagreement. But she guessed when one was gifted with visions of the future, others were sure to follow her words of wisdom.

"Don't worry, Syd," Felix consoled. "We're not going to run in there blind. We'll think of something. This way we can help keep Cali safe as well as help those who might be unfortunate enough to be caught in the crossfire."

The logic appealed to Sydney and seemed to calm her.

They lapsed into contemplative silence that was interrupted when Joel glanced over the business card Cali had handed over. "*Join the Guild of Kratos and help empower the world.* The Guild of Kratos? Really?"

Cali took the card back and stared at it. "What does Kratos mean?"

"In essence it means 'power.' So their catch phrase is a little redundant if you ask me."

"No one's asking you, Joel," said Niella.

He ignored her. "We should come up with our own name if we're going to be combating them. Our own guild."

Felix perked up at the idea like a little boy. "What should our guild represent?"

Joel tapped his finger against the sofa in thought. "They already took power . . ."

"Truth," Cali spoke up.

Joel nodded to himself. "That's not bad."

Cali quirked a brow at him, "Not bad? It fits perfectly. How do you think Collette and Vander got everything they were after? They used Collette's Illusions or Vander's lies. They deceive people like they deceived me. We should represent truth."

"Or justice," Felix added.

Joel shared a boyish grin with him. "Or the American way?"

"We're not goddamn Superman," Niella muttered.

Their grins grew and Cali punched Felix in the arm. "I'm serious about truth."

He held his hands up in surrender. "I'm just as serious as you are about justice."

Joel opened his mouth but Sydney gave him a dark look. "If you say the American way one more time you're going to be sleeping on the couch for a month."

His mouth shut.

"I'm with Cali," said Niella. "Truth. We wouldn't bullshit people who came to us for help."

"Agreed," Sydney added her input.

Joel pulled out his smart phone. "If we're going to use truth then we might as well have a cooler translation of it."

Sydney stifled a yawn. "Why don't you finish that at home?"

Cali hadn't realized how late it had gotten. She was exhausted from the day and starving. She could have gone into the kitchen and made herself something to eat but she didn't want to leave the comfort of Felix's body. His hand was no longer on her thigh, but that didn't stop her from leaning into his warmth.

Joel got to his feet and stretched. "I can do this at home. I can also look up some names for that Jente guy."

"What do you mean look up names for Jente?" Cali asked.

Joel scrolled through something on his phone. "I mean he needs a title. We can't call him an Invisible, doesn't sound right."

Cali didn't get it. Felix came to her rescue. "He means a title like you have the title of Silencer, I'm an Eraser and Sydney's a Shielder . . . get it?"

"You mean to tell me those aren't . . . universal terms?"

"Nope," Niella supplied helpfully. "They just made them up."

"We *all* helped make them up," Sydney defended.

Cali looked between all of them. Unbelievable. "So who made up mine?" Not that she was going to argue. She was becoming accustomed to her title. She liked how it made her sound deadlier than she really was.

There were a few puzzled looks shared between them.

"None of us, actually," said Felix. "Niella had her Dream, and when she told me to go after you she said you were a Silencer, a manipulator of sound."

"Niella made it up?" Joel looked at her as if seeing her for the first time. "No way."

Cali could almost swear that Niella was embarrassed. "I didn't really make it up. I Dreamed about it. I'm sure one of you made it up and I simply plucked the word from my Dream. So in reality, you made it up but because I already supplied you the name you didn't have to think it up in the first place."

Everyone gave her blank stares.

"Never mind."

"Well, there you have it," said Felix, "the origin of your name came from *the future*." He wiggled his fingers to add effect. Cali knocked his hands down, trying and failing to suppress a smile.

Sydney got to her feet. "We'll see you tomorrow?"

*

Felix saw everyone out. As soon as he got up from the couch, Cali had made a break for the kitchen. There was something off about her. Ever since she came back from her "job interview" she'd been acting differently. When they'd been on the couch she'd slid into him like she belonged at his side. Not that he was complaining, but it drew his attention when not even twelve hours ago she was jumping away from his touch after having sex. He'd tried to catch her eye but she'd acted as if nothing were amiss. As if her body pressed into his wasn't a huge deal to him that was distracting as hell.

Was she acting different because of what had almost happened at the Kratos building? He ran a hand through his hair, unable to believe he'd almost lost her. Twice in the same day he'd fucked up. He should have been there for her. At her interview and when Collette attacked. He should have pushed when she'd left her apartment, just like Joel had suggested.

Joel's truck disappeared down the street. He shut the front door to return to the kitchen where Cali was already polishing off the last of her sandwich.

Felix was too antsy to go to sleep. He leaned against the island. "Want to watch a movie?"

They'd done it countless times before over the past week.

Cali put her plate in the sink and said, "I'd like that."

He rearranged the couches so that they wouldn't have to ruin their necks to see the TV and put on an action/adventure film he knew Cali enjoyed.

She was making her way over to the couch when Felix decided to conduct a little experiment.

He waited until she'd taken her seat and purposely sat next to her, making sure to keep a few inches between them. Enough room so they weren't touching. A few previews passed with Cali doing nothing. When the menu popped up, Felix selected the *play* button and Cali made her move.

She was subtle, he'd give her that. She leaned into him to give herself room to tuck her legs underneath her, slowly inching herself closer to him until their arms were pressed together, her knee touching his thigh.

Blood rushed straight to his groin. He clenched his jaw to keep from reaching out for her. Being away from her had been torture. Doubly so when he realized what kind of danger she'd been in. She was his Mirror Mate—it was his job to protect her. And for the first time, Felix believed she was finally feeling the bond too. Why else would she seek out his touch?

He purposefully scooted out of touching distance again.

Unfortunately he was not nearly as subtle as Cali. Her eyes locked on his. He waited for her to say something but nothing came. He craved her but he wanted her to crave him more. She shifted closer. He shifted back.

She gave a frustrated sigh. "Stop moving."

"Why?" *Come on, Cali,* he willed with his mind. *Say it.* "What do you want from me?"

He wasn't going to play this game unless he knew without a doubt that he'd get her in the end. He didn't want another fling. He wanted *her.* All of her.

Tell me you want me just as badly.

She was clearly struggling with herself. "I want . . . ." She gave an exasperated gesture and started again. "I just . . . oh, fuck this."

She shoved up from the couch.

Felix granted himself a small smile. She might not have admitted her need for him but a curse was just as good. He'd learned that when Cali was pitted in a tough situation her only escape was anger. He'd angered her because she didn't want to answer his question. She wouldn't lie to him, either. Cali was better than that. It was a small victory but he'd take it.

"Not so fast." He wrapped his arms around her, taking a moment to revel in the feel of her soft body against his hard one.

"Let go of me." She struggled against him but the movements only pushed her body harder against his erection.

Felix stifled his groan and held back from thrusting against her. Barely.

"Stop trying to run away from me," he gritted in her ear. He pulled her back and dropped them both to the couch where he quickly draped his leg over both of hers to lock her in place. "I'm not going to push you anymore. Relax, Cali. I just want to hold you."

She tried one last time to move but he held firm. She turned to face him. "I don't believe you."

He grinned down at her. "I don't care what you believe because I got you right where I want you. Now stop being a pain in the ass and watch the movie. You scared the shit out of me today."

"I did?"

She settled a little more calmly against him, his big body spooning hers.

He pressed his lips to the back of her neck and felt her shudder. "Yes, I swear it's almost like you go looking for trouble."

That riled her. "I do not go looking for trouble. I'm not some thrill junkie who needs—"

"Easy." He kissed her neck again. "Easy." He loved the way her body responded to his touch. "That's not what I meant."

They got maybe ten minutes into the movie before Cali spoke again. "Felix?"

He tightened his arms around her. "Hm?"

Her body slowly stiffened, her heart racing so hard he could feel it.

He frowned at the back of her head. "What is it?"

"Are you using me just so you can get full control of your powers?"

The question came straight out of left field. Felix blinked before his mind could catch up to the question. Was she serious? Her body was stiff as a piece of wood in his arms so he guessed she was.

Felix ground his teeth. It was all that fucker Tyson's fault. He swore if he ever met the bastard he'd rip his limbs from his body.

He rose up onto his elbow and turned Cali onto her back so he could stare into those dark brown eyes of hers. "Cali, no. I'd never do anything to hurt you."

He could see the indecision warring inside her. "I already asked Niella—" That surprised him. "—and she said I could trust you guys, but I wanted to make sure."

"You can trust us."

She nodded. "Good, because for some reason I'm really starting to like you guys."

He gave a nonchalant shrug, a wicked smile teasing his lips. "It's not every day you have people willing to take on a huge business to protect you," he said with false modesty.

She grinned right back at him, the sight like a punch to the gut. She was so beautiful.

"Well, don't expect anything in return. You guys offered willingly so I'm not holding myself in debt."

He raised both eyebrows at her. "Do I look like I expect anything in return?"

She pushed at him playfully. "You're always looking for something in return."

He pretended to think about that while he adjusted himself more comfortably atop her. "True enough. So what are you going to give me? Last I remember, you were down by two."

He pressed a soft kiss to her collarbone. Her breathing hitched. That small reaction had his cock throbbing.

Slow, he reminded himself. *Take this slow. She's finally starting to trust you.*

He trailed his tongue up her neck, her hands threading into his hair. "I'm only down by two because you're an unfair ref."

"Me?" he asked innocently, his hand sliding up to graze her breast. The air left her lungs in a rush, her breath tickling his neck.

"Yes." Her voice was rougher, lower. It turned his blood to fire. "Y-you don't play. . .fair."

She turned into his kiss eagerly. His tongue slid between her lips before he pulled back. Her grip tightened in frustration. "Sometimes you have to fight dirty to get what you want."

Her eyes were ablaze with desire. He could all but smell her arousal, and it made him crazy.

Slow!

He growled low in his throat.

Cali pulled his head back down to hers for a scorching kiss. She spoke against his lips, nearly cracking his resolve right then and there. "I'm okay with dirty."

He threw his head back on a groan. "God, Cali. I won't be able to control myself if you talk like that." He buried his face in the crook of her neck, his hands cupping her breasts. Her nipples were hard beneath his palm. He squeezed gently. Her body arched into his. "I want to learn every little part of your body. I want to know where you're most sensitive and what makes you go wild." He pulled the material of her bra down and sucked her nipple through the fabric of her shirt.

She bucked beneath him, rubbing against his erection, hard.

"Felix." His name was a breathless plea, and her hands went straight for the waistband of his jeans.

Slow, his mind screamed at him.

With a self-control he didn't think he possessed he pulled her hands back from him. "Wait, wait." My God, he could hardly speak properly. "Slow. I want to take you slowly. Savor you. Be gentle."

She strained against his hands and nipped at his bottom lip. His cock tightened painfully. "I don't want you to be gentle."

Well, fuck.

He crushed his lips against hers. His hands slid possessively along her legs, hiking her skirt up until it bunched around her waist.

An explosion came from the movie but Felix hardly heard it.

Cali made quick work of his shirt. She took a moment to marvel at him. Every time she looked at him like that he became hers more and more. When she gazed at him like nothing else in the world existed but him, he felt invincible.

She yanked him to her, her mouth connecting with his chest, her tongue laving his skin.

He tore her panties from her legs and maneuvered himself

between her legs. She was already wet for him. Felix swallowed thickly as his fingers slid in and around her sex.

She moaned beneath him, her hips rising in unconscious surrender.

Felix clenched his jaw. "I want you naked," he growled.

Her eyes were glazed with desire, her lips red and swollen. She lifted her arms without complaint, and he threw her shirt to the floor to join his. Her bra followed shortly. The only item of clothing that remained was her skirt. It was fitted around her waist like an oversized, purple belt. He didn't mind. The sight of her like that was sexy as hell.

"So fucking hot." He glided his hands up her body to squeeze her breasts then trailed them lower to tease her between her legs.

Her eyes never left his, the connection between them rocketing his arousal higher.

She licked her lips, a hungry glint to her eye. "You have too much clothing on."

Her hands took their time traveling down his chest and abs. She started up again at his jeans and this time he let her. She pushed them and his boxers down in one sweep. He pushed himself up off her as much as possible so she could get his pants down around his knees. He took care of the rest until he was naked atop her. He dropped his body to cover hers like a blanket and they both moaned at the contact.

He rocked his hips against her, his cock sliding against her clit. She grabbed his hips. "Stop teasing."

He gave her a roguish grin. "You forget, I love teasing you." He rocked a little harder against her. Her nails dug into his skin. He took her mouth with his. He thrust his tongue deep into her mouth and kissed her until she was wanton beneath him, her hips arched recklessly against him, seeking. He held out just a little longer.

He snuck a hand between their bodies and toyed with her, his mouth swallowing all her cries of pleasure.

His fingers dipped into her sex. He groaned. "You're so wet, Cali."

She bit his lip and sucked it hard. "I want you."

His control cracked.

"Take me," she begged.

The crack grew.

She undulated against him with a moan. "I need you."

His control snapped.

He kissed her hard. One of his hands slid to her lower back and pulled her up. He rubbed the tip of himself against her sex, coating himself in her cream. Her arms wrapped around his back, her legs clutching his hips. With one powerful thrust he drove himself deep within her.

Cali cried out.

He pulled out to the crown and pushed back in, rolling his hips. Cali went wild. Her nails dug into his back, the small nip of pain adding to his pleasure as he thrust harder and faster into her.

He could feel her muscles tensing, felt the pleasure rising within her. Sweat collected on his brow as he pushed himself to move faster. He pounded into her, her moans of pleasure nearly drowning out the movie in the background.

"Come on, Cali," he urged. "Come for me."

Her inner muscles clenched around him as she climaxed. He rode her through it, thrusting harder and harder until he couldn't hold himself back anymore. His balls tightened, his cock jerked, and he came with a roar.

He couldn't move for a long moment. And he didn't want to. Cali's hands slid along his body at her leisure, as if she were trying to memorize every inch of him. She was positively glowing beneath him. She looked like a woman well loved. Pride filled him.

One of her hands slid through his hair, and he tilted his head into her palm. "Am I crushing you?"

She relaxed further into the couch and shook her head. "Feels nice." As if to make sure he wouldn't leave she wound her arms around his back.

"Don't worry, Cali." He nuzzled her neck. "I'm not going anywhere. You really like me, remember?"

He could feel her grinning.

She pushed him off her. He rolled into the back of the sofa.

"I meant I'm starting to really like the rest of the guild. Not you." Yet, despite her words, she snuggled into his chest and spent the rest of the night in his arms.

Chapter 18

An alarm sounded at three a.m.

Felix.

Cali was going to kill him.

The blaring ringtone came from the coffee table. Cali's thoughts were consumed with needing to stop that horrible noise. She dragged her body from the warmth of the couch with one mission in mind. Pound the crap out of his phone.

Felix grabbed her around the waist and spun her away from the coffee table before her fist could drop. "Whoa, Cali. Not the phone. Not the phone."

She relaxed back into the solid warmth of his body and noticed with some interest that he was already hardening. She rubbed against him.

Felix swallowed a growl. "As much as I'm loving your sleepy and cuddly morning attitude, I have to get ready for work."

It was too early to even think about working. Cali turned in his arms and tried to rub the sleep from her face on Felix's chest. It didn't really work. It was too damn early. Cali hadn't even known this hour of the morning existed.

"Okay," she mumbled groggily and pulled him down for a good morning kiss. It started out innocently enough but slowly gained heat. The sleepy fog that clouded her mind cleared as arousal peaked. It didn't help that both of them were still naked. It only made it easier to crush her body against his, to rub herself against his rapidly growing erection.

Felix broke away. "I have to get ready for work," he repeated though it sounded as if the sentence pained him.

Cali kissed him again. "Morning sex first," she mumbled against his lips.

Felix groaned low in his throat. "Work can wait."

They fell back onto the couch. Cali wrapped her legs tightly around his hips and thrust to meet him. Her body was already wet and ready for him. He slid in to the root.

Cali dropped her head back. He felt so good inside her. Last night had been wonderful—raw, passionate. This morning Felix took her slower, his hips working at an agonizing rhythm as if he thought she were sore from the night before.

She wasn't, but the way he worked against her built such a delicious ache that she didn't dare tell him to move faster. The more time she could steal with him the better.

That sweet tension within her grew. Layer by layer. Each smooth thrust taking her higher.

Despite the slower pace her breathing still increased. She was so close. She tightened her hold on him, driving her hips up so he filled her completely with each forward thrust.

She was right on the edge of climaxing when he kissed her. His tongue tangled with hers. He rolled his hips, and she cried out with the pleasure of it. Felix came a few seconds later.

She kissed along his collarbone, his heart thundering under his skin. She placed her hand over the harsh beating, marveling at how rapidly she was falling for someone like Felix.

She'd never felt like this before. She'd never had morning sex with anyone because she'd never really spent the night with anyone. She always left after the sex or in the morning before her boyfriend would wake up, or before her boyfriend's friends woke up.

Felix kissed her long and deep. "I'm going to be late for work."

"Maybe you should call in sick." She rotated her hips. He was still inside her and his eyes nearly rolled back in his head.

"I . . . " She repeated the motion. His jaw bulged. ". . . can't."

She tried to pout but a huge yawn ruined her. "Fine, fine, but bring me back my cherry pastries?"

"For you, anything."

*

Cali woke eight hours later covered with one of Felix's fleece blankets. She didn't remember falling asleep with it, which meant he'd covered her before he'd left. Her heart warmed just as her stomach grumbled. She needed to feed herself after all that physical exertion, but Felix wasn't home yet. She took a shower to waste away the time before dragging herself to the kitchen table. She pulled out her sketchpad and froze when she saw her nearly completed project.

It was the piece that was to pay for her rent, the one she'd forgotten all about in her haste to win over her fake job interview.

The happiness she'd woken up with evaporated as she dropped her head in her hands. She was going to lose her apartment.

The front door opened. "Cali? You awake? I brought breakfast." Felix caught sight of her in the kitchen. His bright grin dimmed a little when he saw her. "What's wrong?"

Stop being such a downer.

She swallowed her self-pity. There was no need to drag Felix into it. He and the guild were already doing enough for her. It still amazed her that they were willing to fight against Vander to help keep her safe. Granted, they were doing it to help any others like them out there as well, but the underlying concept was that they were behind her all the way.

"Nothing's wrong. I'm trying to figure out what I'm going to do for a job, is all. You know, since my last option was some psycho-ass CEO who was only interested in kidnapping me."

He dropped the white bag of baked goods on the table and stood behind her to knead her tense shoulders. "From what I've seen of your art, you're not going to have trouble selling anything you create."

"Your flattery isn't going to get you anything, you know." She took a large bite of her new favorite cherry pastry.

When he spoke his voice was right next to her ear. "Are you sure?"

She suppressed her shiver of delight and instead shoved some pastry into his mouth. "Yes. Now I've got work to do." And lots of it. She wasn't going to let Vander Donahughe screw up her life. She was going to finish this latest project and make her rent. No psycho asshole was going to ruin her success.

Cali worked straight into the evening. Felix took a nap sometime during the afternoon and woke up to make her dinner. She could get used to this kind of treatment. She didn't think she'd ever been made dinner before.

Felix set a plate in front of her and took the seat opposite. "Joel called while I was in my room sleeping. They want us to come by the clinic. He sounded really excited about something. I was too afraid to ask."

Cali bit into her ravioli. Delicious. "He probably thought up some crazy name for our guild."

"That's exactly why I didn't ask."

*

"Alethcia," Joel proclaimed proudly once they set foot inside Sydney's clinic.

Cali and Felix shared a look. "What?"

"The Guild of Aletheia. It's Greek . . . you know, for truth? You guys don't like it?"

"No." They denied his claim simultaneously.

"It's great, man," said Felix. "Quite a mouthful though."

Cali nodded. "I like it. It sounds . . . strong." She couldn't think of a better word but the name did remind her a bit of Athena.

"That's what I said." Sydney came out of one of her patient rooms. The clinic was closed and she was busy cleaning up.

"I think it's ridiculous," said Niella. "But as long as we're not giving out business cards with the name on it, I guess it's okay."

"That's the spirit," said Felix jovially.

Joel looked as if he didn't know whether or not to thank Felix for his little remark or punch him for it. He chose to ignore him. "I also found a title for that Jente guy you were talking about yesterday, Cali."

"What'd you get?"

"You said his power was invisibility, right?"

"Yeah, by the way, Sydney are you using your powers?" Cali called.

"Yes." Her yell came from somewhere in the back. "I've been using them all day, and I can tell you personally that I'm getting a little crabby because of it."

"Anyway," Joel continued eagerly. "I figured when he turns invisible it's like he's pulling a veil over himself, so why not call him a Veiler?"

Niella shook her head behind the reception desk. Joel didn't seem to notice—he was too invested with Cali's reaction. And when she really thought about it, the name did fit him. It was pretty cool too.

"I like it," she told him honestly.

Joel beamed at her.

"Is Veiler even a word?" asked Felix.

"Nope." Niella stuffed some papers into a file.

"Perfect." Felix slapped Joel on the back. "We're defining our own words."

Cali took one of the seats in the lobby. "I have a question. You guys made up all the terms, right? So where did the term Mirror Mate come from?"

Joel and Felix stared at each other for a few seconds before sharing a shrug. "It just makes sense," said Felix. "If you really think about it, souls that truly reflect one another are destined to find each other eventually."

The way he looked at her with those blue-green eyes left her breathless. She knew he was thinking about her. *Them*. Being Mirror Mates.

But no one in their guild knew very much about how they were supposed to bond. Or when it would happen. Was it possible they weren't soul mates? The idea made her sick.

Car doors slammed outside.

Everyone turned toward the front of the clinic. "What was that?"

Felix raced to the glass door and swore. "Everyone up. Now! Sydney!" He called to the back to warn her then swiveled back to the rest of the group. "Joel, Lock this door. Hurry."

Joel was seated next to Cali. He tried to rise but his chair got caught with hers and he nearly fell. He cursed. Cali jumped out of the way but it was too late.

The door shook.

Sydney came hauling ass from the back of her clinic, hair tied back, a flimsy hospital mask pulled down around her neck. She'd obviously been busy cleaning. Her green eyes spotted whoever was on the other side of the door and she screamed.

Glass shattered.

"Felix," Sydney cried, motioning for everyone to make a run to her. "They have weapons."

"I'm on it." Instead of heading to the back of the clinic like a sane person would, he stepped toward the assailants as they came through the door. They were dressed as regular people, probably so they wouldn't draw attention, and even had a large stuffed dog. Cali tried to get to Felix but Joel pushed her toward the back hallway and Sydney, forcing her to move. She could only catch glimpses of their attackers, but she saw enough to know they were armed with guns. A chill made its way down her spine at the sight of the weapons, but she needn't have worried. One second they were there, the next the guns were gone.

Felix.

Sydney must have dropped her Shield. Felix had started

disarming the men as soon as he saw what they were packing. They didn't look all that startled to find their weapons magically gone, which meant they had to be Vander's men.

Sydney practically pulled Cali's arm off as she dragged her toward her office. "Come on," she yelled.

Cali hesitated. She couldn't leave Felix.

"He'll be fine," Sydney reassured. "He's just waiting to make sure all the weapons are disposed of. Now head down the hall toward the kennels. There's a back emergency exit. These guys are after you, remember? Not us."

Joel hung back in the lobby, and before her view was completely blocked she saw him throw a punch.

"Wait." Cali stopped Sydney. "What about Niella?"

They'd left her by herself behind the reception desk.

Sydney looked pained. "She'll be okay, Joel and Felix will protect her. She has the counter to use as a shield. You're our first priority."

The emergency exit at the end of the hall flew open. Sydney screeched to a halt, Cali running into her. Two more men must have run around the back of the building to block them.

"Shit." Cali backpedaled, bringing Sydney with her.

They made their way to the front where Felix and Joel were engaging two combatants each.

Joel caught sight of Sydney. "There you are. Turn off your powers. These guys were trained for hand to hand." As if to prove his point he got clipped in the jaw and went stumbling.

Sydney called out. "I'm not using my powers." She turned to Cali, her look beseeching. "I'm not using my powers," she repeated in a low, scared voice. Her brilliant green eyes were wide as saucers.

Shit.

What to do, what to do?

Was it possible Sydney really was using her powers and she simply didn't know it? Cali remembered during her training sessions with Felix that when emotions ran high, it was harder to control them.

It was worth a try. She grabbed Sydney by the shoulders. "Listen, just take it easy. Try and calm down. You might be using your powers without even knowing it."

Sydney's blonde ponytail swung as she shook her head. "No, you don't understand. I'm not using them. I'd know. I get this sensation." Her hand fluttered uselessly behind her neck.

The tingling at the back of the neck. Cali knew all about it.

There went that idea. So if Sydney wasn't using her powers that had to mean one of the men had an ability.

"There's another Shielder," Cali told Sydney.

"You think?"

"Has to be." She tried to think as they stayed huddled between the main hallway and the lobby. Then it hit her. The men at the emergency exit. They weren't coming after them. "Chill here," she told Sydney.

"Where are you going?"

"Technically, nowhere. I need to look around the corner to see if those guys are still guarding the exit. If they are, then our best guess is that one of them is the Shielder."

Understanding dawned on Sydney. "You're right, because he'd need his concentration to keep the Shield going."

Cali tapped her chin. "Then all we need to do is cause a distraction?"

Sydney smiled. "A big one."

"We have to move fast." Cali winced as she heard another pained grunt from the front. She hoped it wasn't Felix or Joel. Or, lord forbid, Niella.

Sydney's demeanor changed instantly. Gone was the scared little vet. "Into my office, now. I have an idea."

They flew across the hall to her office. The men at the door fell into defensive positions at the sight of them but still didn't give chase. Cali slammed the office door. Sydney dove beneath her futon. A few seconds later she pulled out a wicked looking golf club. Cali wasn't a golfer by any means, but she was pretty positive Sydney held a driver.

Shit, she'd never beamed someone with a golf club before.

"You didn't tell me you had that under there," she said to Sydney. It would have gone a long way in soothing her nerves that first night she'd slept there, knowing that was under the futon.

"My bad," she said without remorse. "Turn around."

Cali faced the office entrance. "Why am I turned around?" she asked over her shoulder.

Sydney held the club face up and approached her. "Because we're going to pretend to surrender. Now, I need to position this so you or I can reach it easily without it falling through your clothes."

It took a few seconds before she understood what Sydney meant. "Shove it down my shorts but keep it on the outside of my tee," she instructed.

Sydney started to get to work. "What if the club tips to the side from the weight at the top?"

"Counteract that weight by shoving the majority of the handle down so it rests along the back of my thigh."

"Are you going to be able to walk like this?"

"We're about to find out." Cali grabbed the knob. "Joel and Felix can't hold out indefinitely. You ready?"

Sydney pulled her hands back from the club and held them out as they both waited to see if the club would tip out from behind her body.

It tilted, but not by much.

"Good enough," said Cali. "Stay behind me. My height should keep you relatively hidden."

Sydney nodded. "Wait." She sprinted to the mini fridge at the back of her office, grabbed something, and raced back to Cali. She held up two syringes. "Tranquilizers."

Cali couldn't quite mask her surprise. "Damn, Sydney," she said in approval. "Let's go."

They started down the hall toward the emergency exit. Both men eyed them suspiciously.

If you only knew what we had in store for you, Cali thought smugly.

The guard on the left straightened as they continued their advance. Cali kept her pace slow. She didn't want to startle them or jostle the golf club that was shifting precariously in her pants. Once or twice she felt Sydney reach out and steady the club.

Less than twenty feet from the exit, Sydney peaked out around Cali and whispered up to her, "I think the Shielder is the one on the right. Notice how he's distracted, not completely focused on us?"

Cali nodded once to let her know she'd heard.

The brown-haired guard on the left shifted nervously. "Stop right there." She expected the command to be followed by the raising of a gun, but luckily Felix had gotten to these two before the Shielder could take away his power.

She held her arms up in surrender. "We want to turn ourselves in. Please, call off the men in the front."

The man had the audacity to smirk. *Arrogant bastard*. "Are you Cali?"

She continued to step forward.

Just a little closer.

"That's me," she said.

His eyes shifted to Sydney, taking in her scared, cowardly appearance as she hid behind Cali. He dismissed her easily enough. Cali assumed a lot of men didn't take the short blonde seriously. Their mistake.

Her hands shot behind her body to grab the golf club. Cali pulled it straight up and swung straight down.

The guard on the left yelped as she twisted to snag the head of the club around the back of his knee. His leg buckled. Meanwhile, Sydney jumped out from behind her like a bright blonde jack-in-the-box.

"Surprise," she said cheerfully, before jamming both needles into both men's thighs and shoving the plungers down with enough force to make Cali wince.

The guards stared at them in surprise, their eyes already glazing. A few seconds later they fell over.

"Shit, Sydney, how much drug did you shoot into their veins?"

She gave a delicate shrug. "Enough," she said cryptically before yelling to the others. "Hey guys, power's back on." As if they'd been experiencing nothing more bothersome than a blackout.

There was a tired, "Finally," from the front. Cali and Sydney booked it to make sure everyone was okay.

Cali stumbled to a halt when she made it into the lobby, her sneakers slipping on blood. Her stomach twisted. The puddle was small but she still scanned for Felix. He didn't seem to have any major injuries.

Joel, on the other hand, was bleeding pretty badly from his nose. She guessed he wasn't used to fighting as much as Felix. Where Felix dodged oncoming punches with a dancer's grace, Joel waited until the punch was nearly upon him before making his move.

It didn't take long for Cali to realize that Joel wasn't a horrible fighter, he just had to take bigger chances to favor his powers. She watched in fascination as he waited for a punch to be thrown. At the last minute he shifted his weight to avoid it and grabbed the attacker's wrist at the same time. He kicked a leg out from under the man and he stumbled to one knee. Joel slammed his opponent's hand palm down on the linoleum. Cali waited for him to crush the hand under his shoe or something, but all he did was hold on for a second and let go.

The man tried to pull his hand from the floor. He couldn't.

Cali's eyebrows shot into her hairline.

He was Locked to the floor.

Whoa.

She turned to Sydney and found the Shielder watching her boyfriend with admiration.

Cali had to give it to Joel and Felix, once they were able to use their powers they worked really well together. Felix took the brunt of the fighting, mostly to distract the others as Joel snuck between them to Lock their feet to the floor. He even got one guy with his hands Locked together. Within a few minutes all the men were incapacitated.

"Are you okay?" She ran to Felix and gave him the once over. He had a few hits that were going to bruise but otherwise he looked well enough.

Felix rubbed a tender spot on the back of his head. "Never better. Were you guys harmed at all?" His eyes briefly touched on Sydney but his attention was all for Cali.

Warmth bloomed in her chest.

And then in regular Felix fashion he had to go and ruin it by opening his mouth. "I saw you guys running to the back. I have to say, Cali, I didn't take you for the retreating type."

He gave her a teasing smile, and she punched him in the arm.

"We weren't hiding. We took care of the two bastards in the back. One of whom was a Shielder."

Some of the humor left his eyes. "We need to get out of here."

"Where's Niella?"

She wheeled around the reception desk. "I'm here. Don't worry, no one came after the cripple." Her voice dripped with bitterness.

Cali frowned.

"There could be more on the way." Joel's stuffy voice came from the corner where Sydney was busy patching up his bloody nose.

Felix nodded in agreement. "And that could mean more with powers too. We should hold up at one of our places."

"How'd they know about my clinic?" Sydney leaned into Joel once she finished with him. "Felix, you've never told Collette about it."

Cali knew all too well who'd given up their location. "It was

Jente. He's been here and he's also been to your place," she said to Felix, "which means we're not safe there."

Felix looked like he really wanted to punch someone out. Too bad all the thugs were already unconscious. "You're right. Where should we go?"

"Anywhere but here," Niella spoke up as she pulled her attention from the window. "I just saw another black SUV pull into the plaza parking lot."

Sydney and Joel shot to their feet.

"To the back," Felix ordered. The familiar sound of car doors slamming came through the broken glass of the front door. "Now."

Cali ran to Niella but she slapped her hands away when Cali tried to grasp the handles of her wheelchair. "Leave me. I'd only slow you down."

Cali couldn't help the growl of frustration that rose up from her throat. "You have to be fucking kidding me. We're not leaving you, Niella, so you can stop trying to martyr yourself. Now shut the hell up and let me push you. You're just as much a part of this horribly named guild as I am."

Niella stopped resisting. The look in her eyes could have passed for gratitude, but Cali didn't bother trying to figure it out. She wheeled her the hell out of there.

Felix waited for her in the hall. Joel and Sydney had gone ahead to try to clear the two guards from blocking the back entrance. "Jesus, Syd," Joel was saying. "Remind me never to piss you off."

Sydney flashed her teeth like a shark, admiring her handiwork. Felix darted around Cali to help with the bodies and together the three of them locked the men in the dog kennels. Footsteps could be heard from the front.

Cali shot through the back into the cooling evening heat. Dusk was setting in, the ocean breeze kicking up enough to raise goose bumps on her bare legs and arms. She steered Niella to the left to give everyone room behind her to get out. They needed to find their way back to the front of the clinic so they could get to the cars.

Joel was the last one out. He placed his hand on the door to Lock the new arrivals inside.

"No, wait," said Felix. "Leave it unlocked. We need them to chase us. Hopefully, it'll give us some extra time to make it around front without being spotted."

Joel dropped his hand.

"This way." Sydney took the lead and sprinted along the back of the plaza. Her clinic was on the corner, but she didn't lead them through the quick and easy route. There were too many windows on the side of the clinic, and they couldn't risk being seen if anyone was left in the lobby watching over the other men.

Instead they made their way toward the center of the little strip mall. They passed the back exit to Tom's Pizzeria—unfortunately closed—a grooming store, and a Laundromat before there was a narrow break in the buildings where they could run to the front.

Shouts erupted behind them as their pursuers gave chase. Cali could hardly hear their progress over the pounding of everyone's feet.

"Wait a second," she mumbled to herself, then called louder, "Felix, I need you to take Niella."

He was already halfway down the small alley. He paused. "What are you doing?"

Sydney came out of nowhere. "I got her." She took the wheelchair from Cali and high-tailed it down the narrow strip of concrete.

Cali stopped running so she could clear her mind. The back of her neck prickled instantly. She focused on the pounding footsteps of her guild.

Make it go away. Hush the sound.

The noise faded.

"You hear them?" Cali heard a man yell from behind the buildings.

A curse came from another one.

She allowed herself a smug smile and turned to catch up with the others.

Strong fingers dug into her upper arm, wrenching her backwards. "Got you."

Felix's fist came flying into her peripheral vision. "I don't think so."

Their attacker went down hard.

Felix spun to face her, grinning. "Is that four or five, now?"

"That so does not count."

"You're falling behind, Cali," he said as they ran.

"And I just told you—"

"Not now," he interrupted as they poured out of the little alley. "You can bitch at me later."

"Oh, I'm going to bitch at you, all right," she told his back as they raced to the Hummer. "I'm going to make your life a fucking misery."

He spun around, Cali nearly plowing into him. He cupped her face and gave her a quick kiss. "I'm looking forward to it."

She went to punch him but he was already out of reach.

"Felix." Joel called him over to where he was hovering near the enemy SUVs. "Don't think they're going to need these."

"Let's load up first. I'll Erase them on our way out. Cali, can you Silence the car?"

She scrambled over to his Hummer where Sydney was helping Niella get in. "I'm on it."

Felix climbed into the driver's seat. "Ready?" he asked her.

Her grip tightened on the dash. "Let's hope so."

He turned the key. The car rumbled beneath them but there was no sound from the engine.

They shared a grin.

"Everyone in and accounted for?" Felix called to the back.

"Yes, now can we hurry up and get the hell out of here?" Niella said.

They pulled out of the parking lot, but not before Felix Erased the enemy cars.

"What are you going to do about your clinic?" Cali turned in her seat to address Sydney.

She already had her cell phone out. "I'm calling the police. Those bastards are stranded and they're going to pay for my busted glass."

Cali readjusted herself as Sydney reported the break-in. "Where are we going?" she asked Felix.

He glanced in the rearview mirror at Sydney still talking on the phone. He lowered his voice so as not to be overheard by the others. "She can't Shield us all night, and I don't think we should return to any of our houses. Not right now. I'm driving us to the nearest motel. We can bunk there for the night. So if we're being followed, it won't lead anyone from Kratos to another home address."

After Sydney hung up with the police Felix explained his plan to everyone else. There were some grumbles of disappointment about having to sleep at a motel, but everyone understood the reasoning behind Felix's precaution. Even Niella went along with the plan without complaint.

*

"Here we are—home sweet motel room—" Joel slid the large, glass door aside for everyone to enter their tiny room. It was the best the motel had. Three queen-sized beds. Two of which were in the main room as soon as they entered. The third bed was in a small, separate room that only had enough space for the bed and one nightstand.

"Cozy," Felix said dryly as he leaned through the doorway. "Who gets the semi-private room?"

Sydney took a seat on the bed closest to the bathroom and gave the mattress a few experimental bounces. "You guys take it. Joel and I will take this one, and Niella can have the one closest to the door. That way her wheelchair won't block the small walkways." She motioned to the three-foot-wide walking space that surrounded the beds.

Joel came out from his tour of the bathroom. "There's nothing in there but two mini bars of soap and two equally mini shampoo and conditioner bottles. I think I'll run to the closest drug store and pick up some things. This room's got me claustrophobic. Syd, you coming?"

Sydney snuggled deeper into her pillow. "I think I'm going to rest," she said sleepily.

"I'll go." Niella wheeled herself over to the sliding glass door. "I can't stand being this cooped up."

Once Joel and Niella left, Cali and Felix retired to their room, where Sydney's soft snores could be heard even with the door closed.

Cali rolled onto her side, hyperaware of the fact Felix lay less than a foot away from her. "What are we going to do?" she whispered.

The heat at her back grew as Felix shifted closer. He trailed his fingers down the side of her arm. "We're going to keep you safe, find a way to get proof of Kratos' wrongdoings, help the others like us out there, and eventually dismantle Vander Donahughe's company."

The bed creaked as she turned to face him. "We're going to do all that from inside a motel room with nothing but the clothes on our backs?"

He rubbed the hem of her T-shirt between his thumb and forefinger, his eyes dark with lust. "We don't have to wear the clothing on our backs."

Her heart kicked against her ribs.

"Sydney's in the other room, you moron."

His hand slid along the skin of her stomach, ratcheting her pulse up higher. "I can be quiet." He kissed her.

Cali melted against him. His arms wound around her, his legs curling behind hers to drag her closer. She grasped his face in her hands, the stubble along his jaw prickling her palms. She parted her lips in welcome as his tongue thrust deep. Her entire body throbbed with want.

The hands at her back snuck beneath her shirt, drawing it up. His palms slid around to the front of her shorts, one hand dipping inside.

Her head fell back on a gasp.

"Shh." Felix breathed heavily along her collarbone.

One of his fingers pushed inside her and Cali bit her tongue to keep from moaning. Her muscles clamped around him, the heel of his hand pressing against her with the perfect amount of pressure.

"Does that feel good?" he whispered in her ear. His voice was rough, heightening her arousal.

"Yes," she panted as he started to thrust.

He growled in animalistic desire. "I want to be inside you."

Her hands dropped to the front of his jeans. "Then what are you waiting for?"

Her fingers had wrapped tight around his cock when the sound of the sliding glass door opening reached their ears.

"We're back," Joel called merrily.

A low grumble signaled Niella's presence.

Cali instantly released Felix. His eyes spelled murder for Joel. She jumped from the bed and made a dash to the bathroom through their own separate door. She locked both entrances, needing a minute to organize herself. Her skin was flushed bright red, her breathing heavy. If Joel had walked into their room, there would have been no doubt in his mind of what they'd been about to do.

She turned the faucet on and wet her face with cold water. The ache between her thighs pulsed with every beat of her heart. She cursed Joel's timing. He couldn't have waited just a little longer?

She shut the water off and gave herself a couple extra minutes before exiting the bathroom. She stepped out into the main room where Joel was dividing a pile full of toiletries on his bed.

Sydney hadn't bothered sitting up. She watched with half-lidded eyes. Niella was on her bed. She had earphones on and her eyes closed.

No sign of Felix. The door to their room was still closed. Was he trying to collect himself as well? She licked her lips as a different image came to mind. One of Felix bringing himself to climax.

Cali swallowed thickly. Surely he wouldn't do that . . . without her?

She flung the door wide open.

He lay on his back, one arm draped over his eyes, the bulge in his pants still obvious.

"What?" he asked irritably before looking to see who had entered. His expression didn't lighten when he saw her. In fact, it darkened, as if he blamed her for the pain he was in.

You're not the only one suffering from sexual frustration, pal.

After a few seconds of standing there she started to feel like an idiot. "Uh, Joel brought toiletries."

He closed his eyes and dropped his head back on his pillow. "I'm so excited," he deadpanned. "Is he going to be leaving again anytime soon?"

"You need something else, man?" Joel spoke up from behind Cali. He was still seated on the bed, blissfully unaware of Felix's mood.

Felix sighed. "I'm fine, Joel. Thanks."

Everyone went to bed pretty early after rock-paper-scissoring who got to use the bathroom and brush their teeth first.

Niella won. Felix came in last.

Cali took advantage of Felix's time in the bathroom to strip off her shorts and bra and climb under the covers. They had to check out of the motel tomorrow before eleven. Whoever decided on that time should be shot, in Cali's opinion.

They were supposed to be planning Vander's downfall tomorrow, but Sydney had to go in and talk to the police. Niella would most likely go with her. Felix had to work, as did Joel. That left Cali alone the majority of the day. She didn't mind, though not having a car kind of sucked. Felix was worried about leaving her alone and proposed she come to the bakery with him. She shot the proposal of waking up at three a.m. down flat. There was a small park close by that she decided to take advantage of while everyone else was off taking care of their lives. Joel mentioned the hotel's main office carried notepads and pencils. She'd pick up some items after she checked out.

"You still awake?" Felix slipped into bed beside her.

Her body instantly became aware of him. And what they'd left unfinished a couple hours ago.

His arm wrapped around her waist and pulled her flush against his body as if they did this every night. As if they were a couple.

Were they?

For the first time she didn't find the idea frightening. Not even when she considered them to be Mirror Mates. There was a trust she had with Felix that, despite her best efforts to resist, went beyond anything she'd ever had with anyone else, but instead of scaring her, she found herself pressing forward, curious to see where it would take her.

Hopefully somewhere good.

She smiled to herself and relaxed back against him as sleepiness took root. With Felix she'd always be safe.

Chapter 19

Cali woke up the next morning twenty minutes before checkout.

"Shit." She rolled out of bed and rushed to the shower where there was barely enough shampoo and conditioner left for her. "Really?" She pounded at the conditioner. "Guys need to use conditioner?"

She dressed at lightning speed and made it to the check out desk with one minute to spare. Only to realize she didn't have any cash on her to pay for the sketching supplies she wanted to use that day.

"Awesome," she said to no one as she shielded her eyes against the burning summer sun. She made her way over to the park and found a tree to rest against. She patted her front pocket to double-check her phone. Felix had said he'd call when he got off work.

She didn't know how long she sat under that large tree, but suddenly she got a strange, creeping sensation at the back of her neck.

She knew better than to discard her instincts and scanned the park for anything that could be a threat. Children screaming as they ran through the playground were suddenly suspicious to her. Were they Illusions? Was she sensing Collette?

She was sitting off far enough in the trees for Collette to attack without notice.

Not the brightest idea, Cali.

She inhaled deeply to calm herself and focused her power. The tingling at the back of her neck kicked up, and she willed any and all heart beats in close proximity to her to sound aloud.

Lub-dub, lub-dub.

Her head whirled to the left. Nothing was there. Nothing she could see, anyway.

The heartbeat grew louder as she focused on it.

Jente appeared out of nowhere. "Impressive. It's not very often

I'm detected." He was wearing board shorts and a dark hoodie. The clothing allowed him to blend in with the crowds. It also made him look less threatening than Cali knew he really was.

"What do you want?"

He gave her a droll stare and tucked his hands into the pockets of his jacket. "It isn't obvious by now?"

She kept her face expressionless, though her heart was going a mile a minute. "What does he want with me? Why am I so damn special?" If she was going to face down Jente, she might as well try to get some answers. Collette had already established Cali wasn't wanted for the strength of her powers.

Jente shrugged carelessly and took a seat next to her as if he had all the time in the world. He was so young. Sunlight streamed through the tree branches, hitting his hair and lighting it with jets of red. His mismatched eyes watched her carefully.

"Not going to run screaming?"

"I want some answers."

He made a thoughtful noise in the back of his throat. "The brave and stupid route. At least you keep it interesting."

She clenched her jaw. "I'm going out on a limb here, but I think that the combination of your age and attitude means you're the regular pain in the ass of your corporation. Following that assumption, I'm also guessing you don't mind sliding by the rules or ignoring them."

There was a gleam of amusement in his face that hadn't been there a second ago. "You'd assume correctly."

At least she was getting somewhere.

"Then what does Vander Donahughe want with me? I know for damn sure it's not because of my artwork."

Jente scoffed. "His loss. I've seen your work and it's amazing." He sounded like he meant that. Cali frowned as he leaned over and fished something out of his back pocket. His shoulder brushed hers, and she caught the scent of sand and orange blossoms. He held up a small notebook. She knew that notebook, kept one just like it next to her bed at her apartment so she could sketch when the urge came to her in the middle of the night.

"Is that—?"

"Yours?" He held it open for her to see. "Yeah, I helped myself when I searched your apartment. Place looked as if a bomb had gone off. Not much of a cook?"

Cali felt a small prickle of satisfaction when faced with the option of ratting out Collette. "I got a little visit from a friend of yours."

It didn't take him very long to put two and two together. "Collette's a stuck-up bitch. And she's not my friend."

"Don't have many friends, do you?"

"Neither do you," he said ruthlessly.

"How long have you been watching me?"

She could have sworn color spotted his cheeks. "Long enough to make sure."

"To make sure of what?"

He gazed out at the children playing. "That you were the one we were looking for."

This was it. "And why were you looking for me in the first place?"

Jente shrugged. "I'm not high enough on the food chain to know that. All I was told was that Vander had been left instructions by Collette's soul mate, or whatever, about a woman with the power to control sound."

"Collette's Mirror Mate told Vander about me?" Wasn't that guy—Keith? No. Kevin—in a coma?

"Mirror Mate?" Jente laughed. "Is that what you guys call them?"

Cali felt a burning need inside her to defend her guild.

Now wasn't the time. "Well?" she pushed. "I thought Kevin was unconscious somewhere."

"He is." Jente shifted against the bark of the tree, as if trying to find a comfortable spot. *Good luck with that.* "Vander's the one keeping him alive. He pays for his life support as long as Collette does everything he says and doesn't fuck up."

Cali refused to feel sympathy for that psycho bitch or her Mirror Mate.

Kevin shot Felix, remember?

"How did he know about me?" she asked suspiciously.

"He had a vision." There was an unspoken "duh" tacked on to the end of that sentence. "Vander used him all the time to find people. He was the only one I knew of who could see whatever Vander wanted him to."

A full-forced Dreamer.

And somehow he'd seen Cali all those months—years?—ago.

Her fingers itched to reach for her cell. "When did you guys learn about my powers? *How* did you learn about them?"

She hadn't learned about them till over a week ago, when Felix had busted into her life. How could they have known about her when she hadn't even known herself?

She shook her head to clear her thoughts. She could only imagine what it must be like for Niella to have to deal with all that sort of information. Cali would have gone mad long ago.

Jente averted his eyes. "You have a bad habit of using your powers when you work on your art. I was watching you one evening when you were working on that piece for the dental office. Your roommate was blasting music and singing with that God-awful voice of hers."

Cali couldn't help but smile. It was good to know she wasn't the only one who had thought Jessica had a horrible voice.

Jente continued, "You were so focused on your work that the sound of the music faded from your room. It was small at first. I barely noticed it, but eventually it faded to nothing. I kept closer tabs on you after that. It became more and more frequent as your deadline pressed down on you."

The dental office painting . . . that meant Jente had been watching her for nearly four months. She didn't know how she felt about that. Violated? Angry? His obvious appreciation of her work would be a nice sentiment if he hadn't been her own personal stalker for nearly half a year.

"What else was in the Dream?"

Again, he was amused. "Dream?"

This was really grating on her nerves. "Vision, Dream, same thing. Did Kevin say anything more about me?"

"Like if you were some prophetic child come down to save or destroy us all?" He shook his head. "Nah, nothing that melodramatic."

They fell into silence. The tension slowly grew as Cali anticipated an attack and Jente no doubt anticipated an escape attempt.

Cali wiped the sweat from her palms onto her shorts. "What happens if I don't come with you?"

"You're coming with me," he said matter-of-factly. "It's up to you whether that way is comfortable or not."

"Why do you work for Vander?" Would Felix make it in time if she kept delaying Jente? She carefully placed her hand over the cell phone in her shorts pocket, willing it to go off.

Come on, Felix. For once be here when I want you to.

Jente eyed her suspiciously. "Why do you care?"

She didn't. Not really. But she was curious. She understood why Collette still hung around, but she didn't understand why someone so young would work for someone like Vander. Was it only for the money?

She stared him right in the eye, unwilling to back down. "Humor me," she told him.

"I know where this trail of questioning leads. You see the young kid working for the big bad evil and automatically think this was my only option. That I'm here against my will, right? Well, wrong. I'm here because I want to be. I need Vander, and right now he needs me, and that's all I really give a fuck about. I'm using him and he's using me and we're just peachy. Now, are you going to cooperate with me?"

Her muscles tensed as fight or flight started to creep in. "You don't have to deliver me to him."

He sighed as if her comment disappointed him.

Too fucking bad. She wasn't going to be handed to Vander on a silver platter.

Her cell phone went off. She nearly jumped ten feet into the air. Felix.

Her hand shot into her pocket to dig it out when there was a small sting against her thigh. "Ow." She jerked away and noticed Jente pulling something from her leg. A tiny needle.

He caught her expression and smiled. "I heard what you did to those two men at the clinic and thought I'd follow in your footsteps."

He'd *tranqued* her.

Cali's stomach flipped. Her vision was already starting to blur. She blinked rapidly but couldn't seem to shake it. Her mouth felt like cotton. The weight of her phone in her hand was a distant memory, the sound a faint buzzing. "You didn't have to. . .do. . .this."

Jente got to his feet smoothly. "Orders are orders, Cali. You don't understand how badly I need Vander's resources."

She blacked out.

*

Felix hit redial for the seventh time.

Still no answer.

"Dammit." He ended the call and barely resisted throwing his phone across the car. Why the hell wasn't she answering? He felt sick to his stomach, the ache in his chest pulsing worse than usual. Was Cali in trouble?

His foot pressed down harder on the gas.

The park came into view and he swerved into the nearest spot.

Children squealed in the background as Felix searched for Cali. Her dark brown head of hair was nowhere in sight.

He bit back a curse and pressed onward. Cali didn't like people, so it only seemed reasonable that she'd distance herself from them, even at a park.

He trolled the tree line but there was nothing. Maybe he could get Joel to track her cell. He pulled out his phone and on one last-ditch effort he called Cali.

A faint ring came from over his shoulder.

He whirled. "Cali?"

He knew she didn't like to wake up before eleven, but could she really have fallen asleep out here in this heat?

The ringing continued. He ran blindly, his heart in his throat. As the sound grew louder, the sinking sensation in his stomach became worse.

He found her phone abandoned in the grass near a large tree. The blood in his veins froze. Terror and rage warred inside him as he picked her cell from the ground. The screen displayed a candid shot of him in his kitchen baking. He'd never even known she'd taken a picture of him.

His fingers curled around her phone as rage won out.

He was going to tear Vander Donahughe limb from limb. Red clouded his vision. Somehow he made it back to his Hummer, Cali's phone tucked safely away in his pocket. He speed-dialed Joel.

He picked up on the fourth ring. "A little busy here, Felix."

"They got Cali."

Something smashed to the floor. Joel cursed. "You're sure?"

"I found her phone in the park." His teeth ground together. "We shouldn't have fucking left her alone," he nearly roared.

"How'd they find her?"

Felix sped through a yield sign and avoided a collision by a hair. Horns blared at him. He paid no attention. "That punk kid, Jente. He's the only one that could have followed us without our knowing." He vowed pain and dismemberment upon him if he ever saw that fucker.

"We'll find her, Felix." Joel tried to calm him. It wasn't working. "Are you driving?"

"Yes," he gritted through his teeth. More horns blared.

"For fuck's sake, Felix." Joel sounded both scared and exasperated. "You're going to be no good to Cali if you're dead. Where are you going?"

"I don't know," he said honestly. He felt lost. Then an idea hit him. "I'm going to Niella."

"Easy how you tread with her," Joel advised. "You know she can't Dream on command. Too many Dreams, even if they're for good reason, can start playing with her mind."

"It's all I've got right now, Joel."

Cali was all he had. She'd become such a large part of his life in so short a time. He would take on the whole Kratos Corporation single-handed if that was what it took.

Chapter 20

Something sharp pushed into the skin at the bend in Cali's arm. Her body jerked to attention. Multiple pairs of hands pushed her back down.

"Get off me," she screamed. Her struggling did no good. It only exacerbated the pain in her arm as the needle shifted. They were drawing a blood sample. Her eyes latched onto the dark blood pouring into the vial. Nausea rode her hard.

"Keep her steady," someone said. Everything was still fuzzy from that damn tranquilizer Jente had shot her with.

That little bastard was going to pay for that.

"She keeps moving," another complained as Cali freed one of her feet and kicked out blindly. She wiggled and wormed for all she was worth. However, she was too busy trying to get free to pay any attention to what was going on around her. One minute she was surrounded by what felt like a hundred hands, the next Vander Donahughe stood over her.

He regarded her with affection.

She wanted to spit in his face.

His dark, coffee-bean hair was combed back in that rich way men of status wore their hair. His eyes were a deep, mahogany brown. They were intellectual eyes, as if they knew the secrets of the universe. He had a broad forehead and pronounced cheekbones. He was a little on the pale side but at one point in her life, a very low point, Cali had thought Vander attractive. It was the first time she'd seen him, when he'd approached her with the position in his corporation. Now she couldn't look at him without thinking about all the evil he'd probably committed in his life.

What was the point? To see how much money he could make

before he died? Anger flooded her, chasing away the rational fear she should be feeling. She renewed her struggling.

"Sir," one of the people at her feet said. "It'd be so much easier if we could sedate her."

Vander glanced over his shoulder. Whatever expression he gave the person shut them up fast. "Sedation won't be necessary." He was back to staring down at her. "Cali will cooperate, won't you, Cali?"

"Fuck you," she seethed and pulled at her restrained wrists. The woman on her right was due for a manicure, her dirty nails digging into the flesh of Cali's wrist.

The whole room held its breath after she spoke.

A muscle in Vander's jaw ticked but he remained calm, his voice like steel. "You will do as I say because if you do not, I'm afraid I'll have to exercise my own power against you."

"Oh yeah? And what the hell is your power, to look filthy rich?" She knew she was digging her own grave, but she wasn't going to go quietly. "What do you want with me?"

Vander knelt next to her and brushed aside her bangs, his fingers lingering on her forehead. She expected his touch to be cold and clammy, like evil should have its own distinct feel so people would know to watch out for it. But instead his fingers were warm. Gentle.

"I want *you*, Cali," he said genuinely. "You're my soul mate, after all."

All the air left Cali's lungs.

He's lying! He's a goddamned fucking psycho! Don't you dare believe him, Cali.

She blinked, too stunned to do much else.

The needle was ripped from her arm. Someone put pressure on the puncture.

Vander smiled. "There's a good girl."

Those four little words were like a slap in the face. Cali shot up, and a few people yelped in surprise followed by cries for her to be restrained. She barely got to take in her surroundings. She was in some kind of large bedroom. Wood was everywhere. The bed where she lay was a canopy bed with lace drapes hung around the four posts.

Where the fuck was she?

A smooth, warm hand wrapped around her wrist like a vise.

Vander.

"I was really hoping you'd learn to cooperate," he said as if talking to a child.

The nasty retort she had ready died on her lips as a sudden, unexpected pain ripped through her body like a blade.

Her knees buckled. One of the flunkies closest to her caught her before she hit the floor.

Vander's hand didn't release her.

Her heart pounded in her chest as she tried to wrench her arm free from his grip. There was another fierce stab of pain. She cried out. Her whole body shook as her strength left her. Bile rose in her throat as another lance of bone-deep pain exploded. She felt like she was dying, slowly, her life seeping from her body.

"Stop." The plea was a low croak, and distantly she realized it had come from her.

"You see?" Vander was talking to the room at large. "All that is needed is one swift example."

His fingers tightened and Cali screamed as her world went black.

*

"What the fuck is taking so long?" Felix ran his hand through his hair for what was probably the fiftieth time. It'd been two days since Cali was taken. Two fucking days!

The other members of the guild eyed him warily.

Joel looked up from his laptop where he'd been spending all his time trying to hack into Kratos' main database. He was looking for any and all signs of Cali, but so far the firewalls and encryptions had deterred their progress.

Joel got up from his seat and placed a comforting hand on Felix's shoulder. He shrugged it off.

"Look," Joel said in a lowered voice. "You have to keep it together. You're scaring the girls. We'll find Cali, okay? The information we're searching for might be buried in the database I'm cracking. I'll keep looking, and at the same time I'll search for anything that can help bring down Vander. So far I've only found accounting and marketing documents. There's no record of anything illegal, but it's only a matter of time before I find it. You just have to keep it together."

Felix knew Joel was speaking logic, but his brain and heart just wouldn't listen. Somewhere out there Cali was alone, at the mercy of Vander. His hands fisted. "Have you found anything on where Vander Donahughe lives?"

The location of the CEO's home was proving to be as elusive as finding anything illegal in the Kratos database or anything on Cali.

They were getting nowhere.

Joel looked crestfallen. "There's no address under that name. Everything including his electric bill is sent to the corporate building."

Felix's anger spiked a few more notches. "They don't even have a rough guess as to where he lives? Nothing?"

Joel held his ground. "Listen, Felix, I can imagine what you're feeling right now. If anything happened to Sydney—"

Felix's temper snapped. "You don't know what I'm going through. Sydney isn't your Mirror Mate, and one day you're going to have to accept that she'll belong to another."

Sydney stared as if she didn't know him. "Felix—"

It didn't matter what she would have said. Joel's fist connected soundly with the side of Felix's face. The pain felt good. It helped him focus on something else. It eased the hurt inside of him.

He threw a right hook and caught Joel in the jaw.

Everything else faded into the background as they got into it. The closed space they occupied didn't allow enough room for them to really move around.

Felix dimly heard Sydney crying out for them to stop. She tugged insistently on Joel's arm. He could tell Joel wanted to shrug her off, but he let her pull him over to the couch. He watched Felix with angry eyes.

They were both breathing heavily, the tension in the air nearly suffocating.

"What the hell is wrong with you?" Sydney yelled at him, though her eyes were red-rimmed.

He didn't know what was wrong with him. His whole body felt on edge. His nerves were frayed, his temper always at the breaking point. He wasn't normally so temperamental but he found himself unable to calm down. Not even baking calmed him like it once did.

He scooped his keys off the counter. "I need to clear my head."

Niella rolled out in front of him, nearly cutting off his toes. "Hold on there, Del Valle. I don't think it'd be wise to let you go off when you're this riled up." She held her hand out for his keys.

Again he found his temper spiking. What the hell was wrong with him? He never got upset at Ell. If anything she should have been the one upset with him. Especially after he'd demanded that she Dream about Cali's whereabouts the other day. He'd clearly been in the wrong, but she'd brushed him off and acted as if his slip into madness had never happened.

His anger shouldn't be controlling him like this. His keys bit into the palm of his hand. The back of his neck began to prickle.

His animosity gave way to a sudden jolt of terror.

He tightened his hold on his keys even more, unwilling to move any part of his body even an inch for fear of his powers Erasing something.

He hadn't lost control like this in years.

He stared into Niella's hazel eyes. They were hard as granite but turned puzzled when she noticed his shallow breathing.

Joel and Sydney were talking in hushed voices behind them.

"What's wrong?" Niella whispered.

Felix swallowed. "I'm not safe to be around," he said through tight lips.

Niella regarded him for a few moments. "Then go take a lap around the block to cool down," she ordered and wiggled her open palm. "Leave the keys."

"I need you to take them from my hand."

Niella finally seemed to understand the severity of the situation. She carefully reached into his hand and pried his fingers apart.

Careful not to move his hands, Felix made his way out the door to clear his head. The fresh air and warm sun helped ease the tension in his neck. The tingling faded as he gained a little more control over his emotions. His face, on the other hand, was starting to pound and throb as the hits from Joel started to swell.

Good. He deserved it.

He felt like such an ass for what he'd said. It wasn't Joel's fault he hadn't gained complete access to the Kratos database yet. He'd only been trying to help. The only person he was entitled to be pissed at was himself or Vander. A part of his anger stemmed from the unknown of what he was doing with Cali.

They hadn't figured out why he wanted her. Would he brainwash her into working for them? Like he had Collette all those years ago?

Collette . . .

Felix stood a little taller as the wheels in his mind started to work. She'd have to know where Vander lived. She'd know where Cali was being kept. All he had to do was find her.

He jogged the rest of the way back home.

While he no longer knew Collette's home address, he knew the next best thing.

*

Cali was in hell. The hours—or was it days?—passed in a hazy blur. She had no concept of time. She remembered the first time she woke up after Vander had done whatever the hell he'd done to her. She'd been too weak to even feed herself. She'd had to swallow the humiliation of being fed by Vander. Naturally, he'd practically jumped at any opportunity to help her. Of course that help fell short when it came to letting her go.

She'd tried escaping on her own. Twice. The repercussions were to be drained by Vander until she nearly threw up or blacked out.

When she factored in all those instances, she guesstimated her capture time to roughly four days, if not five.

She was unfortunately well acquainted with her new living quarters. The bedroom was filled with wood and historical artifacts. Old tapestries made of dark fabric hung on the walls. They depicted black, swirling demons, raining chaos and ruin among the living while they seemed to suck the very souls from the fleeing bodies.

African masks caught in screams of agony rested on the right, each one crying out in desperation, forever searching for someone to help them. And straight ahead of her stood terracotta statues of gargoyles and mutated half demons, sneering like angry sentinels.

Cali had wanted to scream bloody murder the first time she awoke to her surroundings, but she resisted.

By eavesdropping with her powers she found she was being held at Vander's home. When she'd first found out she was being kept at a home address, hope had flared white-hot in her chest. But it had been days since then and Felix still hadn't found her.

Had something terrible happened to them?

She'd gone over the question again and again as she bided her time pretending to recover from her latest draining session. When others thought her to be weak she was left unattended.

She fell into a light sleep as she debated what to do for her next attempted escape. She was jostled from her nap by the door opening. She didn't know if her fortune had gotten better or worse as Collette strode in like she owned the place.

Rage flooded her whole body.

At least it's not Vander.

She stayed as still as possible as Collette drew closer. She looked down on Cali with pity. Genuine pity.

Cali didn't want her sympathy. "What?" she growled.

Collette jumped as Cali opened her eyes completely. Any trace of sympathy was wiped clean as Collette smiled down at her. "Comfortable?" she asked sweetly.

"What are you doing here?" She wanted to sit up, but was afraid if she showed any sign of improved strength she'd be drained again.

Collette slammed a hand on either side of Cali's head, shaking the entire bed. She leaned so close to Cali that Cali could smell salad dressing on her breath. "I want to know what you're playing at," Collette seethed.

"It'd help if you could be a little more specific with your accusation." Cali reveled in pissing Collette off even more.

Collette drew back with a sneer. "There's no way in hell you're Vander's soul mate. I saw the way Felix looked at you. How he protected you." She sounded disgusted but Cali didn't care.

Holy shit.

Collette knew she was Felix's Mirror Mate!

"Did you bond yet? Did your soul call out to his when you slept together?"

Cali frowned. The bonding was supposed to happen when they had sex?

No. She shook herself mentally. Collette had to be wrong.

But she's the only one who has bonded with her Mirror Mate.

What did that mean, then?

Was Felix truly not her . . . soul mate?

Her throat closed up and her eyes burned with unshed tears. She held them back. There was no fucking way she was going to cry in front of Collette.

Collette had been silently watching Cali, taking in every facial expression. "You haven't bonded yet, have you?" she said thoughtfully. "Could it be you weren't meant for him after all?" A malicious smile curled her lips.

Cali forced calm disinterest into her voice. "You'll never know. But what I do know is that Vander is not mine and never will be. I'm sure if you were the one to tell him, he'd reward you. Otherwise all this—" She motioned around the room. "—is nothing but a waste of his time."

"Is that right?" Collette hadn't bought her act one bit. Cali should have known better. Hadn't Felix told her that Collette had been a theater major? "You want to know what I think?" She was back to leaning in close to Cali's face again. "I think that, for whatever reason, Vander believes you to be his soul mate. And considering the idea came from my dearly unconscious Kevin, there is no reason for me to correct that little misconception. In fact, I rather like the idea of Vander trying his best to get your soul to call out for his. I think I might have a few suggestions to make."

Cali's body went cold at the implication.

Collette must have sensed her dread because she chuckled and said, "Oh, yes, Cali. I'm going to tell him anything and everything to make your soul cry out, so that by the time he's done with you, your soul will weep."

Cali didn't think. She lunged for Collette's throat.

The Illusionist screamed as Cali's fingers wrapped tight around her windpipe. Her cry for help cut off as Cali squeezed.

Footsteps came thundering up the stairs. The door to the bedroom burst open.

Collette's eyes were bloodshot and glazed by the time hands wrapped around Cali's bare arms. Vander hauled her off Collette, and that was only because there was such a vicious pull on her energy that it momentarily had Cali blacking out. She'd barely even felt the pain through her blood rage.

"What is the meaning of this?" Vander bellowed. He tucked Cali against his side protectively. She could hardly stand on her own two feet—otherwise she would have shoved away from him.

Collette was too busy rubbing at her neck to speak.

"Get out of my sight," Vander ordered her.

Collette didn't wait to be asked twice. She shot one more scathing look at Cali before she disappeared, leaving Cali to her fate.

Collette might have been her only chance to convince Vander she wasn't who he thought she was, and now she had completely annihilated that possibility.

Vander led Cali over to the hated canopy bed. He helped ease her down to the mattress despite her trying to push him away. He sat next to her, one of his hands brushing her hair out of her face. She jerked away. Vander never let her tie her hair back, which meant it was a wild mess.

"What happened?" He trailed his finger down her arm. Cali's stomach twisted. She was dressed in a white lace tank top Vander had picked out for her, along with black Bermuda shorts. She hated that he dressed her like a doll. She hated that he'd been in the bathroom with her when she'd showered and dressed. She hated him. Period.

She cleared her throat. "I'm not your soul mate," she croaked. She needed water and food.

Vander ran his hand through her hair. She gritted her teeth. "Is that what Collette told you?"

"Yes," Cali lied, wanting Collette to hurt by any means possible. "But it's true. I knew before Collette told me."

"You've been misled," Vander soothed. He leaned in closer and Cali's whole body froze in terror. He cupped her face and pulled it toward his. She resisted for as long as she could, but Vander didn't take kindly to her reluctance. A small pain slid from her body to his hands as he slowly took her energy until he could pull her face to his and kiss her.

Her stomach revolted.

His tongue pushed into her mouth, and she squeezed her eyes shut tight.

"Surrender to me, Cali," he breathed against her lips.

She imagined that was what the devil sounded like before he took someone's soul back to hell.

He pushed her back into the mattress, his body atop hers. Terror made her heart beat wildly, but when she pushed against his shoulders nothing happened.

He was so close she could see the darkness lurking in the depths of his eyes. It swirled there, not quite the madness that overtook Collette's, but a different kind of desperation.

"Just think, Cali. Once you and I are together, you will never want for anything in your entire life. I'll take care of you. I've had a long time to wait but now I've found you."

She stared up at his face. A face that, if possible, looked younger than when she'd first met him all those months ago. His words echoed in her brain.

"How old are you?"

He couldn't have looked more pleased that she was engaging a conversation with him. Hell, at this point she'd do anything to keep his lips away from hers. "I was born November 16, 1894, in London."

"No fucking way," Cali blurted.

Vander rolled off her and propped his head up on one of his hands. He smiled. "Yes fucking way. Would you like to hear about all the wars I've fought in? About how I was nicknamed 'The Plague' because I'd be sent in to scout out enemy camps, but when my troop arrived there were no more enemies?"

Vander told her the tales of his past. He told her the story of a young man who grew up to value power over everything else. He was a man that fancied himself friends with Death and despite the horrific stories Vander spoke of, after a while Cali could hardly keep her eyes open. His accent got stronger the longer he talked of his home, and Cali fell asleep to dream of battle trenches and famine.

She woke to the sensation of fingertips tracing the contours of her face. She smelled hot soup and warm bread.

"I thought you might be hungry," Vander said right next to her ear.

The nap had helped rejuvenate her but she was still famished. Vander helped her sit up, and she allowed him so he wouldn't be able to guess how much stronger she felt.

There was a tray next to the bed. It had hot soup, fresh buttered bread, a tall glass of water and milk, a fruit bowl, and some kind of deli wrap cut into bite-sizes.

It was a feast in Cali's opinion, and she inhaled every bit she could.

"Feel better?"

She carefully wiped her mouth on the napkin he provided for her. She took her time to carefully consider how she was going to answer. She felt better than she had in days. Stronger. But was it strong enough?

"Much better, thank you."

He tucked a strand of loose hair behind her ear. "You're very welcome." He leaned in to kiss her and this time she didn't pull away. She could feel his surprise at her behavior. He kissed her harder. Deeper. She still didn't resist.

Let him think he has me cowed.

Desire burned bright in his eyes when he pulled away. He got up from the bed to gather all the dishes on the tray, his back to her.

It was her only chance.

She raced for the door. She wasn't as fast as she wished, but it wouldn't have mattered. Vander was faster. He cleared the bed like a hurdle. He loomed in front of her, face purple with rage. "You think to trick me?" he roared. She tried to backpedal but it was too late.

His hands reached for her face. She knew what was coming.

She screamed.

She thrashed beneath his force as the pain enveloped her body. The fight didn't last long. She gave out much faster now that her body could never fully recharge. Everything went black within seconds.

Chapter 21

The hospital room was cold and smelled of antibacterial soap. Felix hadn't been by in years, though it always nagged at his conscience.

The room was well kept; large for only one patient, but when Felix factored in just who had to be funding the care it didn't really surprise him Kevin would have the most luxurious living space. Not that he counted Kevin's current state as living.

Felix rubbed at his hollow chest. Was what he was experiencing being separated from Cali like what Collette felt every day? Was this why Collette acted like she did? Did the restlessness, the on-edge feeling eventually lead to madness? It was as if no matter how much sleep Felix got he was never rested. He was irritable. All the time.

He stared down at the Dreamer's face. He looked peaceful. His limp brown hair had grown out a bit, and his eyes were closed. But behind those lids, Felix knew, was a pair of sad, blue eyes.

He'd felt sorry for Kevin all those years ago. Blinded by his love for Collette, Kevin let her tear him down inside. He didn't really know Kevin, but from the small glimpse he'd been given he seemed like a good man, though weak willed.

"You were lucky enough to have found your Mirror Mate." Felix spoke softly. "And now you're going to help me get back mine."

Right on time, the clipped sound of high heels echoed down the hall, stopping just inside the doorway. "What are you doing here?"

Collette stood in the doorway holding a handful of white roses. Felix had been lurking around the hospital for a few days now, asking nurses about visitors and visiting hours. He'd found out Collette visited almost every other day, always after dinnertime.

"I've been waiting for you, Collette." Felix could feel the anger in him swelling, that restlessness trying his already shortened patience. He wanted to throttle Collette and drag the answer he was searching for out of her. But this operation called for a gentler hand. He had to play by Collette's rules, which meant he had to be ruthless. Callous. He had to hit her where *she* would hurt.

"What do you want?" She stood frozen in the doorway, fingers white around the stems of her flowers.

He stared down at the helpless Kevin. "I was overdue for a visit." He pinned her with his eyes. "Don't you think?"

She swallowed visibly and glanced behind her, but Felix already knew there would be no one she could call. The one good thing about the extravagant care they were giving Kevin was the privacy factor. The nurse on duty wouldn't be checking in on this floor for another twenty-eight minutes.

He ran his hand along the edge of Kevin's bed. "Tell me, Collette, do you still feel Kevin? Is the bond between you still there? Would you be able to tell if he died?"

She licked her lips and lifted her chin stubbornly, but he'd already seen the flash of fear in her eyes. "You can't threaten me with him," she lied boldly.

He fingered the cord clipped to Kevin's finger to monitor his heartbeat. "Because you don't think you love him." He dropped the cord and waved his hand carelessly. "But you do."

The heart-rate monitor vanished along with the cord and the finger clip.

Collette stopped breathing momentarily.

Felix could feel the anger burning through his eyes. "Where's Cali?"

"I don't know," she said smoothly. Too smoothly.

He gave a tense smile, saw the color drain from her face. "You're lying." He flicked his hand, and the IV connected to Kevin's arm disappeared. "How long do you think he can last without that? Or without that?" He looked pointedly to the life support on the other side of the bed.

Collette's whole body was shaking.

He took two steps to the end of the bed and then paced back up. "Do you remember me telling you I had no idea where things went when I Erased them?" He spared a fleeting glance at her. "What do you think would happen if I Erased Kevin?" He stopped his pacing to give her a questioning look. "I know you still feel the bond between you. It wasn't severed completely when I knocked him out, but what would happen if he died? What would happen to you? Just think, whatever it is you feel connecting him to you, gone." He shrugged. "He might live. I've never Erased a person before. You could tell me whether he lives or dies once he vanishes. You can put to rest the one question I've been plagued with for years."

Collette finally found her voice. "You wouldn't."

Fury took root in his gut and spread like a deadly virus through his blood stream. He held his hand out above Kevin's chest. "Where's Vander holding Cali?" He didn't recognize his own voice, but he was beyond caring.

It looked as if it took everything Collette had to stay where she was. "She can rot in hell for all I care— No!"

Felix waved his hand.

Collette dove across the room to cover Kevin's body with her own. Felix stared down at her with dead eyes.

She stared up at him with a mixture of horror and hate, her eyes rimmed with red. "You've always accused me of being capable of horrible deeds," he whispered to her as he knelt. "How does it feel to be the one to bring it out of me?"

Her hold tightened around Kevin's thin shoulders.

"Where. Is. Cali?"

A tear leaked from her eye, but she didn't release her hold on her Mirror Mate. She glared for all she was worth and finally in a broken voice said, "She's being kept at Vander's home."

He stood and pulled out his phone. "What's the address?"

She rattled it off. He started to make his way to the door when her voice followed him, threatening. "You better watch that you don't bring my wrath down upon you."

He turned on his heel and made it to the bed in two easy strides. He dropped down so he could stare into her face, close enough he could see the flecks of gray and blue swirling together in her eyes. "No, Collette," he hissed softly. "It's you that should watch out so you don't bring my wrath down upon yourself."

*

The bread was stale when Cali bit into it. She had no idea how long it had been sitting out, or how long she'd been unconscious. All she knew was that when she woke up she was blessedly alone. There had been food next to her bed, and she'd eaten as much as she could. She felt better after she finished eating.

She experimentally got to her feet. Her legs shook slightly, but she was able to hold herself up. She wasn't back to full health by any means, but she had enough strength to try another escape. She made her way over to the door and leaned her ear close to it. She inhaled deeply and felt the familiar prickling at the back of her neck. She reached out carefully with her powers, searching for any sound throughout the house, but she couldn't stretch her powers very far. A headache was already making itself known, and she needed as few distractions as possible. She'd just have to take it on blind faith she wouldn't run into anyone.

The door was unlocked.

She peeked out into the hall and, like everything inside her room, everything she saw in the hall was made of wood: the floor, the banister directly across from her room, the walls, and even the decorative tables that lined the hallway. Sconces in the shape of faux candles were the only light besides the few rays of sunlight that spilled in through the half moon window facing her. She crept out to the banister to scope out the bottom floor. The thick curtains did a good job of blotting out a majority of the light, but a few stubborn rays pierced through, adding a hallowed feel.

There wasn't a soul in sight.

Where was Vander?

She closed the door to her room so that if anyone walked by they wouldn't know she was missing. Over the banister, she kept an eye out for any movement and her ears open for any sounds. She was tempted to open some of the closed doors she passed on her way to the stairs, but the risk of running into Vander was too high.

The stairway was lined with original eighteenth century oil paintings that looked to be framed in pure gold. Cali stood there in astonishment before slowly making her way down step by step. The paintings got older the farther down she went, but halfway down was when she heard the footsteps.

She turned and tripped, falling hard on one of her knees and hissing silently in pain. She scrambled the rest of the way up the stairs and barely made it when Vander appeared from a room on the right. He looked tired as he ran a hand down his face. He passed the stairs and Cali exhaled in relief. He went through a doorless threshold and disappeared from sight.

She strained her ears to hear where he'd gone. There was a creak from a door, a brief moment of silence, and then the soft clip of a door being closed.

Cali didn't waste any more time. She took the stairs down two at a time, nearly jumping down the last four. The landing jarred her knee, which was already throbbing from her fall. She nearly lost her footing as a wave of dizziness hit her. She was pushing her body too hard, too fast, but it was better than the alternative. Being stuck here.

When she reached the solid mass of wood that posed as the front door she cursed. There, mounted on the wall next to it, was a keypad.

Son of a bitch.

She could try messing with the pin and risk sounding an alarm, or she could check for other exits.

She went with the second option and followed Vander's path through the arched threshold. It opened up into a formal dining room. Straight ahead was a door in the corner, a brilliant white beacon in a home of despair. Vander must have disappeared through there.

Did the door lead to a garage? Was this her only way out?

There were more rooms branching off from the dining room but she didn't see any backdoors. If she followed Vander she'd be able to study what he was doing and gauge how much time she'd have to look for an alternate escape.

Hell, she might even luck out if Vander had left and all she had to do was follow him out the garage.

But of course luck never was on Cali's side when she needed it.

The door opened soundlessly, thanks to her powers, to nothing but a long metal walkway, complete with railings. At the end it looked as if it opened into a large space but Cali stayed where she was.

Did she really want to spy on Vander when he could potentially spot her?

The idea terrified her. Already she could feel her limbs weakening as phantom hands cupped her face. Her stomach gave a sick twist. She backed up until she hit the wall and closed her eyes.

"Breathe," she told herself.

All she had to do was get through this, and she'd never be at the mercy of that man again.

She opened her eyes and caught sight of a computer screen inside another little room across the way. The small area housed a computer monitor, drawers, and old-looking books stacked neatly in a bookcase. An office.

Would there be a phone?

Cali made it halfway across the dining room before she realized she hadn't memorized any of the guilds' numbers. The only number she knew by heart was her parents'. She could call

911, but the thought of regular people coming into contact with Vander sounded like an all-he-could-eat buffet.

No.

She needed to keep pressing forward. She'd be useless on Vander's computer, anyway. She wasn't a technical genius like Joel.

She made her way back to the white door and stepped into the metal hallway. Maybe whatever was in this room with Vander could be used against him. It helped build her confidence and she pressed forward, using her powers to steal the sound from her feet.

She was almost to the end of the hall when she realized she was inside a giant green house. The scent of plants was overwhelming, a mixture so broad that she couldn't pin down a specific scent for any one plant. The arched hallway opened into a large, domed room. She found herself on the second floor. It acted as a balcony, wrapping around the circular structure. She stepped back toward the safety of the dim hallway and caught sight of Vander. He was down below, in the middle of the greenhouse, surrounded by potted trees.

Cali had never seen so many plants before. They were everywhere, and in their center Vander stood like the sun. She didn't notice the dead ones on the outskirts until her second sweep of the room, they blended so well into the shadows. The amount of dead plants was almost as startling as the amount of living ones. They were piled atop one another, their dead branches and leaves reaching out like rotten hands grasping for a second chance.

She shivered.

Vander was watering a particular large flower with a brilliant red and yellow blossom. A potted tree sat next to him, nearly too large for the container it resided in. The roots were starting to crack the plastic. He finished with his watering and moved to cup the tree like he had her face so many times before.

The blood chilled in her veins.

At first nothing happened and then the changes started. The leaves started to darken and shrivel. The green coloring of the tree faded. Brown took over, the texture of the tree going from smooth to dry and crisp.

Vander's head fell back, his chest expanding as if taking in a huge lungful of air.

Cali hadn't realized she'd walked to the edge of the second floor until her fingers tightened over the railing.

He was sucking the life right out of that tree. She stood motionless as the plant withered and died before her eyes.

That was when hands grabbed her from behind.

Chapter 22

Cali gasped against the hand at her mouth, her powers dropping away as she flailed.

Her foot shot out and stubbed the railing with a horrifying *ping*, the sound echoing out into the dome.

Vander's eyes snapped open, his head swiveling to stare straight at her. Cali's heart momentarily stopped beating. The arm around her waist tightened, pulling her closer to a warm, firm chest.

The jig was up. She'd been caught. It'd be back to her prison room where Vander would continue to suck the life right out of her. Despite her best efforts to remain fearless, her body trembled.

She opened her mouth to say something. What that something was, she had no idea. Would Vander go easier on her if she lied and said she'd been looking for him? Her stomach rebelled at the idea of pretending to actually like this man.

Lips pressed against her ear.

She caught the scent of sand and orange blossoms when a voice—Jente's voice, whispered, "Don't make a sound."

Caught completely off guard, she turned her head fractionally to stare into his mismatched eyes. They were burning with concentration.

What was he playing at?

She turned back to Vander, whose gaze was now flickering from place to place.

He couldn't see them, she realized.

She stared down at her legs. She could still see herself but apparently he couldn't.

Jente's attention never left Vander. She continued to stare in amazement as he used his power to make them invisible.

After searching his greenhouse and failing to find what had

made the noise, Vander went back to his plants. He moved away from the dead tree and turned his sights on the beautiful flower he'd been watering earlier.

Cali couldn't watch anymore. The idea that he had done that to her left her feeling nauseated.

Jente must have sensed her need to get away. He slowly guided her backward into the hallway. His boots made the slightest *thunk*, but she was too overwhelmed to get a handle on her powers to even try and help make their escape easier. He didn't release her until they were back at the door. She waited for him to open it but he just stared at her. He held a finger to his lips, then pointed down to the handle.

Cali frowned at him.

He rolled his eyes and forced her hand to the knob. *"Use your powers,"* he mouthed.

Right.

She needed to focus. She calmed her mind and waited a few painful moments until her neck started to tingle.

The door swung open without a sound. Jente followed her through and shut the door behind them.

Cali let out a breath she hadn't known she'd been holding. Once her heart eased into a less frantic rhythm she whirled on Jente, fists balled at her sides. "What do you want? Why'd you do that back there?"

Jente blew her off and grabbed her elbow to propel her to the front door. "Isn't it obvious what I'm doing," he huffed. "I'm saving your ass."

She ripped her arm from his grip. "I don't believe you. You're the one that delivered me to him in the first place. You're probably moving me to a more secure location." *Shit!* She started to back away. Jente caught her hand before she got out of reach. His fingers laced with hers. His hand was warm and dry.

"I'm not moving you. I'm helping you. I had no idea that when

Vander wanted you, this is what he would do to you."

Her temper spiked. "Oh, you thought I'd be staying at a five-star hotel with full room service? Bullshit. You knew what was in store for me."

Genuine shame flashed briefly in his eyes. "I don't have to prove myself to you. All I'm saying is that no one should have to endure what you have. I didn't know and now that I do, I'm getting you out."

He typed a code into the front door too fast for her to see.

"I thought you weren't up high enough on the food chain to know super secret things?"

He shot her a mischievous smirk. "You'd be amazed how many 'super secret things' I learn when no one thinks I'm around."

The light on the control turned green, and Jente gestured for her to precede him through the front.

Fresh air had never smelled so good.

Cali hadn't realized just how musty the inside of Vander's home was until she sucked down lungful after lungful of cool, salty air. The sun was setting, the breeze kicking up to ruffle her hair.

"Come on." Jente re-laced their fingers and towed her down to the street where a sleek, black motorcycle was parked one house down.

She pulled her hand from his, uncomfortable with how easily his hand seemed to fit in hers. "Why are you doing this?"

Jente gave her an exasperated look. "I thought we'd been over this."

"So you saw what he was doing to me?" Somehow that knowledge made her feel worse. She might have screwed up in her life when it came to Tyson, but at least there was no one there to witness her humiliation. Now she'd always know Jente had seen her at her weakest, at the mercy of a man trying to claim her as his own.

Jente had the grace to look away. "I wasn't there for all of it. I had . . . work to do."

"And what was that? Spying on my friends?"

"Do you really want to spend your time yelling at me? Right

here in front of Vander's home where he can hear or see us at any moment? Or do you want to get the fuck out of here?"

He threw one of his black jean-clad legs over his cycle and eyed her expectantly. With the way his hair was styled he looked like some kind of anime or *Final Fantasy* character come to life.

"Clock's ticking, Cali."

She hopped on behind him and made a valiant attempt to ignore the way his body stiffened when she wrapped her arms around him. "So now you're a villain with a conscience?" she asked as he kick-started his motorcycle.

The engine started with barely even a rumble.

Well, it wouldn't do for a spy to have a noisy mode of transportation, now, would it?

Jente took off down the street. "I could leave you here, you know," he retorted over his shoulder.

Cali didn't bother answering that. She knew he didn't mean it.

As they continued driving, Cali took in her surroundings to get her mind off the fact she was pressed up very firmly to a man who wasn't Felix. They were on Irvine Avenue in Costa Mesa, the Upper Newport Bay out on her right. The sight was beautiful, and for one fleeting moment Cali wanted to spread her arms out as if she could fly.

Freedom.

It was like being released from the detention facility back in high school all over again.

"Where to?" Jente asked when they stopped for a red light.

She stared down at her clothes. She was going to burn them as soon as she stripped them from her body. "My apartment."

She really should have had him drive her to her parents' so she could pick up her car that she'd left there, but the drive was too far and she wanted out of her clothes as soon as possible.

It wasn't until her building came into view that she remembered her overdue rent. Her heart sank at the idea of all her belongings being dumped. Would there even be anything left?

She knocked hesitantly on Mrs. Deder's door. When she didn't hear anything after a few seconds she knocked again. Louder.

"I'm coming," came the grumbled response. "Keep your fucking panties on."

The door opened.

"What do you want, criminal?"

Jente bristled behind Cali, and she prayed he wouldn't say anything to ruin this for her. Jente was just the type to stand out on Mrs. Deder's radar. Hell, she probably thought he was a fellow criminal.

She clasped her hands in front of her and prepared to grovel like she'd never groveled before. "Mrs. Deder, I'm so sorry I missed my rent, and I swear I'll move out as soon as I can, but can I please be let into my apartment? Please tell me you haven't dumped my stuff."

The wrinkles in Mrs. Deder's forehead deepened. "What are you rambling on about? Your rent's been paid."

Cali must not have heard right.

"What? By who?"

Mrs. Deder was already shutting her door. She waved her hand carelessly. "By the same man that came by and replaced the locks. Some tall, good-looking fellow. He had dark, slightly curled hair, held himself like a real man, most definitely not a criminal." She eyed Cali. "Don't know how he got tangled up with you."

Cali didn't even care that Mrs. Deder had checked Felix out more than anyone her age had the right to. He'd paid her rent.

Suddenly there wasn't enough air in her lungs.

Mrs. Deder shut her door. "Wait." Cali lodged her foot before it could click closed. "Can I have a key? I misplaced mine . . . again."

There was a tirade of grumbling as Mrs. Deder vanished behind her door. It didn't take her very long to collect the spare. Once it was in hand, Cali raced up the three flights of stairs to her apartment.

She reached her door, wheezing. The burn in her lungs felt good. It meant she wasn't trapped, helpless, or dead.

"You okay?" Jente asked as she unlocked her door.

"Fine," she lied. She took a step into her apartment, but her leg buckled after the exertion up the stairs.

Jente caught her. Desire flared in his eyes, a quick flash he couldn't hide fast enough.

Cali scrambled from his arms. "Why are you helping me?" she asked again.

Jente followed her into the main room. "Are you suffering from some kind of memory loss? We've been over this . . ."

"But that's not the only reason, is it?" She stared him down, waiting for him to look away in embarrassment.

He didn't.

Kid had guts. He didn't accept or deny her claim.

"I need to change," she said abruptly when it was obvious neither was going to step down. "You can stay in here, visible." She pointed down at the floor like Jente was a dog she was ordering to stay.

In lieu of an answer he gave her that up-to-no-good smile.

"I mean it," said Cali. "If I so much as hear you anywhere near my door I'll kick your ass right out my third-floor window."

His smile deepened. "I solemnly swear not to go into your room." He crossed his heart and took a seat on one of her barstools.

It was the best guarantee she could get. She slammed her door shut and stripped her clothes off. She hadn't planned on taking a shower, but even with the clothes removed she felt dirty. She could still feel Vander's hands on her, his lips on her.

After showering she brushed her teeth. Twice.

She threw on a pair of jeans and a plain black tee on the off chance Jente would take her to Felix's.

He was rummaging through her fridge when she came out of her room.

"You got anything besides rotten food in here?"

She took the closest barstool and leaned over the counter. "Try the cupboard. There might be peanut butter in there or a box of instant something or other."

He unearthed a microwavable kid's dinner from the freezer.

Cali watched him as he cut the plastic covering and shoved it in the microwave. He moved with a martial arts type grace. She couldn't help but think of how much good they could do if they had someone like Jente on their side.

"Is there a reason why you're watching me so intently?" He didn't even bother glancing at her.

"Why don't you help us? The Guild of Truth could really use someone like you."

He laughed. "The Guild of Truth? Is that what you call your little band of misfits?"

"Technically, we're the Guild of Aletheia or something like that. But that's not the point. The point is—"

"The point is," he finished for her, "that your little guild couldn't do squat for me. You're made up of, what? Five people? You have no power, no resources, no nothing."

"Why do you need such fancy resources? Who are you searching for?" It was a shot in the dark that he was actually looking for someone and not something, but she knew she'd hit true when his mask cracked, and for just a moment she saw the raw hate behind his eyes.

"That's none of your business."

"So it's fine that you know practically everything about me and I know nothing of you? Fine. Get the fuck out of my home."

He motioned to the microwave. "My food's not done yet."

She didn't know if she wanted to hit him or laugh at him. She decided to stay on course and try and pump him for more information.

"Why does Vander have you search for people with powers?"

The microwave beeped and he pulled out his meal. "Lots of reasons. The most recent one being that he's looking for another person like Kevin. What did you call them?"

A chill swept down her spine. "Dreamers?"

"There you go. He's searching for Dreamers. He's been looking for one ever since his last one died. Old man was useless, anyway. Vander kept him so doped up on drugs I don't think the poor man knew what was real and fake anymore."

Her hate for Vander doubled along with her fear.

Did Jente know Niella was a Dreamer?

She could ask, but she didn't trust Jente enough to risk Niella. She didn't trust Jente, period. One act of good did not wipe away all the wrongs. She wasn't going to fool herself. Just because it looked like he had a crush on her didn't mean he'd confide in her or protect her. In fact, she had to keep her guard up even more around him. It'd be too easy to forget this kid worked for Vander.

"What about the fights he makes you and Collette participate in?"

Jente's fork froze halfway to his mouth. Something dangerous passed over his face. "How do you know about that?"

She tapped her ear. "You'd be amazed by what I hear when nobody thinks I'm listening."

He continued eating. "Fair enough," he said around a mouthful of mashed potato. Cali waited, but he wasn't forthcoming with any more information.

She pressed on. "Does he use you to find new people to fight for him? Is that how he guarantees his wins? By using those with powers?"

It'd be the perfect illegal scheme to nail Vander with.

Jente finished his meal and dumped the plastic container into the trash. "You'd best be careful where you tread, Cali. I helped you escape from Vander's home, but if you're caught again and sentenced to the arena there's nothing I can do for you."

"Nothing you can do or nothing you will do?"

"Both. I wouldn't keep sniffing around someone like Vander Donahughe. You won't be able to escape his clutches twice."

"And how is it fair that all the people you've helped him capture haven't even escaped his clutches once? How can you save me and not feel guilty about leaving countless others?"

"Easy." He turned to her as he opened her door. "I'm a

villain, remember?"

"Trust me." A new voice came from behind Jente. "I'll never forget it."

Felix's fist slammed into Jente's face.

Chapter 23

Jente staggered back.

Felix wound up for another hit.

"Felix, wait." Cali grabbed his arm. The shock of his skin against hers after so long sent a jolt all the way down to her toes. His eyes latched onto hers, the blue and green of his eyes filled with too many emotions for her to filter them all, but she knew he'd felt the shock too. "Don't hurt him. He helped me escape."

"He was also the one who put you there." His voice was fierce. How had he known that?

Cali had never seen Felix this worked up before. He was terrifyingly beautiful in his rage, but underneath it all she could see the dark circles below his eyes. His five o'clock shadow was darker than usual, and his hair looked as if he'd woken up scant seconds ago.

She cupped his face. Her lungs could barely get enough air to breathe. "I'm okay."

He opened his mouth to say something but quickly shut it. He whirled around, Cali following his gaze.

Jente was gone.

"Fucking little bastard," Felix growled. "How do we know he's not in here somewhere?" Cali closed her eyes and strained her ears, searching for that low rumble. Her neck tingled, and far off in the distance she heard the start of Jente's motorcycle.

She felt an unwanted pang in her chest but pushed it firmly aside. Jente wasn't some puppy that needed to be coddled. He made his own choices, and she wasn't going to bemoan the idiocy of them.

"Are you sure you're okay?" Felix pushed the door closed behind him and stepped closer until there was hardly a breath between them.

Her heart lodged in her throat. Heat pooled low in her gut as need consumed her.

"I went looking for you," he continued. "I got Vander's address out of Collette but by the time I arrived no one was there."

A spike of fear. "You went to Vander's home?"

He could have been captured.

His arms wrapped around her waist, pulling her tight to his hard body. "I had to find you. I'm so sorry I ever left you, Cali. So sorry."

She pressed her fingers to his lips to quiet him. "You paid my rent." She let her hand drop to trail down his chest. His heart thundered beneath her hand.

He frowned. "Of course I paid your rent."

"That's the nicest thing anyone has ever done for me." She pressed her lips to the pulse in his neck.

Felix hissed. His arms tightened around her.

"Cali," his voice was strangled. "I've been driven mad this past week. I don't think. . ." He swallowed. "I want you so bad."

She could feel the moisture gathering between her thighs.

"But—"

She cut him off with a hot, open-mouthed kiss. "No buts," she spoke against his lips. "I need you, Felix. I need you to erase all the memories I have. I need you to erase every touch, every taste. . ."

Felix pulled back, his eyes dark with the promise of death. "Did Vander. . .?" His gaze dropped below her waist, the question left unspoken.

She shook her head. "He never got a chance to go that far."

His tongue delved between her lips.

Her head spun, her hands getting caught in the tangle of his hair.

She pulled back to tear his shirt from his body. She wanted to erase every memory of Vander and replace it with Felix. She wanted to taste every inch of him. She kissed a trail down his chest as her hands worked the waistband of his jeans.

"Cali . . .?"

She shoved his pants down along with his boxers. His cock stood thick and erect. Her hands wrapped tightly around him.

His head fell back on a groan.

"I want you, Felix." Her breathing was ragged and she sank to her knees.

"What . . .?" His words were cut off with a shout as she took him deep into her mouth. His hand shot out to steady himself against the wall as she sucked him. He was too big for her to take completely so she used her hand to pump him hard and fast. He was trying to keep still but after a while his hand slid into her hair, his hips thrusting to meet her. He was helpless under the power of her mouth, and maybe that was exactly what she wanted. After being held at someone else's mercy for so long, she wanted to be in control of something. Someone. She loved the idea of Felix helpless against her, but what she loved even more was the man himself. He'd saved her countless times, he'd taught her how to control her powers, he'd paid her rent. She wanted to show him just how much he meant to her. She took him as deep as she could. His body shook as he moaned her name.

When she finished, she kissed a trail back up to his mouth. He crushed her against him and lifted her until she wrapped her legs around his waist.

A few seconds later her back hit her mattress. Her jeans were magically gone, and Felix replaced her panties with his tongue.

At that first, wet stroke electricity shot through her veins. She jumped but Felix held her thighs open to him as he pushed his tongue inside her. Her body was aflame as he worked a finger into her, his mouth settling over her clit. She arched her back as pleasure exploded. He rode her through it, not stopping his assault until she was boneless.

He crawled up her body, his knee wedging her legs apart. She must have been laying there in a daze for some time because he was already hard again.

She sucked in a quick breath as he slid the tip of himself into her. He didn't go any farther. He gave short little thrusts that had her biting back her cries of pleasure. When she thought she'd go mad, he slid in a little farther and repeated the same torture.

"Felix, I can't take it anymore."

Their eyes locked and she felt a quiver all the way down to her soul. His face was tight with held-back desire. "You want it hard and fast?" The words were practically a growl.

"Yes."

He pulled out of her. She nearly cried out at the loss. He flipped her onto her stomach and pulled her hips up. He pushed in to the root from behind.

Cali's scream was muffled by the blankets, and she fisted the sheets as he thrust into her just like she wanted him to. The bed rocked beneath them as sensation built higher and higher until she couldn't take it any longer. Pleasure ripped through her.

Felix came a second later before nearly collapsing on top of her. His body was so hot it was like a furnace. She wanted to lose herself in the protective heat of his body and never resurface.

He rolled onto his back, taking her with him so that she was snuggled against his side. She still had her shirt on but was too lazy to take it off. Instead she wrapped one of her legs around his and rested her palm over his heart. It beat strong and fast beneath her hand and, unbidden, her mind went back to that day Collette had visited her at Vander's.

Could it be possible that Felix wasn't her Mirror Mate?

They'd had incredible sex a handful of times now and still there was no shining light from above, no chorus of angels.

Does it really matter if you're soul mates or not? You want him, yes?

More than anything.

And just like that, it didn't matter what anyone said. She was going to stay with Felix for as long as he'd have her.

"What are you thinking about?"

She picked her head up to stare him in the eye and noticed for the first time the fading bruises along his jaw.

"What happened?" She touched one that was still a little yellow.

He caught her hand in his and laced their fingers together. "Are you trying to avoid my question?"

"Is it working?"

He mirrored her grin before his face grew serious. "You don't have to talk about it if you don't want to."

"It?"

"You're time with Vander."

She didn't say anything for a few moments. She didn't want to talk about it but suddenly she was. She confessed every little detail, starting from the first moment she'd woken. She thought retelling it would make it worse, but with every word gone from her lips it was like a weight was lifted from her shoulders. Felix remained silent as he listened. Every now and then he'd give her a reassuring squeeze to let her know she wasn't alone. When she finished, Felix still didn't say anything. He simply rolled her beneath him and kissed her. Soft and gentle. It melted her insides and made her throat close up.

Afterwards all she could do was stare into his endless blue-green eyes. Raw emotions swirled, hinting at all the things that remained unspoken between them.

Felix opened his mouth. "I . . ."

From the front of her apartment, Felix's cell phone went off.

He swore, the moment between them broken. "It might be the guild." He disappeared out her door, and the sound of his phone cut off as he answered. The conversation didn't last very long. He stood in her doorway with his clothes in his arms. "Joel needs us." He dropped the clothes at the end of her bed and dug for his boxers.

She sat up, her head only spinning slightly from the exertion. "Did you tell them about me?"

"At the end, but I ended the call before Joel could blow my

eardrum out." He threw her panties and jeans onto the bed, and she pulled her underwear on.

"So who gave you those bruises?"

She sighed in disappointment as Felix covered all that rippling muscle with his shirt.

"Joel and I had a bit of a disagreement while you were away."

"Joel gave you those bruises?" She shimmied into her jeans and searched her room for a hair tie. "Did it have anything to do with going after Vander? I understand if they don't want to continue with their plan to take down the Kratos Corporation. Vander's a bad man."

"What was your first clue? When he kidnapped you, tried to kill you, or tried to steal your soul?"

"I'm serious, Felix. You don't know the kind of power he has, both physically and through his company."

"And if our plan pans out the way we're hoping it will, we'll be eliminating one of those powers." He gave her a quick kiss. "Now come on. We have a major conglomerate to dismantle."

Chapter 24

Felix opened the door to the clinic for Cali.

A blonde blur shot past him and nearly bowled her over. "Cali!"

Cali's expression was priceless, and Felix had to bite the inside of his cheek to keep from laughing. She had no idea what to do as Sydney hugged her for all she was worth.

Finally he decided to help her out.

"Where's my hug, Syd?"

His question had the desired effect. Sydney released Cali to put her hands on her hips. "You weren't missing for a week."

Cali stealthily moved away from Sydney as if she were afraid she'd be hugged again. Felix held his hand out to her, and his jaw nearly hit the floor when she made her way to his side. She didn't take his hand, but Cali wasn't one for public displays of affection. Which was why it was so fun to lace his fingers through hers when she least expected it. She jumped away from him, snatching her hand back. He could have hung on but they had more important things to do.

Joel was behind the reception desk with his laptop out, Niella right next to him.

"It's good to see you back, Cali," Niella said with genuine sincerity.

The two of them shared a smile that had him wondering just when that friendship had blossomed.

Joel came around the reception desk to give Cali a hug that had Felix biting back a growl. His didn't last as long as Sydney's but a handshake would have been just as effective. "I'm glad you're okay."

Cali managed a stiff nod. She was anything but okay, he knew, though she wasn't going to tell the rest of the guild that. Heat bloomed in his chest every time he thought of Cali confiding in him rather than another. He wanted to be the one she went to, always. For anything.

"What'd you find?" he asked Joel once he was back in front of his laptop.

Cali leaned over the counter and Felix mirrored her move, only he pressed up behind her, a hand on either side of her body.

She inhaled sharply. No one else seemed to notice.

His body stirred to life but he managed to drag his focus away from her and listen to what Joel had to say.

"I broke the encryption surrounding all of the Kratos Corporation's documents."

"You broke into the Kratos computer system?" asked Cali.

Felix pushed a little harder against her. "Joel has been working on it ever since you disappeared."

Joel nodded. "I was trying to simultaneously find your whereabouts as well as anything incriminating we could use against the corporation."

Cali's astonishment was palpable. "You guys did that for me?"

"Well, duh," said Syd. Her voice was thick with emotion, but she did a good job covering it up with her usual bubbly attitude.

"Now," Joel said, breaking the heartwarming moment. "Let's see what Kratos is hiding."

As Joel continued to systematically dig through all the files, the guild unconsciously gravitated closer and closer to him until they were all clustered behind the reception desk.

Every once in a while someone would point out a file name that caught their attention, but so far there was nothing incriminating.

"Wait." Cali pointed to a folder. "What's that?"

"Blood work?" Joel double clicked on it.

A whole slew of files popped up.

Joel sifted through a few of the documents. "These aren't your average medical records. It's as if they're looking for some kind of signature."

"Search for my name," said Cali.

Joel looked over his shoulder at her. "You?"

Cali swallowed. "They took my blood, so they must be looking for some kind of power signature, right?"

He typed her name into a search screen. A few seconds later, a scanned file appeared with her information.

"Doesn't look like they found anything," said Sydney. "According to whatever tests they were running you came back negative."

"So does that mean our blood isn't any different than anyone else's?" asked Felix.

"According to this," said Joel. "Damn, look at all these blood samples." He pulled up another window that was covered with nothing but names and strange symbols. Felix had no idea what the symbols were, but he could make an educated guess based on the colors used.

The list was in alphabetical order. Felix's eye caught on a name closest to the top: Kevin Bauer. His name was in green along with a red symbol that looked suspiciously like a blood drop and some other symbols. Felix pointed them out on Joel's screen and nearly had his hand slapped.

"Don't touch it," Joel snapped at him.

"Do you know what those mean?" He pointed again, making sure his fingers stayed a good six inches away from the screen.

"Not sure," Joel said, distracted, as he scrolled through the list of names. A lot of names were in black. Some in red.

Felix's stomach knotted when he saw Cali's name scroll past in green followed by his own.

Joel stopped in the K's. "Shit. My name is on here."

And he was green.

How much information did the Kratos Guild have on them?

Joel shot to the bottom of the list where the S's were. Sydney's name lit up green. Niella's was black.

"Well that's a little comforting," said Niella.

Felix noticed Cali's name was the only one with the blood

symbol next to it. "Do we know what's happened to all the people with green names?"

Fuck, had Vander gotten a hold of them all? Was that his plan for their guild? Abduct everyone with powers and kill them if they didn't join? There could only be one reason why there were names in red. How else would Vander know that a person didn't have powers unless he tortured it out of them?

His hands balled into fists at his sides.

Joel clicked around on his laptop. "I can't find anything about person whereabouts. That might be in a different folder. I'll keep this window tabbed so we can cross-reference. Let's keep looking."

A few seconds later a folder caught Felix's eye. "Stop. Go back. Click on that." He had no idea why the file caught his attention—maybe it was just idle curiosity, or maybe he wanted to see what Kratos was hiding in plain sight.

"The building blueprints?" Joel hesitated.

Cali backed him up. "Do it."

Joel obediently scanned through the documents. "This looks like any other building."

"I don't think any other building has cells built into their basements." Niella pointed to another window that was half covered by scanned files.

"Watch my screen," Joel warned.

"Bite me." Niella tapped the computer screen for emphasis. "Click this."

"Don't tempt me, Niella. I will Lock your hands together if you ruin my electronics."

She arched her brow in open challenge.

"I think we just found the arena Niella Dreamed about." Cali leaned over the back of Joel's chair to get a better look.

Felix and the rest of the guild hunched in.

"Look at that layout," said Sydney. "You've got a medical ward, isolation cells, regular cells, prep rooms, confined rooms, some kind of living quarters. . ."

"Can't forget the restrooms." Niella pointed them out.

"And of course there's the giant arena built toward the back of the building." Felix stared at the large, circular space on the computer screen. It dominated nearly a third of the map.

"Okay," Cali thought aloud, "so the cells nearest the arena make sense. Vander's keeping his unwilling fighters close by, but what the hell are these aisles and aisles of cells for?"

"Looks like a collection," said Felix.

Cali's hand sought his and she gripped it tight.

"What is it?" He asked.

The rest of the guild turned to stare at them.

"I think I know what those cells are for," said Cali. She pointed to a spot on the map. "See how there's this comfortable living area set up with a back door that leads to one of the cell aisles? Vander's harvesting these people." She used her finger to designate the entire section. "I bet you they're his backup energy source."

"Energy source for what?" asked Sydney.

Felix locked eyes with Cali and gave her an encouraging nod. The rest of them had the right to know just what Vander could do.

"For his power," Cali told them. "Vander Donahughe's a Diverter." Felix hadn't expected the title but as determination shown in her beautiful dark brown eyes he felt a swell of pride that she'd accepted herself into their group. They'd accepted her but it was her decision if she really wanted to join them. And now she had. He grinned.

"He redirects life energy into himself to lengthen his existence. The man is one hundred and seventeen years old but doesn't look older than his late twenties. From what I've seen . . . and experienced, he can pull as much or as little from a host as he wants, but I'm pretty sure he could kill a person if he wanted to."

Joel gave a low whistle. "Fucking fuck. That's quite a person to go up against."

"And you said he used his powers on you?" Sydney asked.

Cali's spine stiffened fractionally. "Yes." She didn't elaborate and no one pressed.

"We still need to find something to use against Vander." Niella redirected the conversation.

Joel went back to his computer. "I've got nothing here." He flipped through more files for at least another half hour.

The rest of them got comfortable around Sydney's lobby.

Felix drew lazy circles along Cali's jean-clad thigh and watched with amusement as the browns in her eyes darkened with desire.

From across the clinic Joel cursed.

Felix's relaxation quickly changed as adrenaline shot through his veins. "What?"

"I found a schedule."

"And that's significant how?" asked Niella.

"Because there's no list of workers, just times like tonight at midnight and two a.m."

"You think they're fights?" said Sydney.

Cali's body went still beneath his hand. "They are," she said.

He glanced at her. "How do you know?"

"When I went to the Kratos building for my fake interview, I overheard Jente and Collette talking. Jente mentioned Collette having a match that night at two a.m. I bet you anything they're having another event. Tonight."

Felix could read her thoughts through her eyes. Tonight there would be another innocent with powers forced into a battle that might kill them.

But that couldn't be right because if their fighter died then Vander would lose the match. Then something clicked in his brain. Collette. Of course. One of the fighters probably wasn't even real when she was called in to work her powers, which meant they could win or lose without any repercussions.

"This has to stop," he said.

"I agree." Joel's voice echoed the same fierce emotions Felix felt tumbling around inside him.

"We have to make a move. Tonight."

Everyone looked at him like he was crazy. Everyone except Cali.

"You want to storm the Kratos Corporation tonight? After just getting Cali back?" said Sydney.

"She'll never be safe unless we put an end to him. Besides, what good are powers if you don't use them toward something worthwhile?"

"You do realize that going up against someone with Vander's power could kill you, right?" Of course Sydney would be the voice of logic.

"I've never wanted to live to a ripe old age anyway," he said blithely.

Sydney scowled.

He shrugged at her. "It's the only way, Syd. We have to do something. Now's our chance to do more than rescue stray kittens and limping puppies."

Her scowl deepened. "We've never saved stray kittens or limping puppies."

He grinned.

Joel swiveled in his chair to face them all. "We could wait it out. There's another schedule posted for two weeks from now."

Sydney seized the information. "Then we should wait. We'll have more time to prepare, to plan things out."

"We can't wait," said Cali. "I'm guessing those red names don't show up on that list on their own. People are suffering, and I'm not going to wait around for another name on that list to turn up red after tonight."

Joel rubbed a hand over his face in defeat. "So how are we going to do it?"

Sydney's face flashed briefly with outrage at Joel's sudden flip.

"In teams," Cali spoke up. "Felix and I can go in first. We stand the best chance."

Joel crossed his arms. "How do you figure that?"

Felix could tell Joel's opinion rested with sending in the two men, but the look on Cali's face said she'd be damned if she would sit back and do nothing.

Cali crossed her arms over her chest. "I've already been inside. Plus, I can make us soundless so no one will hear us approaching. I can Silence alarms, and Felix can Erase cameras as well as anything else that could be a potential threat."

Again Felix felt a swell of pride as Joel huffed. Cali's points were all valid, and there was no arguing her logic.

"Sorry, man," said Felix. "You can be our next wave with Syd. You'll be the emergency backup."

"I don't like the sound of that," said Sydney.

"Well, too bad." Felix got to his feet and stretched. He pulled out his phone to check the time. "We have a little more than four hours until midnight. We should rest up as much as possible."

"And if I don't hear from you guys by two a.m., I'm calling the police," said Niella. "I'll be the real emergency backup."

Felix didn't want to contemplate the event of their failure. But there it was, hanging over all their heads like a dark cloud threatening rain. Were they ready for this?

There was only one way to find out.

"We'll all meet at my place," he said.

Everyone nodded.

Sydney, Joel, and Niella loaded up in Joel's truck and before they pulled away Felix leaned in through the window. "Stay safe," he told Ell.

It wasn't a goodbye, but there was a rare flash of emotion behind her eyes that said she felt as if that was exactly what he was saying.

"I will," she promised.

They'd agreed that Niella would stay at her own place until she heard from them. His house wasn't safe, and after they headed out for the Kratos building they didn't want to run the risk of leaving Niella there by herself.

When he and Cali pulled into his driveway he knew he should

spend his time resting, catching up on all the sleep he'd missed when he'd been mad with worry and anger over Cali. But once they stepped foot inside, alone, just the two of them, sleep was the furthest thing from his mind.

Cali looked at a loss for what to do. Felix took the decision from her as he wrapped his hand around hers and led her to his bedroom where he spent the rest of his time slaking his lust for her. Again, and again, and again.

Chapter 25

Cali took her time in the shower as Felix raced to let Sydney and Joel into the house. The water felt so good sluicing off her well-pleasured body. Despite the amount of energy she'd just burned she felt renewed. Cali was satisfied in a way she'd never thought possible.

A chill danced up her spine. *Enjoy it while you can.*

The minutes until they willingly went to Kratos were dwindling. It was only a matter of time before she'd be forced to look into the eyes of the one who had kept her locked up for his pleasure. If Jente hadn't saved her. . .

She never let herself finish the thought. Just like she never let herself finish the thought of what Tyson would have done to her had the police not shown up.

She'd been through this before, knew what to expect and how to cope. It was her turn to help another. Somewhere in that building's basement was a person like her—unlucky, defenseless, and with no way to fight back.

She might have been scared shitless at the idea of what they were going to do tonight, but Felix had been right. She'd never be safe if she didn't take Vander down. Tyson had left her alone out of fear of the authorities. There were no authorities Vander feared. He'd been around for over a century. The man had faced fear over and over again.

She didn't expect him to fear her. That was a pointless fantasy, but she did want to destroy something he held dear. Money and power seemed the only options, and she'd take what she could get.

She shut the water off before it started to cool and toweled herself dry. She made a quick dash into the guest room in nothing but her towel to get to the duffle she'd left at Felix's when she'd lived with him. She dug out comfortable dark jeans, sneakers, and a dark T-shirt. She pulled her hair back into a ponytail and tucked as much of her bangs as possible behind her ear.

In the living room Joel and Sydney were dressed in a similar fashion. Dark pants, dark shirts. Sydney even carried a black beanie she said she'd use to cover her golden hair.

Felix was dressed in black jeans and a dark blue tee that strained over the muscles of his arms and chest.

Cali's body warmed as she remembered all that muscle taut over her, pushing against her, pressing her harder into the mattress as her muscles clamped around the length of him.

As if he read her thoughts, Felix's eyes caught hers.

The air left her lungs and heat pooled low in her gut. She clenched her thighs together, amazed that after everything they'd done she was already aching for more.

Soon, his eyes seemed to say and Cali shuddered with anticipation.

"Are we going in two separate cars?" asked Joel.

Felix tore his eyes from her. "Yeah, Cali and I will make our way in. If you don't hear from us by 12:30 we need you to come in as backup. Follow our path—it'll probably be the easiest. I'll Erase all the doors we can't open, and Cali will Silence any and all alarms." He went over to the counter that separated the kitchen from the living room and picked up a print out of the building. "We'll go in through the back. The only way to access the basement through the front entrance is by way of the elevator, and that'll be too much of a hassle. Plus, I'm hazarding a guess that all the match attendees come in through some back way to avoid detection."

Cali's heart rate started to kick up.

"You're right," said Joel as he pulled something from the back pocket of his pants. "I dug around a little more when we parted ways and found a satellite photo that leads me to believe there is a possible underground garage the patrons are entering through."

Felix took the paper and scanned it. Cali made her way

over to him, careful not to touch him. Once she gave in to that temptation, she'd never relinquish the feel of his skin on hers. She was as addicted to the feel of him as she was to the sound of his voice, the rumble of his laugh, and the glitter in his eyes.

"This'll be our best bet, then." Felix held the picture out for her to see. Amusement sparkled in his eyes, as if he knew what she was trying to do by keeping her distance.

Bastard, she thought affectionately.

She pointed to another parking lot that was cut off at the edge of the paper. "We can leave the Hummer here where no one can see it and make our way through the bushes to the garage."

Felix nodded. "Joel, you and Sydney should stay there too. That way you can watch as people arrive and call us if anything looks suspicious."

Joel tucked his hands into his pockets. "It's an underground, illegal cage match. What constitutes as suspicious?"

Felix grinned. "I guess anyone who looks like they're packing real weapons. I'm sure there's going to be quite a few power players attending this thing. Vander wouldn't have been able to accumulate this much money if he didn't have some high-paying supporters."

"Those people are sick," said Sydney. "If I see any I'm going to snap pictures and send them in anonymously after we get all those people out. Let them fall right along with Vander."

That was their plan. They were going to sneak in and free anyone unfortunate enough to have been captured by Vander. The last thing they needed was for the police to question captives and accidentally learn about the existence of people with powers. The chances a prisoner would confess the real reason behind their capture was very slim, but Cali had a feeling a regular person wouldn't mind throwing everyone under the bus. A wailing witness confessing to the authorities that they'd been kidnapped because some wacko thought they had super powers was not something they wanted to deal with.

"I don't care what you do with pictures of those sons of bitches sick enough to attend this, but just stay out of sight. I'll try and Erase as many parking lot cameras as possible, but that might draw attention in itself."

"You can leave the cameras in the parking lot. They won't be able to see us behind here. Focus instead on the ones that will witness your mad dash to the back of the building," said Joel.

"Will do," said Felix before looking around to gauge all the faces. "Is everyone ready?"

Cali's stomach cramped. Her heart pounded painfully against her ribs, and she almost couldn't hear Felix over the sound of its beating.

Calm down, she ordered herself. She wasn't going to be any good to anyone if she couldn't access her powers. *They're counting on you. They* need *you.*

It was an amazing feeling to be needed, to be accepted, and to know that this group of people would have her back no matter what for the rest of her life.

The beating in her chest calmed. She held her chin just a little higher. "Let's go get this fucker."

*

"I count four cameras that'll catch sight of us high-tailing it to the back of the building," Felix pulled back in behind the safety of the foliage. "What about you?"

"Same, although that one in the far corner has me worried. I can't tell if it sweeps this far over."

Felix stared at the camera in question, watching as it made its slow progression from right to left. "We should be good."

He turned to her, determination and a reckless glee shining in his eyes.

"You ready?" He started to get to his feet but Cali put a hand on his forearm to stop him.

"Felix." For a moment her courage failed her. She wasn't good at this sort of thing, but what if they were captured? "When I told you about my time with Vander, there was something I left out."

"Cali, you don't have to confess anything to me that you don't want to."

She pressed onward. "It was when Collette came to visit me."

Felix went still. "Did she do something to you?" That dark, murderous look was back in his eyes.

She held his gaze. "No, but she did tell me something. She told me that she and Kevin bonded after having sex."

She waited for it to sink in. Felix's forehead slowly creased. "What are you saying?"

Her pulse started to race. Shit, she was fucking this up royally. "What I'm trying to say is that even though we didn't bond, even though we might not actually be Mirror Mates . . . I still want to stay with you."

For a moment she couldn't read a damn thing from his expression. He was as blank as a fresh canvas. Was this it? Was he going to tell her that if they weren't Mirror Mates then he wanted nothing to do with her?

She didn't care. There was only one way to get what you wanted. You had to chase after it. And she'd chase after Felix until the end of time if that was what it took to convince him that she belonged with him.

Finally he smiled. It was a slow, deep curl of his lips that flashed the white of his teeth in such a way that it stole her breath. He grasped her shoulders, his thumbs rubbing gentle circles. "We are meant to be together, Cali." He kissed her. "And I'm glad you want to stay with me, because I wouldn't have let you go anyway."

Warmth enveloped her. Felix wanted her to stay with him. The only obstacle was Kratos.

She kissed him once more—a fast, fierce kiss with a teasing stroke of tongue. "Let's move."

They made their way across the dark, deserted parking lot. Felix's hand waved at his side, taking all the cameras that would have reported their movement.

At the back of the building they found a large driveway sloping down. Joel had been right; there was an underground entrance. One definitely big enough to house cars.

"Think everyone's already inside?" Cali asked from beside Felix as they debated their next best course of action.

"Let's hope so," said Felix. "Because once I Erase this door, it ain't coming back. Someone might get suspicious that the entrance is gaping open."

Cali searched for any other way in, but there was nothing that guaranteed access to the basement. "We'll have to risk it."

Felix moved his hand. Cali focused her powers, letting them spread out in a wave to suck any unwanted sound away. She didn't know if there was an alarm attached to that door but either way no one would hear anything.

They made it to a utilitarian type door without any problems. That alone had Cali's suspicions rising. It was almost too easy. Was security really this lax because of the event?

Felix tried the handle. Cali readied her power again. The door opened.

Felix pushed Cali behind him as he fell into a defensive stance, but there was no one waiting on the other side.

"Something's wrong," he whispered to her.

The door shut behind them with a soft hiss. Bright bulbs burned overhead, a startling contrast to the dimness of the garage. Cali blinked to allow her eyes to adjust.

Blue-grey walls and hard, concrete-floored hallways spread out before her like a giant maze. "Which way?"

Felix pulled the blueprint from his pocket. "Where to first? The isolation cells or the ones nearest the living quarters where you think Vander is feeding off them?"

"The second option."

He tucked the map back into his pocket. "I figured as much." He raced along ahead of her. Cali focused on their footsteps, Silencing them.

The halls wove left and right so much that Cali found herself lost within seconds. Felix's directional skills never faltered. "We should be getting close," he called over his shoulder and took the next right.

He came to an abrupt stop. Cali slammed into him thrusting Felix into the back of a guard who stood before them unaware. There were three of them spread out along the hall.

The man Felix had bumped spun on him. Cali threw her hands up, Silencing his shout of surprise. The other guards remained ignorant.

The man was nearly the same height as Felix. His suit was tailored to emphasize his broad shoulders and muscled frame. He frowned at them, opened his mouth to speak. Nothing came out.

Felix didn't hesitate. He clipped him hard and fast in the side of the head. The man smashed into the wall, crumpling at their feet.

They crept down the sterile-looking hallway. The smell of antiseptic grew the deeper they traveled inward, tickling the back of Cali's throat.

Felix had the second man in a choke hold before the last guard caught sight of them. He tried to shout for help but it did him no good. He went for the radio on his belt. Cali jumped him, thrusting her elbow as hard and as deep as she could right under his rib cage.

Cali coughed as putrid breath whooshed across her face.

She swung for another hit but the guard was a fast little fucker. He shoved Cali with all the strength of an ox. She stumbled back, nearly tripping over the other fallen guards.

He had his radio out in seconds, one of his hands wrapped tight around his abdomen where Cali had nailed him.

Felix lunged for him. The radio went flying to crash noiselessly to the ground.

"You're bleeding." Cali rushed Felix once he'd taken care of the last attacker.

Felix licked his split lip. "Bastard sure packed a punch."

He swiveled his jaw a few times as if to test that it wasn't broken. When he was satisfied he pulled her along, down more twists and turns. "We need to get as far away from them as possible. I don't know how long they'll stay out, and someone might come across them."

They maneuvered down a few more hallways before they braked in front of a pair of double doors.

"Is this it?" asked Cali.

Felix nodded, his fists tight at his side. "I think so."

The doors were locked. No surprise there. Cali scanned the corners for cameras but couldn't see any. She doubted Vander would have cameras here. If anyone hacked into the system like Joel had, then they'd see the people being held. Vander must either be very cautious or very arrogant to think no one would dare break into his facility.

Felix readied his hand. Cali stopped him. "Wait. Can you Erase the lock? Only the lock?"

That way if anyone happened to walk by, they might not notice quite as quickly what was happening.

"Sure thing." Felix's gaze bore into the handle. He flicked his wrist, and the handle vanished along with whatever bolt held the doors closed.

A chill like death itself danced along the nape of Cali's neck as soon as she set foot past the doorway.

This wing of the basement looked like a hospital, with door upon door lining both sides of the hall. The temperature was cold, the air both stale and crisp. Electronic security locks were attached to every door, buzzing softly. Small windows allowed Cali to look into the rooms, and bile rose in the back of her throat at what she saw.

People were confined to rooms no bigger than eight by eight.

Some were sleeping, while others sat on their beds, knees curled up, arms wrapped around themselves. Some rocked back and forth as if the motion comforted them. But what Cali noticed most was the lack of hope that rested in all of their faces. Some of the prisoners looked to be seniors.

Or was that a side effect of being drained by Vander?

Dread settled in her stomach. Was that going to happen to her? Had Vander taken years off her life by doing what he'd done?

She pressed her hands to her face as if she could feel the wrinkles already forming.

Felix scanned the other side of the hall. A new curse left his lips with each window he passed.

"Quite a collection, isn't it?"

They both whirled.

Vander stood at the head of a large group. "Back so soon?" he asked Cali.

Felix started toward him, his face a dark mask of retribution. Vander's black gaze shot to him. Vander motioned with his hand, and his own personal army came forward. Terror shot through Cali's veins.

She went to grab Felix so they could make a run for it, but Vander's men beat her to it. Felix threw a punch at the closest one, sending him careening into the others. Shouts erupted.

Two men came toward her. The majority joined in to restrain Felix. Cali stayed her racing heart and focused her energy on the shouts and grunts around her. She amplified the sound, pulled it toward her, and shot it forward.

The wave hit the men with a startling burst.

Now what?

Vander carelessly sauntered toward them, his calculating gaze devouring Felix as he fought.

The men at Cali's feet started to rise. In quick succession she kicked them both swiftly in the jaw. Their teeth snapped shut, their heads flying back.

"Hold him," Vander ordered as Felix took an especially hard hit to the gut.

Cali rushed toward him, throwing sound left and right. Her concentration wasn't fully behind it. The men pursuing her only staggered back a few steps.

She had to get to Felix. She knew what that look in Vander's eyes meant. She knew what he planned to do once he got close enough to touch Felix.

She jumped between two men and got a few more steps before arms grabbed her from behind and wrenched her body backward.

She screamed at them, the sound echoing loud within the enclosed hall. The hands released her as the men went to cover their ears. "Felix!" She was tackled to the ground. Pain erupted in all her joints. "Erase him," she yelled.

Their eyes locked through the sea of bodies.

She saw the answer plain as day in his eyes.

He wouldn't do it.

Felix wasn't that kind of man. He was better than that, better than Vander.

Felix was smothered with guards. They forced him to kneel. The split in his lip bled anew. Vander reached a hand out and touched him with one finger on the forehead.

No!

Cali squirmed for all she was worth. Felix tried to jerk back but too many hands held him.

She watched in horror as she saw the exact moment Vander unleashed his power. Felix's entire body jerked. A cry tore from his throat.

"Stop!" Cali screamed. She focused her power to resonate through the building but her emotions were too wild.

Vander turned to her with a sickening smile on his face.

The veins in Felix's neck stood out as he thrashed.

Cali's whole body went numb. Her vision darkened. "No," she shouted.

Felix!

Cali! Felix's voice sounded clear in her mind. White heat burst from her chest and then everything went dark.

Chapter 26

Cali awoke to a sterile-smelling room. Her body was chilled to the bone, and she shot to her feet as memories assailed her.

"Felix." His name slid from her lips. She could feel him but he was nowhere in sight. She was stuck inside one of the rooms she'd been scouting. She moved to the door and turned her head to look through the small window. The hallway was empty on the other side. She tried the handle. Locked.

She swore and kicked the door. She succeeded in nothing more than making her toe ache.

"Felix?" she called through the door.

There was no answer. But she could *feel* him.

She remembered struggling with Vander's men. Remembered Felix at the mercy of Vander's touch. She remembered trying to reach him, protect him. She'd cried out for him.

No. Your soul cried out for him.

No way . . . But Collette . . .

Collette was one experience.

That didn't make her all-knowing.

Cali stepped back from the door, afraid whatever she was feeling could be seen from the outside. Did everyone else know what had happened? Had that been why she'd blacked out?

She shut her eyes and focused inward like all those yoga, hippy types told her to do when she was experiencing a block with her artwork.

The heat that seemed to be radiating inside her was like a mini sun. The warmth was dimmed, as if it knew it was away from Felix. She wondered if this brilliant, indescribable feeling would increase when he was near.

She had to find him. She stepped back up to the window

and pushed her face as close to the glass as possible to look out. "Hello?" she yelled. The sound of her voice echoed in her room. Could no one hear her out there?

She strained her ears. The back of her neck tingled. Far off in the distance, she could hear the sound of heavy footsteps followed by light taps of bare feet.

Someone was escorting a prisoner back to their cell.

Cali pressed her ear to the cool glass, pushing out farther with her powers. The foot falls stopped and she waited.

There. A distinct series of four beeps. The access code to unlock the doors.

Cali prayed the security on the doors wasn't like that on a computer that would freeze up after so many attempts. She couldn't waste any more time. She had no idea how long she'd been out. Were Sydney and Joel already on their way?

She and Felix had gone in a half hour before midnight. They had to check in after an hour. Had that hour passed?

She started to press the numbers on the keypad in order. She kept her eyes closed and focused on the distinct noise each key made.

1? No.

2? Yes.

3? No.

The keypad didn't lock her out, and eventually she had the code. 2847. She punched it in. The little red sensor turned green. Cali threw open the door.

No one in the hall. She froze and listened for heartbeats. Footsteps. Any sign of life nearby. They were all far off in the distance. Cali worked her way back toward what she hoped was the right direction, willing herself to be silent as the grave.

She had to get to Felix.

She chanted the mantra over and over.

She didn't realize a heartbeat had snuck up on her until she turned the next corner.

Hands gripped her shoulders before she could run head first into a firm chest.

Her fist shot out.

"Fucking hell," gasped Jente. He hunched over and clutched his middle. "That's quite the jab you have there, Cali."

She held her ground.

You can't trust him, remember?

She waited while he sucked in the air she'd expelled from his lungs. "Where's Felix?"

His mismatched eyes glanced up at her. "Jeez, you guys are like broken records, you know that? Is that all you guys care about? Yourselves? 'Where's Cali?' 'Where's Felix?'" Jente mimicked. "There are more than two people in the world, you know."

There was no mention of Sydney or Joel. Cali took that as a good sign. She still had time. Felix obviously wasn't that hurt. She would have felt it otherwise. Right?

"Where's—?"

"Yeah, yeah." Jente stood to his full height. He was a couple inches taller than her. Probably six foot even. "Felix this and Felix that."

"What has Vander done to him?"

His grey and green eyes went carefully blank. "He's been scheduled for the arena."

*

Felix groaned as the pounding in his head woke him from blissful unconsciousness. He threw his legs over the edge of the bed he'd been placed on and cradled his head in his hands. "Motherfucker." He rubbed his temples until the pain ebbed.

Once the nausea settled and the room stopped spinning, he got to his feet. His hand pressed to his chest. "Cali."

They'd bonded. Holy shit.

He grinned, the pull on his lips reopening his cut. He didn't even feel the sting over the swelling heat radiating from inside his chest. He could feel Cali in a way he never had before.

He had to get to her.

He surveyed his surroundings. His room was small but it lacked the sterile, white color scheme of the cells he'd been exploring with Cali. Which meant he was being held in the other containment rooms on the opposite side of the basement nearest the arena.

The door to his room vanished with a wave of his hand. No room could hold him.

He halted when he came out into unknown territory. Left or right?

A low siren started to sound. Men flooded in from the left.

Right it was then.

He passed cell after cell, a few of the captives crying out to him when they caught sight of him.

"Hey, help me!"

It tore at Felix that he couldn't stop to help them. "I will," he shouted over his shoulder at them. "You'll be free soon."

"Or dead." Vander stepped out from fucking nowhere.

Felix skidded to a stop. He changed directions before Vander could get within arm's reach. He understood on a completely different level now what Cali had had to endure when she'd been at Vander's mercy. When he'd touched Felix and sucked the life right out of him, it was a pain like nothing Felix had ever experienced before in his life.

He was going to do everything he could to avoid that life-draining skin.

Guards bore down on him. He calculated his best course of action. They were all tall, well-built men, which meant they'd least expect an attack from below. Increasing his speed, he slid like a baseball player into home plate.

He banked on sliding between two of his pursuers, but they closed ranks and instead he bowled right into them. Heavy bodies crushed down on his shoulders as hands went to grab for him. The questing fingers couldn't find purchase with all the flesh he was buried under. A hand skimmed his wrist, and he elbowed back blindly. A grunt. Pressure around his ankle. He kicked. Missed.

"Hold him," the voice at his feet yelled.

The bodies standing overhead cleared, and he caught sight of Vander watching him. Waiting. Gaze hungry. "You're power is vast, yet you hold back your potential. No prison could hold you, so why do you allow my men to?"

The last thing he was going to do was try to explain morals to a sick bastard like Vander. It was a waste of both their times.

"Go on," Vander urged. "Make them vanish."

There was a maddening glaze to his eyes.

"No fucking way." Felix struggled but there were too many hands holding him. Every time he so much as tensed, fingers dug into his flesh. He was going to be sporting bruises for the next two weeks.

Vander sighed in disappointment. He crouched down next to him. Felix's heart tripped, but he kept himself still. He wasn't going to show fear in the face of this monster. Bastard could suck his own dick for all he cared.

"I admire your fighting spirit. You're very talented. I could simply deal with you my way." He tapped a finger to Felix's forehead. Felix's blood froze as he waited for the pain. Nothing happened. Vander removed his finger. "But I think I'd like to extend the invitation to my arena instead. You will fight for me—"

"Fuck that," Felix cut him off. As soon as he was released he'd be out of there. Vander was right, no prison could hold him. The only thing that could were people. Once that was removed from the equation nothing, would get in his way.

Vander's jaw bulged. Man didn't like to be interrupted. Too fucking bad.

"You *will* fight for me," he repeated with deadly venom, "and put on a good show for my audience, or my dear Cali will have to pay for your mistakes."

Rage bubbled inside him. "She's not yours," he growled. "And if you damage so much as—"

"Threaten all you want." Vander smiled smugly. "You can't get to her fast enough to stop the pain I'll unleash upon her." He leaned closer, his face inches from Felix's. "You're the reason she resisted me. You're the one who brainwashed her."

"I didn't do shit. Cali's not yours. She's not a piece of property to be owned. She makes her own choices, and she chose me. We were meant for each other. Kevin lied to you."

The comment hit hard. Vander pulled back from him. "Your lies will cost Cali dearly."

"I'm not lying," he gritted. "Kevin lied to you because he was a weak son of a bitch and probably couldn't take the punishment you would have dealt him if he didn't deliver what you wanted. Kevin hated me because Collette hated me. You don't think it's convenient that Kevin gave you the name of the woman who was destined to be with me? Newsflash, Vander—you were played. Kevin was never working for you. As soon as he set eyes on Collette, he was hers body and soul. It was nothing but a revenge gig. Plain and simple."

Of course he wasn't one hundred percent sure about that, but he wasn't going to share that bit of information. Kevin *had* hated him. But Felix also got the strange feeling that deep down Kevin had led Vander astray because of what he might've Dreamed if Vander became full-forced.

The idea was more than a little frightening.

Vander remained silent as he took in Felix's words. His face was hard as granite. The perfect mask. His bottomless eyes were devoid of any emotion. "Get him ready for the arena. The next match will be starting soon. Change out the fighters. And keep a close watch on Miss Crazar. In fact, take her from her cell. I think she might like to witness this match."

Felix ground his teeth. His muscles bunched. He sprang into

action, but Vander had been waiting for it. His hand came down on Felix's arm. There was a powerful tug, and Felix's knees buckled, unconsciousness took him.

*

"What?" Cali dug her hands into the front of Jente's shirt. "Where's the arena? Where is he being held?"

Felix wouldn't last in a cage match. Not if Vander Diverted enough of his energy.

Jente very calmly pulled her hands from him. He didn't drop them right away but held on a fraction longer than necessary. "He's probably being transferred to the arena as we speak. The next match is in . . ." He pulled out his cell. "Soon." There was a soft *bing* from his phone, signaling a message. Jente frowned as he read it. He pocketed his phone. "I'll take you there."

Cali went instantly wary. "Why?"

Something flashed in his eyes too fast for her to read then his face went carefully blank. "Do you want to wander around aimlessly yourself and get caught or be led without disturbances?"

She didn't really have a choice.

"Fine. Take me."

There was a brief flare of lust in his expression.

Cali could have smacked herself in the forehead. *Better censor your phrasing, Crazar.*

Jente led her without incident to where the halls opened up wide. The arena was close by, the sound of people and cheering rumbling through the cement halls like distant thunder.

"In here." Jente motioned to a pair of opened double doors.

Inside the arena, the sound was nearly deafening. The layout resembled a baseball stadium. The seats angled downward until they dead-ended into the edge of the cage that sprouted up out of the bottom to reach to the ceiling.

Cali whirled on Jente. "Why the hell did you bring me up here? I need to be down there." She pointed to the bottom level.

Jente blocked her way. "I'm sorry, Cali, but I've told you before, orders are orders. Vander wants you here."

She tried to get past him but he was strong. He propelled her down the stairs. Attendees watched as he forced her down the aisle. They were all dressed in fancy clothing as if they attended nothing more than an opera. Five rows up from the bottom the seats were half empty.

"In there," Jente directed.

She wanted to hit him. She should have run as soon as she saw him. Instead she'd let herself believe he'd help her again. She'd been an idiot. The message he'd read on his phone had to have been Vander's orders for her to be taken to the arena. He was going to make her watch.

Her stomach knotted.

Felix.

She took her seat and scanned the packed crowd. She thought she recognized other famous CEOs but she couldn't be sure. She didn't have time to watch the news or the money to afford cable.

Across the way, in an elevated booth, Vander sat like a king on a throne.

He was staring right at her. There was no tenderness in his gaze. Nothing but raw malice. She tilted her head to spot Jente out of the corner of her eye. He was seated next to her but he was the only one. She might cringe at the idea of having to hurt Jente, but he'd made his choice.

Through the speakers an announcement of the next fight came.

The crowd cheered with blood lust. Below, through the bars of the cage, Cali watched as Felix was thrust into the center. A few seconds later another man of equal size and height was pushed out.

A bell sounded without preamble. Felix's opponent lunged for him.

The floor of the ring was roughly twenty feet in circumference and was covered in some kind of gravel. Once or twice Felix slipped when he moved too quickly.

Cali's fingers dug into the armrests. Jente's hand weighed heavy on her shoulder. A constant reminder that she wasn't to move.

Where the hell were Sydney and Joel?

Felix caught a punch along the jaw that sent him staggering into the bars. People roared with appreciation. Cali willed him to bounce back but she could tell from here, could *feel* it within her, that Felix wasn't up to full strength.

Her eyes sought Vander across the way. His black gaze watched her intently. At her look he offered up a smug smile.

He'd weakened Felix. On purpose.

"Jente," she said very carefully. "You can't let this happen. Vander fixes the matches. Felix doesn't even stand a chance down there."

He didn't say anything.

The crowd cheered again. Cali turned to the fight to see a spray of blood. Felix's blood.

He couldn't take much more of this. She had to do something. Anything.

Jente's fingers tightened on her shoulder. She didn't give him any warning. She whirled in her chair, fist flying. There was a satisfying crunch as she connected with his nose. Blood poured. Jente cried out, but it was drowned out in the sounds of the crowd. People were on their feet now, scenting the end of the match.

Cali pushed through the rows as Jente tried to follow after her.

"Out of my way." Cali shoved patrons to get through. People cried foul as she elbowed her way to the front where a crowd was already gathered to see the outcome of the fight below. Cali wormed her way in.

Felix blocked a kick to the gut, but he was on the floor. He looked sickly, weak. Cali felt her throat tighten.

As if he sensed her, Felix's eyes lifted and locked with hers.

She pressed her hand futilely against the bars. Felix held her gaze as his opponent wound up for the final blow. Felix dropped his head in defeat.

Cali railed against the bars. "No!"

Felix's hand moved.

His opponent vanished.

Chapter 27

Cali's heart caught in her throat. The crowd around her shot to their feet in outrage. Chaos exploded. Someone pulled her back from the cluster of people. Jente's face was filled with rage. "You fucking broke my nose." He sounded nasally.

Cali opened her mouth to retort when a bright blonde head of hair caught in the corner of her eye.

Sydney.

They'd come.

Relief and hope sprang from her, and she smiled sweetly at Jente. "I'm sorry," she apologized without remorse. "Does it hurt?" She slammed the heel of her hand into the damaged bone. Jente fell back with a curse.

Cali booked it for the stairs. "Sydney," she tried to call over the building chaos. The noise was too great. No one seemed to even notice Sydney, but the guards at the doors sure as hell noticed Cali.

She took the steps two at a time and plowed through the doors into a sea of bodies as people fled. Fights had broken out among the audience. Apparently the gamblers weren't happy with this new turn of events.

The back of her neck felt iced over. She ran blindly. "Come on, Sydney. Come looking for me." She pressed through a group of woman and overheard the word "cops."

Shit.

Their time was running out.

"Wherever the hell you guys are you better hurry. The cops have been called." She glanced behind her to see the guards still followed but at a much slower pace. She swerved through hallway after hallway until she was well and truly lost.

She plowed past the first unlocked door on her right that she found.

The sound difference was astounding. She had to be in some kind of restricted zone or medical wing. The smell was acidic, the low whine of fluorescent light bulbs the only noise.

Ahead was a pair of swinging double doors.

She exhaled. "If you're out looking for me, Sydney—" She spoke to no one. "—I went through the scary double doors with biohazard stickers."

Once through the swinging doors she steadied them so they wouldn't give her away if anyone happened to come by. She peered through the little glass window to watch the chaos outside. No one came through the door. And why would they? It clearly wasn't an exit.

A pair of guards stepped in. Cali hid before she could be seen and prayed they'd think she'd run for the exit like everyone else.

She stood stooped beneath the little window in the door for at least ten seconds before she realized that if they did come this way, she was screwed. She needed somewhere to hide in case they checked the windows.

She made a mad dash down the hall, noticing for the first time that the flooring was tile and not cement. The smell of bleach grew stronger. All the doors had little windows and key-coded doors. That wasn't going to help her. She needed some kind of storage closet but instead found a small, pharmacy type cubbyhole. She jumped over the counter as the double doors *swooshed* open. Upon her landing, her foot hit a wheeled cart. The drugs that sat atop it tumbled, the clank of glass loud enough to make her cringe.

Fuck.

Light footsteps grew closer.

She balled her hands into fists, ready to catch whoever was on the other side by surprise.

"Cali?" a female voice whispered.

"Sydney?" She shot up and smashed the top of her head into

the counter that hung over her. She landed back on her ass, both hands covering her head where it felt like she'd cracked her skull.

Sydney scrambled over the counter and dropped down beside her. "Are you okay?"

Cali winced as she rubbed the top of her head. "Dandy," she said dryly. "How the hell did you find me?"

She grinned and raised one shoulder in a half shrug. "As strange as this is going to sound, I followed your voice. I could hear you, like a whisper on the breeze. When I came to this hallway I saw a pair of guards. They came in here then left cursing under their breath. I decided to follow, and when I saw the big, hospital-looking doors, I knew you'd be here because you said so. Weird, huh?"

Cali stared at her in amazement. She'd never been able to do that before. Manipulate the sound to travel to only one person. Could that be part of her strengthened powers?

She shook herself mentally. She could figure that stuff out later. "Where's Joel?"

"He went looking for a way to bust Felix out. What happened?"

"Vander."

"He put Felix in the arena to fight?" The green of Sydney's eyes sparked with an anger Cali had never seen before.

"Yeah, after he drained Felix so he'd be at a disadvantage."

"And Felix?" Sydney gripped her arm. Cali felt a twinge of jealousy and pushed it away when she realized how absurd it was. Sydney loved Felix like a brother and vice versa.

"He Erased his opponent."

Sydney's hands dropped. "He did?"

Cali nodded. He'd broken his one rule for her. For them. "Look," she said after a tense moment of silence. "We need to get out of here. I overheard a group talking about the cops coming. We need to find Felix and Joel and get the hell out of here."

"What about the others?" Sydney's gaze was drawn to the doors that lined the far wall beyond the pharmacy.

Cali's heart constricted. "We have to abort the mission and hope like hell no one believes them about being questioned about super powers."

Sydney nodded but she still made her way over to the doors, like a moth drawn to the flame.

Cali followed. She could understand the need to peek inside. She'd forever remember all those hopeless faces, but hopefully this would be the end of their torment.

The lights inside were dimmed due to the late hour. Sydney stopped a few feet from the little window but Cali continued forward.

She didn't remember the name of this wing of the basement. The containment rooms here weren't like the others. They had more security.

Which meant that whoever was on the other side was more valuable.

Cali swallowed.

Could the cells be holding people with powers?

Sydney found her courage and came up beside Cali. They shared a glance as if they both were thinking the same thing and dreaded what they'd find behind this window. Together they glanced through the glass.

In the dead center of the room was a chair. A man sat slumped forward, head down. His arms were secured around his back and he was dressed in scrubs. An IV was attached to one of his arms. The dimmed lights cast shadows all around the room, causing the man's inky black hair to stand out where it hung around his head. Cali squinted against the near darkness, and as if sensing their presence, he lifted his head. He had eyes like ice.

Sydney gasped, taking a step back from the window, her eyes locked with his.

The prisoner's gaze never wavered from Sydney but his head swayed as if drugged. Cali's heart went out to him.

"We shouldn't have looked," she whispered. It was too much to see and not take action. She stepped back but Sydney seemed rooted to the ground. "Come on, Sydney. There's nothing we can do for him. Cops are on their way—they'll take care of him." She tugged on Sydney's arm. She didn't budge. Cali tugged harder and she stumbled. Cali grabbed her by the shoulders to steady her. "Are you okay?"

Sydney blinked. Her breathing was shallow, her cheeks flushed. What the hell?

"Sydney?"

She snapped back to attention. "I'm fine."

Cali didn't believe her, but she could press her for more information once they were out of there.

Sydney led the way. Cali was glad at least one of them remembered the way back to the arena.

"I saw two different entrances leading to the bottom most level. I'll take the farthest one in case Joel and Felix go out that way. You take this closer one and we'll meet in the middle. Got it?"

Sydney didn't give her time to answer. She moved those short little legs of hers and disappeared down the hall. The crowds had thinned. No one was even giving her a second glance. Perfect.

The stairway was cramped, but once Cali hit the ground level it opened up to a similar layout as the top. She made her way toward the center of the arena.

There were more people down here but Cali didn't see any sign of Felix.

She passed some kind of locker room and reached out with her powers. "Felix, where are you, you cake-baking pansy?"

A reply came from behind her. "Easy, C. All those endearments might give someone the misconception that you actually care about me."

Felix grinned as she bulldozed into his arms, the heat in her chest nearly bursting.

She stared up at him. "C? Really? And what do I call you? F? Lix?"

His expression turned thoughtful. "Licks? I could work with that."

She punched him in the arm. "Where's Joel? He was supposed to be looking for you."

The grin left his face. "I haven't seen him. Where's Sydney?"

"She went down the other set of stairs to try and cut you guys off. We're supposed to meet in the middle somewhere. Come on, we're running out of time." She laced her fingers with his and felt whole once more.

Felix squeezed her hand and followed after her. "What do you mean we're running out of time?"

"Someone called the cops."

"Niella?"

That gave Cali pause. "I don't know. What time is it?"

"No idea. My phone was confiscated."

Cali patted her pockets. "Mine too."

"What about the people in the cells?"

"No time."

His hand squeezed hers again. "That's not your fault."

The guilt that weighed heavy on her heart lifted fractionally.

"How do we get back to the cage from here?"

Felix took the lead. "This way." He led them around a large curve before a set of doors came into view. Cali hadn't even realized the bottom level of the arena had seats for the matches until she stepped foot on the ground level. It was nearly deserted except for one female sitting near the cage bars.

Collette.

Had she been sitting there the entire match?

Her eyes spat gray and blue fire.

Felix went still. "Let us pass, Collette," he said calmly. On the other side of the floor, Cali saw Joel and Sydney pass by a doorway. Shit. They needed to get to them before they went too far. Collette didn't seem like she'd be too much of a difficulty. She looked exhausted, but the mad gleam in her eye was a wild card.

"You weren't supposed to win, Felix," she said just as calmly.

Felix slid his hand slowly from Cali's and took a step forward. "But I did. Now let it go. Vander's company is busted. All his prisoners are going to be set free, and all the employees are going to be investigated. I'd take this time to get as far away as possible."

"You forget I can create anything I want. You think the police will be able to pin anything on me?"

It was a sad but true fact. And suddenly it hit Cali. Just like she'd never be free of Vander, Felix would never be free of Collette.

"You, on the other hand," Collette said, "would be held by the police for questioning, and it'd be all too easy to place the perfect evidence against you. Especially now that Vander doesn't want you." Her eyes bored into Cali's.

Cali had no idea what had caused the abrupt change of heart, but she wasn't going to knock it. Vander didn't want her anymore? Fine by her.

"She's right," Felix said to her out of the corner of his mouth. "We can't be caught here. You go right, I'll go left."

Cali gave the smallest of nods before they broke apart and made a run for it.

Collette sprang into action, her faceless mannequin-type bodyguards appearing out of thin air. Those faceless, featureless creatures were creepy as fuck, but Cali remembered a time when Felix had been telling her about Collette and her powers. He'd told her that the more insubstantial the Illusion the easier it was for her to hold onto it. The more details, the harder it was, and the more power and concentration was required.

Collette's attention was divided momentarily as Cali went around the other side. But instead of splitting her men she focused all her energy on Felix. That wasn't like her. Cali hesitated while Felix was intercepted. Collette always went after Cali, but the rage burning on her face was all for Felix. He'd done something to draw her anger.

Felix did his best to Erase everything that came his way but he was beyond exhausted, and Collette was like a mad conductor. Things flew at Felix too fast for Cali to even make out the shape. Something knocked into his stomach. The air left his lungs; he hunched in on himself, but a backhand from one of the mannequins sent him backwards.

Red began to cloud Cali's vision. She scanned the area for something to use. With every grunt from Felix her blood boiled hotter and hotter. She was sick of Collette harassing them. She was tired of having to constantly look over her shoulder because Collette was obsessed with someone who had no feelings for her. Collette had stood over her while she'd been helpless at Vander's and promised her nothing but pain. Well, no more.

Her gaze caught on a fire extinguisher held safely behind glass. Bracing herself for the pain, she thrust her elbow back and shattered the casing. A high-pitched wail came from overhead, and Cali grinned at the sound of it.

She pulled the tank from the glass and approached Collette from behind.

Her neck tingled. "Joel, Sydney, come back to the cage." She sent the message out, hoping it'd find its target. Then she directed all her focus on the fire alarm blaring from the speakers. She stared at Collette, willing the sound to pitch higher and higher in her ears. She wanted Collette to feel all the pain that she'd dealt them. Her rage was a brilliant fire inside her that she unleashed without mercy.

Collette screamed. Her Illusions vanished. She fell to her knees, cupping her ears and ducking her head as far into her chest as possible. But Cali didn't stop. Covering her ears wouldn't help. She wanted Collette to hear everything, all of it, as loud as it would go.

Blood leaked from Collette's ears. It took her a moment before she noticed Cali standing over her. She looked up at her, dazed, and Cali waited, waited for the recognition.

It didn't take long.

The hate and anger boiled to the surface, but beneath that she saw a flicker of fear and Cali smiled down at her.

"Who bested you now?"

Collette squinted in confusion, as if she was having difficulty hearing the words.

Cali slammed the bottom of the fire extinguisher into the back of her head. She collapsed like a doll.

She ran to Felix. He was holding himself up on one of the armrests, staring at Collette's unmoving body.

His gaze jerked to Cali as she came closer. She was breathing heavily, her limbs trembling. She couldn't believe what she'd done.

"Feel better?" he asked, a spark of pride lighting his eyes. "I hear taking out your rival can be very therapeutic."

She held up both her hands. "That's seven, you know."

He stared at the fingers she held up. "Seven?"

"All those guards she had wailing on you? They count."

Felix's jaw went slack. "Those should all count as one," he said indignantly.

"Nope." Cali kissed him gently on the mouth.

Felix hissed from the split in his lip.

"Holy fuck." Joel and Sydney stopped at the sight of Collette. Joel glanced from Cali to the blood in Collette's ears. His hand rose to his own as if in sympathy. "Remind me never to get on your bad side."

"We have to go," Sydney interjected. "The cops are here. They're full on S.W.A.T. teaming the whole place."

Shouts came from the set of double doors Cali and Felix had entered through. Cali dashed to close them but there was no lock. "Joel," she shouted.

"I got it." He pressed his hands firmly against them. "Let's go."

Cali ran alongside him. "How long will that last?"

Pounding and more shouts came from the other side.

Joel gave her a cocky smile. "We're about to find out."

The beating grew louder, the door shaking on its hinges, but somehow it stayed closed. Cali marveled at the world she'd been incorporated into and left the arena without a backward glance.

Epilogue

"Cali, I swear, if you light my house on fire…" Felix left the threat hanging as she laid out the fireworks along the sidewalk in front of his house.

"Nightfall isn't for another hour at least," said Niella as she tore into her hamburger.

"I'm making sure we're prepared," Cali defended.

It was the Fourth of July, and the guild was gathered at Felix's where he'd wowed everyone with his ability to burn the shit out of everything he put on the barbeque. Joel had blessedly taken over.

The events at the Kratos Building had come and gone. The newspapers had a field day ripping apart the company piece by piece. Their stocks dropped exponentially, and Cali thought for sure they'd go under, but some executive in a different branch made the statement that Vander Donahughe had been running his underground events behind the rest of the company's back.

Kratos wasn't as destroyed as Cali would have wanted, but the building closest to them was now abandoned. She'd take any victory she could.

She grabbed a beer from the cooler and made her way over to Sydney. She'd been affected the most after everything that had happened. She was a lot quieter than usual and visited the hospital where all Vander's victims were said to have been dispatched. Cali went with her most times, which meant she knew who Sydney was searching for and not finding.

The man with eyes of ice.

He wasn't among the rescued, and it sat like a bitter stone in her stomach to think that perhaps Vander had been able to transport some of his prisoners before the police had arrived.

Collette had been one of many who were taken to the hospital. She had joined Kevin in his lush hospital room as the world waited for them to come out of their comas.

Cali didn't feel sorry for the Illusionist. She was with her Mirror Mate. That was where she belonged. She wouldn't suffer anymore, and she'd never be able to harm another.

She bumped shoulders with Sydney to draw her attention. Felix had been rubbing off on her. She found she engaged in more physical contact with others than she would have previously. "You okay?" She lifted her beer and Sydney tapped it with her soda can.

"I'm fine."

"What were you thinking about?"

Sydney ducked her gaze. Cali took a sip from her beer and watched as Joel and Felix threw a football back and forth, Niella making snarky remarks about their form. "That guy again, huh?"

Sydney's fingers tightened around her drink. "The authorities never found Vander. He could have gotten away, could have taken some people with him."

"I know. Joel said he'd look through their database again. If we spot any kind of strange activity, we'll go after him. We're the Guild of Truth, remember? It's our sole purpose to vanquish the Guild of Power." She exaggerated her voice, lowered it to a deep rumble.

A reluctant smile graced Sydney's face, and Cali bumped her on the shoulder again.

"Now enjoy the day. Fourth of July is for celebrating. Dump that soda and get a beer." She finished off her own drink and chucked the can at Felix.

"Hey." He dodged it and rushed her. His arms banded around her, locking her own arms down against her sides. "I cry foul," he whispered into her ear.

As for Felix, there was a darker edge to him now. One Cali only noticed when he dropped his guard around her.

They had rehashed the match Vander had forced him into again and again. Cali told him about her sneaking suspicion that his opponent had been nothing but an Illusion, yet Felix still felt the guilt. He told her it didn't matter if the person he'd Erased was real or not, the fact remained that he would have done it either way.

His lips skimmed her ear, bringing her back to the present. Her heart thundered. She grinned at him and licked his jaw. "Pansy," she teased. She'd help him get over his guilt. She'd do everything in her power to protect her man.

"At least I'm not soaking wet," he said calmly.

Cali tilted her head. Felix dropped her back on her feet just as a water balloon burst above her head.

Water drenched her hair and shirt. The white tee stuck to her black bikini, and Felix admired his handiwork, eyes flashing with desire.

"You jerk." She raced for the nearest balloon barrel and went after him.

He disappeared through the side gate. Cali hesitated before pursuing him. She tucked another balloon into the back pocket of her shorts and dashed after him. He was waiting in the middle of his backyard for her.

She stopped a scant foot away. "Got any last words?"

He crossed his arms. "I've got plenty, but the most important ones are 'better luck next time.'" He waved his hands and the two water balloons she held vanished.

Her fingers curled as if she could hang on to them. "You cheater." She pounded a fist into his broad chest.

He laughed before grasping her shoulders and kissing her. "You want to know my second most important last words?" He spoke against her still tingling lips.

She kissed him again. "Mm?"

He trailed his mouth over to her ear. "I love you."

Cali's lungs couldn't get enough air. A stupid, giddy smile came over her, and she couldn't have stopped it even if she wanted to. She cupped his perfectly healed face and smashed her mouth to his. "I love you too," she breathed into him. "You know what I love even more?" she purred.

Felix growled low in his throat. "What?"

"You soaking wet."

She smashed the balloon in her back pocket on the top of his head.

In the mood for more Crimson Romance? Check out *Soul Seducer* at CrimsonRomance.com.